POLITICS NOIR

POLITICS NOIR

Dark Tales from
the Corridors of Power

Edited by Gary Phillips

VERSO

London • New York

First published by Verso 2008

1 3 5 7 9 10 8 6 4 2

Verso
UK: 6 Meard Street, London W1F 0EG
USA: 180 Varick Street, New York, NY 10014-4606
www.versobooks.com

Verso is the imprint of New Left Books

ISBN-13: 978-1-84467-161-8

British Library Cataloguing in Publication Data
A catalogue record for this book is available from the British Library

Library of Congress Cataloging-in-Publication Data
A catalog record for this book is available from the Library of Congress

Typeset in Goudy Old Style by Hewer Text UK Ltd, Edinburgh
Printed in the USA by Maple Vail

CONTENTS

CONTENTS

INTRODUCTION

Lust. Greed. Arrogance. Power.

Congressman Randy "Duke" Cunningham kept a price list for specific bribes for specific favors; President Richard Nixon authorized a burglary of his rivals; water-boarding isn't torture to many in the Bush Administration; former Prime Minister Margaret Thatcher was linked to suspect golf and theater junkets for American GOPers; Senator Gary Hart, after daring reporters to "Follow me around, I don't care . . . you'll be bored," was caught with Donna Rice, not his wife, sitting on his lap on a dock where his boat *Monkey Business* was secured; straight out of Compton, Mayor Omar Bradley retained a traveling chef because he was worried about being poisoned; Vice President Dick Cheney accidentally shot-gunned a hunting buddy in the face; Secretary of State Condoleezza Rice shopped for shoes while New Orleans flooded; and President Bill Clinton was impeached for lying about getting a hummer in the Oval Office.

Politics is a blood sport the public follows 24/7. Drop in on a blog, tune the AM radio dial to any number of blowhards, or channel surf through the myriad programs on your TV, and you'll inevitably find the punditry ponti-ficating about the latest foible of one of our elected officials, and the spin they spin to explain such behavior. We can't help but be fascinated with the men and women involved in this too often surreal pursuit. Recently some eggheads wired a group of potential swing voters under a functional magnetic resonance imaging scanner, asking them to answer various questions about their political proclivities, and monitored their brain activity. Part of this experiment tracked which presidential candidate evoked empathy, positive feelings, anxiety or disgust. A further step in the refinement of imaging and messaging, as future campaign hacks will no doubt study these readouts, galvanic responses and the like to tailor-make their candidate to meet all your expectations.

Given all that it seemed the time then was right for this anthology, *Politics Noir*. When I asked the talented crew of storytellers in this book to contribute original short stories, I didn't have to explain the theme once I told them the title. We all have jaundiced views on the character and nature of politics. It was natural for these hardboiled practitioners and social observers to offer their takes on the arena of which satirist Mark Twain noted, "In religion and politics people's beliefs and convictions are in almost every case gotten at second-hand, and without examination, from authorities who have not themselves examined the questions at issue but have taken them at second-hand from other non-examiners, whose opinions about them were not worth a brass farthing."

What you'll find in the following pages is an assortment of dark, funny, cynical, twisted, and punch-to-the-gut tales that you'll find thought-provoking but, most importantly, entertaining. I do think once you've started to read these stories, you'll give more than a brass farthing about this collection, lovingly entitled *Politics Noir*.

Gary Phillips, Editor

NEGATIVE NIXONS

Mike Davis

1. THE HAWAIIAN SHIRT

"Holy shit!"

Sullivan winced and his hand began to tremble. Like other Guadalcanal vets, he still got the malarial shakes—sometimes at embarrassing moments like now, when he needed all of his gravitas.

"Well Jimmy, don't have a fuckin' heart attack." Myers mocked his partner. "It's only a blow job. Ain't you ever seen one before?"

Sullivan, still trembling, held the photo negative closer to the light, like a doctor examining an X-ray that he knew contained a metastasized tumor.

Even out of focus, the image was unmistakable. A heavily-built, middle-aged man in a bathrobe leered down at another man, his face invisible, who knelt before him, almost reverentially, his hands wrapped around the first man's hips.

Sullivan shook his head. "Blow job? This is a goddamn atomic bomb. It's like stolen plutonium. Think what the Commies would do with this. Lock the fuckin' door."

Myers fiddled for a moment until he found the key to lock the "third-degree room." "OK, Jimmy, relax. Our nuclear secret's safe."

"Are you kiddin'? *You* fuckin' relax." Sullivan sneered and laid the negative next to the front page of a week-old local newspaper.

On the cover, three of the most powerful men in the United States—the Vice President, the FBI Director, and the chairman of the House Armed Services Committee—were relaxing in the California sun, toasting each other with highballs.

One of the men—his famous bulldog face with the slanted, brutal mouth—was instantly recognizable in both photographs.

"So who the hell is on his knees?" asked Myers.

Sullivan again held the negative to the light. The Hawaiian shirt—identical in both photographs—was the give-away. "Christ, it looks like Nixon."

2. SMITHTOWN

Tourists loved the pretty town with its perfect harbor, white beaches, and famous racetrack. Those who could afford it came back to retire in pastel stucco bungalows where they slowly shriveled up like prunes and died of indigestion and boredom.

But it was the Fleet that had built the city, not the wizened old people in the hills. With 100,000 young sailors and marines—not to mention the Okies working overtime in the aircraft plants or the movie stars on weekend junkets—came a rowdy, insatiable demand for sin.

The Stingaree south of E Street offered sleazy hotel sex and stand-ups in the alley, while Sailortown along lower Broadway was a vast emporium of peepshows, tattoo parlors, all-night movies and a hundred games of chance. Tijuana, with dozens of $10 brothels and the raunchiest floor shows east of Macao, was a twenty-minute cab ride from downtown.

Until 1938, when President Cardenas closed the casinos, Tijuana also boasted Agua Caliente, a West Coast Monte Carlo for movie royalty and other wealthy gringos. But he didn't shut the racetrack, and it still attracted half a million punters each year, as did its posh gringo sister, Del Mar, 30 miles north. And if the ponies brought the Mob, they also brought distinguished Easterners, including the Director of the FBI, who visited every year.

Other vices and gambling greased the region's wheels. Sure, the Social Registrer business elites sat piously in their pews while their ministers denounced the reign of Satan in the city, but sin had purchased half the bricks in their Mission Hills and Point Loma mansions.

When Smith arrived in the city, unheralded, during the Depression, a flashy hotelier named Baron Long fronted the vice industry with the support of the city's powerful newspaper. Like both his father and brother, Smith was a professional grifter and swindler. With the help of a handsome pimp named Digiorgio, he mined gold for a while in the Stingaree's sewers and then used the money to buy a little bank.

During the hard years, when local tuna fishermen were starved of credit, Smith's bank offered them money and then punctually repossessed their boats. By the end of the war, he owned most of the fleet, as well as the local shipyard and the major cannery.

With Digiorgio as a front, he also muscled his way into control of the Caliente track and its subsidiary tourist services. The skim from the track helped finance his takeover of Downtown gambling, in the course of which he inherited ownership of the Vice Detail and two ambitious detectives—both decorated veterans—named Myers and Sullivan.

Smith—ceaselessly trying to pyramid his wealth—poured the profits of fishing and gambling into the local and national Republican Party. A chancer, he backed a dark horse named Dick Nixon and won big. Bluebloods ceased to make jokes about Mr. Tuna.

Indeed, one day, when *The City's* wealthy publisher was back east, sitting next to one of the mummified Cabots or Mellons at the Newport Regatta, he was asked where he was from. He proudly named the pretty city with the perfect harbor.

The ancient Cabot (or Mellon) nodded and said, "Oh, yes, Mr Smith's town."

3. AN ERRAND

"Nixon? Don't even think it. That's not a place you want to visit."

Myers kicked away the chair as he stood up, absent-mindedly adjusting his belt, moving the 45 in its swivel-holster back under his coat.

Sullivan threw the negative on the table. "OK, Babe, it's Liberace and Rock Hudson, if that'll make you happy. Where the hell did you get this work of art."

"Smith gave it to me. He bought it from Digiorgio."

"Digiorgio's a rat-fuck piece of shit."

"Yeah, but you gotta admire his balls." Myers lit a cigarette. "Tired of picking up dog turds for Smith, he decides to make his own crazy move. He somehow sneaks a spy camera under the very noses of the Feds, into the old prick's bedroom. Rigs up some kind of automatic shutter. Probably hopes he'll catch the great G-man shtuping the maid or Dorothy Lamour."

6

"Come on, in the boudoir of the FBI Director? And the hundred lackeys in Hoover's entourage don't find the camera?"

"They're the FBI, Jimmy. In case you don't remember, that stands for 'fucked-up bastard idiots.' They can't wipe their own asses."

Sullivan recalled the comic incident two years before, when Myers led the heroic G-men on a wild goose chase through the Stingaree while Sullivan negotiated a sharp hike in baksheesh from frightened Broadway hopheads. "OK, Babe, so how many negatives does Digiorgio have?"

"Smith doesn't know. Digiorgio is holed up in T.J. or maybe Rosarito. The insane fuck is waiting for Smith to make him an offer."

"What's his back-up?"

"Not much. Smith owns most of the muscle in Mexico. Digiorgio's already in his coffin."

"Will Smith tell Hoover?"

"Don't be a fool. Tell Hoover that he was set up by Smith's own director of security? Smith's frantic. He's trembling worse than you are, and pulling all the hairs out of his nose. If any of this crap leaks out, especially the Hawaiian shirt bit, this city will be a ghost town. No fleet, no swabbies, no tickee, no laundry."

"So it's just us?"

"Big boy rules. We take the punk down tonight. South of the border."

Sullivan shook his head. "As if Digiorgio's carrying the friggin' negatives up his ass in a suppository and hasn't buried them or locked them away in a safety-deposit box."

"Well, that's the interesting part." Myers was now relaxed and sly.

"What the fuck do you mean?"

"Smith's orders are to send pretty boy straight to hell as soon as possible. I don't think the boss has a clue what to do if he doesn't have the negatives. That's Smith's up-shit-creek dilemma—but it could be our golden retirement opportunity."

All Sullivan could see of Myers was his cheshire cat grin. "Jesus, Babe, what are you thinking? Oh holy fuck."

4. NIXON'S DADDY

The Director held the mortgage on America: like God, he knew the secret sins of an entire Nation. Every president had utterly despised him, but in public each had been forced to glorify him and the phony legend of his invincible G-Men. Three administrations had been held hostage by the notorious secret files in the Director's safe.

In FDR's case, the file was called "Lucy Mercer." Truman, the former bagman for the Pendergast machine, was vulnerable on many fronts, but it was the file labeled "Daughter Margaret" that kept his thin lips pursed when the Director hunted Reds in the very shadow of the White House. Eisenhower, for his part, might have been impregnable, except for a pretty wartime secretary named Kay Summersby.

Yet the supreme blackmailer himself lived in terror of being blackmailed. The master intruder, whose microphones were under half the beds in Washington, had a servant look under his own bed every night, and his home on Thirtieth Place was swept for bugs once a week.

Even then, both Washington and New York were too dangerous for the Director. Too full of his enemies: Jews, liberals, Communists, and Democrats. In the East, he had no private life; his bedroom simply accumulated dark, unfulfilled fantasies.

That's why he loved Smithtown, especially the wealthy beach suburb near the racetrack whose restrictive covenants excluded "Jews, Negroes, Mexicans, and dogs." It was a sanctuary for his pleasures—the horse races, hobnobbing with movie stars, and, sometimes, discreet encounters with men. He vacationed there every year.

He knew how ironical it might sound, but he trusted the tough, corrupt cops who worked for Smith more than he did his own sycophantic agents. The Director had long been convinced that the Russians had penetrated the Bureau, and he was especially suspicious of the ambitious underlings who pawed at his door in Washington.

But he could relax with Smith, even if he didn't particularly like him. They shared a profound investment in Dick Nixon and his future presidency. Smith had been there first, financing Nixon when he was a nobody running for Senate against a movie star's wife. But the Director had given the young California Republican the anti-Communist celebrity that had made him Vice President.

Still, Dick had become a smart ass lately. He was starting to brownnose his way up Park Avenue. The Director despised the Rockefeller wing of the GOP, and he was determined to remind the Vice President who his real Daddy was. That's why he had insisted on a tête-à-tête in Smithtown.

5. CAR COLORS

Sullivan and Myers were arguing over which car to borrow from the Impound Lot. Jimmy wanted the black 54 Buick, while Babe—perverse as always—insisted upon the brand-new powder-blue Impala.

In Los Angeles and perhaps other big cities, it would have been illegal for the detective squad to use Impound as their undercover motorpool. But in Smithtown, it was a venerable custom.

The Impound sergeant was hungry and impatient. "You two suits been married too long. So make up your friggin' minds, so I can go to dinner." The detectives ignored him.

"For Christ's sake, Babe, this Chevvy belongs to that interior decorator from La Jolla that we busted in the john at the Greyhound station."

"Well, he has cute taste . . ."

"Cute? You outta your mind? Everyone's gonna notice this car."

"Not Digiorgio, Jimmy."

"What do you mean?"

Myers looked behind him. The pissed-off sergeant had gone back to his office. "Look, Einstein," he said softly. "What color car do you drive?"

Sullivan frowned in the almost certain expectation that he was about to play the fool again. "Black. I drive fuckin' black cars. So do you. We're dicks. We drive black Buicks and Chryslers, just like in the movies. Cops always drive black. Not pussy blue convertibles."

Myers laughed. "So what will Digiorgio be on the lookout for? Black, Jimmy, black. Because he knows we're dumb-ass dicks and we watch too many movies."

Sullivan rolled his eyes. Myers punched him in the shoulder. "Come on, you stupid Mick, I'll drive. Digiorgio won't know what hit him."

6. THE PREY

"I fucked Rita Hayward."

The acne-faced kid continued to pick his nose.

"You goddamn punk. I FUCKED Rita Hayworth." Angelo shook with so much anger that his toupee started dancing down his right ear.

The punk just laughed. "Look Mr Digiorgio, I believe you. Take it easy. You fucked Rita Hayworth. You fucked Betty Grable. You fucked all those old broads."

Angelo wished he could kill the insolent snot-eating kid, but then he remembered—God help him—that this was one of his bodyguards. This pile of pimples and the obese pederast in the other room were all that protected him from the wrath of Myers and Sullivan. "Maybe I should just blow my fuckin' brains out," he mumbled.

"What ya say Mr Digiorgio? Is it about Rita Hayworth again?"

"No, nuthin' I am going upstairs, kid—don't you think you should watch the front gate?"

"Sure, Mr Digiorgio."

Upstairs Angelo kept the biggest wardrobe on the coast. It was a shrine to his glory days in the Thirties and Forties, when he turned out more girls than Louis B. Mayer. He had run cheap whores for Smith, but he had also purveyed quality.

Angelo looked at a long rack of old-fashioned double-breasted suits. One of them had been a gift from George Raft. Yeah, he had known all those Hollywood guys. He had pimped for them, sold them drugs, and then given their secrets to Smith.

And, hell yes, he had screwed Rita. She'd just been some little number in a dance act with her father at Caliente. He couldn't even recall what the fuck her original name was. But he remembered her lips.

And he remembered the other pretty actresses who had invited him to their bungalows. They always needed a little coke, maybe pills or some hemp, or just some old-fashioned stick work.

In those days, Digiorgio was Smith's partner and shared the glory. But after the war Smith became more interested in owning banks and tuna fleets and baseball teams than in nickel bags and industrial-strength pussy.

Angelo became just another employee. Yea, he had a fancy name, Mr Security Director, but his main job was keeping Smith's old businesses as far away from the new ones as possible. He entered the mansion in Point Loma by the back door, and kept out of the limelight as much as possible.

Women quickly sensed his diminished power and no longer returned his calls. He lost his hair and gained both a paunch and an ulcer. The bookies started laughing behind his back, and the transvestites spit in his face.

Smith turned to real muscle—the scary duet known as Myers and Sullivan—and Angelo was soon running their errands. His time was almost over.

Then he had the idea about Hoover. It was suicidal but he didn't care. The Director was surrounded by a double ring of security—the Bureau's and, inside of that, Smith's—and he thought himself invulnerable.

But Angelo, with his impressive title, came and went, and no one paid any attention. He got a goofy kid who worked for the Navy lab, some kind of top-secret photo-reconnaissance deal, to rig up the miniature camera. The setup was a cinch.

He had no idea of what he might catch. Maybe just the old bastard spanking the monkey in bed. Instead he landed

Leviathan. He drove down to his beach house in Rosarito, and did nothing but stare at the negatives for maybe thirty-six hours.

Then he realized that he was probably dead anyway, so why not go for the gold ring? He sent Smith a print with a note. Your future's for sale, ole pal. Ante up, or I'll sell this to the Democrats, or, hell, just send it to the KGB.

Smith bought a negative. For a few days, Angelo fantasized about palaces, private islands, and comely young princesses with Rita Hayworth lips. Then he realized that Myers and Sullivan were coming.

Panicked, but too tired to run, he looked for muscle. But nothing was for sale except for the two perverts below. A pair of big poodles would have made more sense. What was left to say?

"Too bad I don't have a picture of Rita Hayworth to show Babe and Jimmy," Angelo jabbered to himself.

7. SULLIVAN HATES BOATS

Myers raced to the border with the top down, swigging Jack Daniel's from his hip flask and giggling like a joy-riding teenager. He gave Sullivan an unusually generous smile.

"Jimmy, how come you don't like fishing?"

Sullivan winced. "I told you a million times, Babe, I don't like boats. I spent half the war puking off the decks of goddamn troop transports."

His face darkened. "Once, when we were being ferried across Savo Strait to Telagu, I saw the remains of a PT boat crew. They had been in the water for maybe a week. The sharks had torn them limb from limb. Just some bloody headless torsos in the water."

Sullivan was now fierce. "So I don't like boats and I don't like fish. I golf and eat steak and fuck barmaids, not mermaids. So quit trying to convert me. You're the great fisherman."

Myers shook his head. He had never understood why his partner was still such a haunted house of combat horrors. He himself had crawled up the leg of Italy, from Anzio to the Arno—brain-splattered rock to bloody rock—with two Purple Hearts and a Silver Star. But he had loved the war.

Not just the whores in Rome, but the war itself: the power and excitement it conferred on a twenty-two-year-old master-sergeant from Shithole, Texas. And tonight was a little like the war—going after that scumbag Digiorgio and whatever muscle protected him. The prospect of combat made Myers happy: it would be even more fun than driving a blue convertible.

"I am sorry Jimmy, but before the night is over I'm going to have to take you fishing." Myers was genuinely sympathetic.

"Rotten corpses in the water," Sullivan muttered. He now had a clear idea how the evening would end.

Suddenly they were in San Ysidro. A minute later, an elderly customs guard in a gray uniform that looked like it was left over from the Porfiriato was flagging them across the line.

"For Christ's sake, Babe, he's laughing at us."

Myers chuckled. Instead of following the traffic into the Zona Roja, he made an abrupt right turn on a corrugated dirt track that ran along the bank of the Tijuana River.

Sullivan's teeth chattered as the Impala vibrated violently. Below the embankment, the bed of the river was full of shanties made from the huge cardboard boxes that they shipped new refrigerators in. It was called Colonia Carto-

landia, and every winter the rains swept the shanties away,
drowning a few kids and drunks; and every spring, when the
riverbed was dry again, its desperate inhabitants rebuilt it.
Myers slowed to a crawl. Ahead they could make out the
dark outlines of a military jeep and a large fancy car. Myers
flashed his headlights. The searchlight mounted on the jeep
flashed back.

"Señor Inspector Gonzalez," Sullivan muttered.

They stopped and got out, brushing dust from their suits.
Three men approached—two young soldiers, expressionless
with M-1 carbines, and an older man, almost as tall as Myers
and strikingly handsome, in an impossibly expensive and
perfectly tailored Italian suit that you might buy in Rome or
maybe Beverly Hills, but definitely not in Tijuana or Smithtown.

"Señores Babe and Jimmy, Bienvenidos," he bellowed in
mocking politeness. "Welcome to my poor city."

Sullivan bit his lip, but Myers loved to watch Gonzalez in
action, Tijuana's de facto dictator and Smith's local ally. He
was doing his imitation of Mexicans he had seen played by
Italians pretending to be Mexicans in Hollywood pictures.

"So what service—por favor—may I provide to your
employer, Señor Smith?" Gonzalez's eyes twinkled. He
had preemptively cut the two detectives down to the size
of mere lackeys.

Sullivan reddened, but Myers took it in stride.

"I am told that you have an envelope that contains an
address of interest to Mr. Smith."

"Sí, and I am told you have an envelope that contains
something that will interest me." Gonzalez grinned.

Myers handed him $2,000, and Gonzalez handed back
Digiorgio's location. His partner showed the slip of paper to
Sullivan. A beach house in Rosarito. "Does he have backup?"

"Nothing that will spoil the evening for you and Señor Jimmy. Just two *chulos* with a shotgun and an old revolver. But would you like some professional assistance? Perhaps my jeep with a 50-caliber machine gun?"

Babe laughed. "You're very kind, Inspector, but Mr Smith wouldn't employ us if we couldn't button our own flies. We would appreciate, as usual, some help with garbage disposal."

"Does that include Señor Digiorgio?" Gonzalez's eyes sparkled.

"No, just the bodyguards. Digiorgio will come with us. We're inviting him on a fishing trip."

"Oh, yes, I remember now, Señor Babe, you are an avid fisherman. Perhaps one day we will go fish together. I like shark and barracuda best."

"So do I," smiled Myers. He shook Gonzalez's hand. Sullivan mumbled something that might have been polite or not. Gonzalez tipped his hat. The bi-national summit conference was over.

Myers turned the key in the Impala and it roared back. He waited for a moment to see if the Mexicans were going to move, and when it became apparent that they weren't, he began slowly backing up the narrow embankment.

8. THE DOUBLE DATE

Rosarito was only a half-hour drive and Sullivan could feel his adrenalin pumping. Then suddenly Myers braked to a stop and made a quick U-turn.

"What's wrong?"

"Don't sweat it, Jimmy, I got a swell idea."

"Yeah?" Sullivan was skeptical, as usual.

"Let's pick up some girls for the party at Digiorgio's."

Sullivan hovered at the verge of another "For Christ
sakes," but he was tired of being made foolish. "Why not? If
it makes you happy, Babe."

Myers slowly cruised the edge of the Zona Roja for a few
minutes, sizing up the local talent with the connoisseurship
of a vice cop. "Those two." He pulled over.

Pretty but very nervous sixteen-year-olds with too much
make-up.

"Poor kids, amateurs, probably from Cartolandia," Myers
mumbled. He pulled to the curb and got out. Sullivan
waited in the car.

The girls came back with Myers. They tried to smile,
but their nervousness bordered on terror. The big gringos
were obviously powerful, dangerous men—just the kind
their mothers had always warned about. On the other
hand, they were obviously rich and their car . . . well, *que
bonito*.

Myers ordered Jimmy in the back with "Soledad," and
Sullivan reluctantly complied, although he was very careful
to leave a good foot of space between them. The *pobrecita*
shrunk into her seat.

Babe, on the other, put his arm around "Lourdes" and
pulled her across the seat. He turned the radio to a loud local
channel and rolled down the roof. He let out a wild mariachi
cry and hugged Lourdes even closer. His insanity seemed
fun-loving, and the teenager laid her head on his arm and
giggled.

In the back seat Soledad dutifully snuggled closer to
Sullivan, who patted her, rather paternally, on the head.

"Hey, Jimmy, lay back and enjoy the drive," crooned
Myers. "Just pretend it's the summer of 1940, prom night,
and her name is Patricia."

Sullivan was incredulous. Here we are on the job, he thought, about to kill three men, or maybe get betrayed by Gonzalez and get whacked ourselves, and fuckin' Babe has turned it into a double date.

9. MURDER IS EASY

Digiorgio was bunkered in a big Miami Beach-style complex in the wealthiest part of Rosarito Beach. On one side was a well-known *marisco* joint favored by Tijuanenses; on the other was another large house, lit up like a Christmas tree with a live band blaring Perez Prado, perhaps for a *quinceañera*.

The tactical problem was considerable. A twelve-foot-high wall made assault from the rear difficult without more gear, while the busy restaurant and wild party in progress made attacks from the side impossible.

Myers told Jimmy to slide down in the back seat with Soledad. He took his hat and coat off, unbuttoned the top button of his shirt, and told Lourdes to bury her snout in his chest. He told both girls that their services would be needed only for a few minutes more, and that they would be well paid, and could return home with virginities intact. The girls were perplexed, but agreed.

Myers turned up the mariachi music even louder and slowly cruised past Digiorgio's expensive bolt-hole. One of the pimps that Gonzalez had mentioned was standing nervously by the gate, attempting to watch everything, and thus seeing nothing.

Babe brazenly pulled into the parking space directly in front of the house. The acne-faced guard, surprised, lurched a little, then pretended to avert his gaze.

"Kiss me, sweetheart," said Myers softly. Lourdes was confused. "Venga, besame mucho," Babe demanded. He pulled the girl to his lips and kept her there.

The guard was having a nervous breakdown trying to figure out who was in the car and what they were up to. He reached inside the gate and fondled the muzzle of the shotgun for reassurance. Then his nerve broke and he bolted for the house, leaving the gate open.

Instantly, Myers, who had been watching from the corner of his eye, pushed the girl away, threw some $20 bills at her and snorted "Get lost! Afuera!" He and Sullivan flew from the convertible.

At times like this, Myers was always astounded by his partner's instantaneous transformation from nagging old woman into a superb instinctive killer. It must have been all those nights on the 'canal waiting for the Japs to crawl into your foxhole or banzai you while you were taking a crap . . .

Sullivan caught the pimply-faced guard just inside the door of the house, and simply wrestled him to the floor and snapped his neck. Digiorgio's other bodyguard—older and overweight—came running right into Myers' silencer. Babe shot him in the mouth and again in the brain.

There was some gurgling and flopping around, some final passing of wind from dead men's rectums, then the house was silent.

Myers smiled and shook his head. "It shouldn't be this easy, Jimmy."

Sullivan just shrugged his shoulders as if to say, so what? He started to reach for his shoulder holster, but had second thoughts. Instead he pulled out the knife he kept in the scabbard taped above his left ankle. It had been standard issue to Carlson's Raiders.

He and Myers just sat quietly. Digiorgio was cowering somewhere upstairs, so they'd just wait patiently for him to make his move. The party din next door rattled the windows, and through the open door they could hear people drunkenly singing in the street.

10. THE INVITATION

Babe quickly grew bored. "Jimmy, I gotta check the car. If Digiorgio comes down the stairs, be kind. Don't cut his ears off or any of that other crap you learned on the 'canal."

Sullivan shrugged his shoulders. "I don't need any new souvenirs, but if you're so worried, don't be long."

The girls were gone, but the Impala's radio was still blasting *norteño* music. Babe turned the racket off, rolled up the roof, and locked the doors.

A good-looking middle-aged woman in a beach dress came outside from the party next door for a cigarette. She saw Myers and offered him one.

He accepted and lit them both. They small-talked for a minute or two, and she asked if he would like to join the party. They were a wealthy family from DF with *yanqui* friends, celebrating a nephew's graduation from San Diego State.

Myers explained that he was with a friend. Bring him, too, she said. Well, he could probably use some relaxation. They had some repair work left to finish—but maybe in another hour?

"Absolutely, this will go on late. I am Margarita O'Connell. And you?"

"Nixon, Edgar Nixon, mucho gusto." He shook her hand. "See you in a little while."

Myers returned to the house. The blood was still draining from the bodies, so Sullivan had dragged them into the kitchen.

Jimmy shot a look at Babe like, "Where in the fuck have
you been?"

It was Myers' turn to shrug his shoulders. He pulled out
another cigarette and lit it for Jimmy. He took two drags,
and suddenly Digiorgio was in front of them.

"Please, you guys, don't shoot!" Digiorgio whimpered.

"Relax, Angelo," Myers hardly looked at him. Sullivan
picked absent-mindedly at a nail with his Marine bowie
knife.

An interminable minute of silence and mental torture for
Digiorgio passed before Myers suddenly exclaimed, "Hey
Angelo, let's go upstairs and see your famous wardrobe."

"Huh?"

Sullivan grabbed Digiorgio by the elbow and pressed the
point of his knife into the small of his back.

They went upstairs.

"Quite a haberdashery," complimented Myers. "What
about shirts, Hawaiian shirts?"

"Yeah, we like Hawaiian shirts," echoed Sullivan.

For a moment, Digiorgio took them literally and opened
up a closet full of expensive sports shirts. He pulled out a
rack of the kind of monogrammed, flowered shirts that are
only sold in the men's store at the Royal Hawaiian Hotel.
Then the penny dropped.

"Oh," the trapped man said.

"Boy, aren't we eloquent tonight. Oh." Sullivan threw the
combat knife into the closet door about half a foot from
Digiorgio's head. It continued to quiver for almost a minute.

Digiorgio fell to his knees.

"Hawaiian shirt. How many negatives?"

"Eight," Digiorgio stammered.

"Well, Angelo, what kind of medieval shit is it gonna take
to get those negatives? The iron maiden, perhaps? Or maybe

some pliers and knife foreplay by my partner here. That's his specialty, you know."

Digiorgio was already a ghost. "Under the pillow."

"You're kiddin'!" snarled Sullivan. But he immediately found the briefcase.

"Go take a look," Myers told him.

Sullivan went into the bathroom and closed the door. He held each negative carefully up to the mirror. To his surprise, his hand didn't tremble, and the images—shit, who cared who ran the world? Four images were completely out of focus or smudged by light—worthless; but the others were gold bullion.

Sullivan went back into the bedroom. He nodded at Myers.

Myers exploded. He grabbed Digiorgio by the scruff of the neck, threw him on the bed and pushed the silencer of his 45 into his mouth, cracking several teeth.

"OK, slime fuck, where are the rest?"

Digiorgio went to pieces—blood trickling out of his mouth, snot out of his nose, tears out of his eyes. He shook convulsively. "That's all. I swear to God. That's all."

Myers looked at Sullivan. Sullivan looked at Myers.

"OK, I believe you," said Myers softly, and turned to browse amongst Digiorgio's myriad sports shirts. He picked out a rich Arnold Palmer and threw it on the bed next to Angelo's shivering mass.

"Try that on, Jimmy. We're going to the party next door. You need a drink and some fun."

Digiorgio suddenly tried to bolt for the door, but Sullivan smashed him to the floor. He and Myers bound and trussed him like a terrified deer.

"I don't want this fuck to spoil our evening." Myers went downstairs and out to the car. In the glove compartment he found the bottle of chloroform that they had borrowed from the county jail infirmary. He took it back upstairs.

"OK, Jimmy, keep your face away. This shit can cause a nasty headache." He spilled half the bottle onto one of Digiorgio's monogrammed handkerchiefs and held it over the prey's face. He went out in five seconds.

There was a Persian rug in a second bedroom, and they rolled Digiorgio up inside.

"OK, brace yourself. This fat fuck is heavy." They carried Digiorgio's mummy downstairs and into the small yard, behind the front wall.

Myers looked outside.

"Gonzalez's undertakers here yet?" asked Sullivan.

"Naw, they won't come until the morning," yawned Myers. Although the party next door was still going full bore and the restaurant was full of customers, the sidewalk was temporarily empty.

Myers opened the trunk of the Impala and ran back to help Jimmy brazenly lug Digiorgio to his temporary crypt. No one had seen them; or if they had, no one cared.

They returned to the bedroom. Sullivan put on the Arnold Palmer shirt, and Myers—insane as always—picked a Hawaiian shirt closely resembling Nixon's in the negatives.

The two left their blood-smeared coats and shirts on the bed.

"Check your pants."

Sullivan found a few splashes of pimp hemoglobin and applied a little cold water to the spots.

11. RIGOR MORTIS

"Edgar Nixon" and "Dick Hoover" thoroughly enjoyed themselves at the neighbors' party for an hour or two.

Someone asked about Señor Digiorgio. "Oh, he's on his dream fishing vacation," Myers offered pleasantly. "Won't be back for a long while."

One of the gringo guests—a middle-aged high-school principal—eyed Sullivan. "Mr. Hoover, I am sure we have met before. Are you an Elk?"

Sullivan recognized him as one of the johns that he and Myers had busted a few years ago in a raid on Mame Zell's in Banker's Hill. Quite a haul of ministers, teachers, and insurance salesmen in their skivvies. As usual, Smith had them sprung in return for their undying support.

"No, sorry, I am a Moose. But maybe we attended the same church in Banker's Hill." The principal blanched and excused himself to a far corner.

Eventually it was time for the two political impersonators to excuse themselves as well, although Myers managed to leave with Señora O'Connell's phone number in his pocket.

It was about 2 a.m., and the car lines at the border were full of drunken teenagers and sailors. Every so often a door would open and someone would barf on the last twenty yards of Latin America.

Myers was haggling with a street vendor over a black velvet painting of a huge-breasted naked woman when something started to thrash around in the trunk.

"Oh, shit!" said Sullivan.

Five minutes later they were at the Border Patrol booth. Digiorgio's exertions were now reaching a *grand mal* crescendo, and Sullivan was convinced that the heaving and thumping could be heard for blocks.

"Do you have something in the trunk, sir?" the nervous agent asked Myers.

"Cadavers always do that during rigor mortis," Babe observed matter-of-factly.

The agent's eyes bulged.

"He's pulling your leg, son." Sullivan leaned across and handed him an FBI badge. "There's nothing in the trunk, but we are in a hurry. Mr Hoover is expecting us in La Jolla."

The flabbergasted agent carefully examined the badge and then handed it back. "You can proceed immediately, sir."

Digiorgio made one last, heroic effort and dented the trunk with a mighty kick. But the Impala was already speeding north on 101, headed for Harbor Drive.

12. ON THE BRIDGE

It was half past three in the morning.

Babe's little gill-netter was the mascot of Smith's tuna fleet, and was moored next to his magnificent flagship, *Southern Cross*. Smith sometimes used the big clipper as a second office, and the lights were on in the bridge.

Myers backed the Impala out onto the pier and Sullivan opened the trunk. Digiorgio was raving and wild-eyed. Sullivan slapped him.

"Buck up. Better not slobber on Smith. He's not in a good mood."

Getting Angelo up to the bridge of the *Southern Cross* was like trying to coax a condemned coward to the gallows. Ultimately they just carried him. They started to dump their captive at Smith's feet, but he motioned them to deposit him instead in the corner.

Smith, hawklike and thin, wearing a yellow windbreaker and a blue commodore's cap, was sitting at the chart table. He poured Jimmy and Babe each a full shot glass of J.D.

"To your health," Smith toasted them.

Myers handed his boss the briefcase. "The original negative is inside as well."

Smith pulled out the negatives, counted them one-to-nine, and laid them across the glass-topped chart table.

"Are you sure this is the whole kit and caboodle, Babe?"

"Absolutely, Mr Smith. Jimmy terrorized poor Angelo's imagination a little with his stunt knife. He's not holding out. This is the lot."

"Excellent." Smith flipped a toggle and the photos were illuminated from below.

He studied them with a deep frown. "Who could have suspected? To think that bastard actually has the power to compel Dick to degrade himself like this."

"Happens all the time in prison." Sullivan instantly realized he should have kept his trap shut. Smith's father, after all, had died in prison.

Smith's face twitched. "Yes. The ultimate submission of slave to master, ruled to ruler." Smith was still peering over the photos. "A future president—my president—at Hoover's feet. I have never seen anything so disgusting."

Smith poured himself another shot. "Well, Babe, what do you think the Boy Scouts will make of these pictures?"

"About the same as the Daughters of the American Revolution or the Knights of Columbus. Lincoln's jaw will probably drop off Mount Rushmore."

"You've been on vice too long, Babe," Smith chided.

"Yeah, but catching the mayor in bed with a hooker is a little different from seeing the Vice President punked by the Top Cop."

"Indeed," said Smith. "This wouldn't be scandal. This would be the end of the country."

He turned sharply to Sullivan. "You both realize that, don't you?"

Sullivan met Smith's gaze straight-on. "We've carried the flag, Mr Smith. You know that."

Smith softened and smiled. "Why, of course you have. You boys are heroes. And as distasteful as you may find tonight's work, it was just as necessary as anything you did during the war."

Smith walked across the bridge. He craned his neck over Digiorgio's slumped figure and then gently squeezed one of his shoulders. He turned back to Myers and Sullivan.

"Angelo and I have been together for almost thirty years. He never had any real talent, just a small-time chiseler and gigolo, but he was loyal and I elevated him far above his natural station. I now see the enormity of my mistake."

Digiorgio was conscious but inanimate, making no response, offering no defense.

"Yes, he reeks of doom and decay, boys. Better to put this fish in the water quickly."

Myers poured the rest of the chloroform on a new handkerchief.

"But you do understand this is patriotism, not business?"

Sullivan wanted to retch. Smith had no more scruples than a moray eel. Nixon was simply a lucrative investment, like his tuna fleet, call girls, and racetrack.

"Yes, sir, for the Boy Scouts," Babe smiled as he again gagged Digiorgio with the chloroform.

"Make sure no one sees you on the way down. Thanks boys. And remember, no more mortgage payments. You've just paid off the principal."

Myers winked, and Sullivan doffed his hat as usual. A gesture that could be interpreted in two ways.

13. THE FISHING TRIP

The breakwater beacon blinked at them while a buoy cried in the distance. A tired Navy garbage scow trundled by. But the new diesel (courtesy of the Broadway hopheads) in Myers' little boat scooted it along at a smart speed. The bow was slapping the water like an expensive speedboat.

"Ain't this the life of Riley?" Myers exulted at the wheel.

"Must be, Babe. First the queer convertible, then the two little girls, now the fuckin' boat. Obviously your idea of heaven." Sullivan, true to his word, was about to lose his dinner.

Digiorgio, mercifully anesthetized, was stowed in a huge Marine sea bag.

"Come on, Babe, let's dump him now."

"Not a chance," Myers laughed. "He'd just wash up in front of the Del Coronado, with crabs crawlin' outta his ears. Then those society bitches would be pukin', not you."

Sullivan gave his partner a deadly look.

"Come on, Jimmy. Go below. Sack out. I'll wake you when we get to Iwo Jima."

Sullivan went below, climbed into the bunk and immediately fell into a fitful sleep. He dreamt he was back in a Higgins boat, skirting the surf break off a claustrophobic coral beach, hemmed in by decaying mangroves. Star flares turned night to day, and Japanese tracer rounds skipped across the water until they found their range. The face of the handsome young Marine next to him disintegrated.

"Hey, Jimmy, come on, we're there." Myers was shaking him.

Sullivan grimaced and rubbed his eyes; to his surprise, his nausea was gone.

It was dawn and the sea was furrowed with alternate swales of velvet and blue. The boat was facing the huge, brooding cliff of a small island. From nearby rocks, sea lions barked at them to leave.

"Where the hell are we?"

"North Coronado—the leeward side, where we're invisible."

Los Coronados were wild-looking skerries twenty miles offshore of Tijuana. But their nationality was often mistaken by sailors, and during World War II, L. Ron Hubbard, the future founder of Scientology, caused a small diplomatic crisis by ordering the crew of his destroyer escort to open fire on the Mexican Marines he had mistaken for Japanese on South Island.

Jimmy looked at Digiorgio; he was starting to thrash around again.

"The poor fuck's awake again. He's probably had a worse nightmare than I did."

Myers frowned. "Yeah, this is no longer much fun. I am beginning to feel sorry for the tormented bastard. Let's do this quick."

With a deftness that suggested practice, they wrapped rope and chain around the sea bag and attached a 100-pound boat anchor. It took some time, however, to manhandle both Digiorgio and all the heavy metal over the side.

"So tell me," grunted Sullivan, "why did we have to come all the way out here? What's so special about this spot?"

Myers sucked in air, dead-lifted the anchor, and heaved it over the side. "Biggest damn barracuda I've ever seen," he gasped. "Seriously, right here."

Jimmy smirked, but as he watched the chain-weighted sea bag sinking, something that looked like a small whale suddenly struck at Digiorgio, then both disappeared from sight.

"Holy fuck!" Jimmy jumped back from the rail.

"See what I mean?" said Myers triumphantly. "Monster barracuda."

14. THE STING

It took two hours to return to port. Jimmy wasn't seasick any longer, but he was still in a black mood. Each man tried to give the other some space. One of Smith's regal tuna clippers passed by, bound for the Galapagos.

Myers decide to try some humor. "Did you know Smith's cannery mixes barracuda and dog fish with the albacore and calls it all tuna?"

"Fuck Smith," Sullivan grumbled.

"Yeah, Jimmy, that's exactly what we've done. We've fucked Smith."

"What do you mean? He's got his goddamn Nixon photos. Digiorgio will soon be a can of tuna. Come on, we're just day labor. For ten years we've sucked that arrogant bastard's dick."

"Not this time, Jimmy. Go below and look in the little galley."

Sullivan found a large manila envelope. Inside was one of the Nixon negatives—the clearest of those they had confiscated in Digiorgio's house. Sullivan was astonished.

"How, Babe?"

"Simple sleight of hand, Jimmy. I just substituted a bad negative of one of those blackmail photos we keep on Mame Zell's. Probably the goddamn school principal back in Rosarito. Too blurred to tell one way or another."

Sullivan suddenly gushed. "Look, I am sorry I've been such a pain in the ass."

"Don't get sentimental, Jimmy. It was more fun surprising you."

"So how do we play this? What do we do next?"

"Not much. Let Smith pay off our mortgages and clean up the Digiorgio mess. We'll wait. Maybe next year, when Hoover returns to the races, or if Nixon becomes president. Or when we're ready to trade in our wives for some sixteen-year-old whores, or when we're simply too sick of wading in filth. We'll know when the time's right. Meanwhile, this is a million in the bank."

"Yeah, I suppose we now own the fuckin' Republican Party," said Sullivan, with some awe.

15. THE LEGEND

Director Hoover ended his annual vacation the next day, and flew back to D.C. for a secret meeting with the President about the Communist subversion of the civil rights movement. He had big plans for unmasking Martin Luther King, Jr., and the other Negroes in the pay of the Kremlin.

Meanwhile, a week went by before anyone noticed Digiorgio's absence. Smith called in some auditors, and there were soon rumors that his security director had fled the country with a trunk full of stocks and bonds.

Smith finally asked the police to investigate, and then the FBI. A warrant was issued for Digiorgio but he was never apprehended. Cleverly instigated reports appeared nearly every year, sustaining the myth that he was hiding out in Mexico, or working for Somoza in Nicaragua. No one suspected that he was just a tuna salad sandwich somewhere.

Myers and Sullivan, for their part, were promoted to the homicide squad, but Jimmy was killed one afternoon in June 1960. He was standing at the corner of Market and Eighth, across from Victory Liquor Store, talking to two Negro patrolmen from the Logan Heights detail. They were arguing over the odds on the Patterson-Johannson rematch, when Sullivan noticed a young white couple emerging from the liquor store. The male hesitated when he saw the cops across the street.

Sullivan recognized him instantly. It was Floyd Meriwether, the punk from Kansas who had been murdering his way across the Southwest for two weeks. The kid fired wildly, winging one of the black cops, before Sullivan nailed him with a slug square in the forehead.

No one paid attention to the girl. In the press accounts, she was Meriwether's hostage. In fact, she was his girlfriend and muse. She shot Sullivan in the groin with the sawed-off shotgun that she kept concealed under her coat. He bled to death before the ambulance arrived.

The loss of his long-time partner grieved Myers, but it also bought him sympathetic attention in the local press. After the elections the following June, the new mayor (another Smith bagman) appointed Babe interim police chief.

His star soared, and by the mid-Sixties he was the second most powerful man in the city. In 1968 he was a Nixon delegate at the Republican National Convention. A year later, he brutally quelled a small riot in Logan Heights, and there was talk that he might be Governor Reagan's next attorney general.

But Babe was content with the throne he possessed. He now owned a yacht that had once belonged to the Chicago gangster Johnny Rosselli, and had remarried a rich heiress from Mexico (Margarita Ramirez, ex-O'Connell).

In 1970 an overzealous DA tried to indict the mayor and most of the city council for a payback scam involving the local cab franchise. Myers undermined the investigation with the help of the Nixon Justice Department.

Six months later, while struggling to reel in a huge marlin off Los Coronados (some said it was actually a barracuda), he had a catastrophic heart attack. He died a few days later in Mercy Hospital.

Vice President Agnew attended Myers' funeral at Rosecrans National Cemetery, and was photographed consoling Margarita. At exactly the same moment, some of the future Watergate burglars were turning Babe's house upside-down. But they didn't find the negative.

Maybe it didn't really matter. In the aftermath of Watergate, and the parallel scandal that exposed Smith as one of the greatest swindlers in American history, there were no virgin Boy Scouts left to worry about.

Yet, periodically, the old rumor resurfaces. An older cop tells his rookie partner a story that he, in turn, had been told as a rookie; or a cub reporter is taken under the wing of a veteran of the city desk, who confidentially recalls a tale he once heard from one of Smith's pimps.

Whatever the provenance, the recounting of the legend always has the same beginning: "Once upon a time there were two cops, angry war heroes named Babe and Jimmy. And there was this photograph. Actually, a negative . . ."

THE LEGEND OF BAYBOY
AND THE MEXICAN SURFER

John Shannon

It's no longer possible to tell a single story as if it's the only one.

John Berger

Brandon "Twitch" Dedrick finds the strange beige window-envelope from the county health department on the hall table in his parents' house above Lunada Bay, Palos Verdes, at the exact moment in time that 670 miles southeast, Jaime Olivares gets himself booted off the chicken ranch where he works in Huépac, Sonora, for calling the *patrón* a *gran pendejo* to his face, which isn't really that much stronger than calling him a big jerk, but still.

He folds the envelope and sticks it into his pocket, and then walks into the kitchen where his mom is stuffing Oreos into her mouth, brown crumbs dribbling all around her. Jesus. It's been like this since his dad left. She's already puffing up toward Shelley Winters-ville.

"You're lucky to be so thin," she says. "But it's a lot of unnecessary crap."

"It's smoking dope keeps me light on my feet. You ought to try it." He does a little tap dance toward the fridge to get a Corona. A hit of crack would help her, too, he thinks. Some meth. Any upper, anything but the endless G-and-Ts, each with its goddamn sprig of mint. He's begun to hate the nose-wrinkly smell of mint.

"Make me a gin-mint, Sweet Brand."

"That stuff's poison."

"Will you play Scrabble with me later?" A peacock screams somewhere outside, the Palos Verdes plague. Brandon Dedrick is one week short of sixteen years old and is the unofficial leader of the Bayboys, a group that is well into its third generation of keeping the best surfing spot in California for locals only, by whatever means necessary.

"Tide's at six-oh-six and there's a weak onshore so it won't be blown off. I gotta go out with the guys."

"Just one game. And what about your lessons?"

Everybody up on the Hill has to have lessons. Tennis, dance, piano, whatever. He's quit the violin months ago but she doesn't know it. "Gotta represent, mom. The damn surfline is announcing eight footers here."

He digs through the chest in the back room he shares with three sisters and his little brother, who sleep every which way on the two old mattresses on the floor. His father has been dead just a year, found too late by the *Migra* on the edge of Organ Pipe Cactus National Monument, Arizona, during a five-day run of unseasonal 100-degree-plus weather. The family learned that his fellow migrants argued hard with the coyote against leaving the foot-lamed Santiago, but in the end they gave him most of their water and hurried on to highway 85, where a truck was waiting.

There isn't much in the way of necessaries for Jaime to collect into the little backpack.

"*Mijo!* Why did you insult Don Ignacio?" His mother stands in the doorway, brown, round, almost breaking his heart with her cross-armed look, both hangdog and accusing at once.

How can he tell her that Don Ignacio insisted he recruit his sister Maricruz to work as a maid in the *patrón's* house? Don Ignacio, the town boss. His household is famous all over Huépac for losing its *mozas* one after another, and Jaime is pretty sure he knows why.

"He began with me, mother."

"You're too hot-headed."

"You know I'm not. I am a rock. I will always have my control. It's just my turn to go to *el norte* for us now."

He doesn't say "Father can't do it any more," but they both hear it and they cross themselves.

"It was about Maricruz, wasn't it?"

He chooses the cleanest of his socks from the dresser and rolls them and piles them in on the white Jockeys.

"*Mijo*, wait," his mother insists. "You think because you speak good *Inglés* and you know maths and I am ignorant, that I'm simple. Nothing is simple in *la vida*."

That gets his attention and he squats on his heels, waiting, a little shamed. He has, just then, thought her a little simple, rural, *una pueblerina*.

"*No seas inhumano y ten caridad que el dios de los cielos te lo premiará*." Don't be inhuman, and have charity, and God in heaven will reward you. It's a line from the *Posadas* reenactment of Joseph and Mary's search for refuge that every Mexican knows by heart.

"Yes, mother."

He notices that she has begun to cry. "How do you think we bought tortillas and beans when your father was gone the last time and couldn't send money?" she asks.

Jaime feels a terrible chill on his spine, but he doesn't know why.

"Don't blame Don Ignacio. I went to him of my own free will. You must learn this—it means nothing at all if you feel nothing."

From the top of the cliff Brandon can see that several of the girls have come out to watch because they've heard there are going to be some good sets, and they are arrayed on the regulation Bill Blas towels, catching the setting sun. It's 100 feet down but he can also see the double line of surfers waiting turns, the regulars positioned for the best take-off and the outsiders in a line-up that has somehow been elbowed to one side and is being ignored in the rotation. He saw the sheriff's car parked up on Paseo when he carried his board across the street, and he can see Deputy "Dawg" Gordon with his hands on his hips nearby, watching the scene developing below.

"Twitch," Gordon calls when he notices Brandon. "No trouble tonight, *please*. I don't feel like climbing all the way down there."

"Sure thing, Dawg. We'll just have to leave those ol' grommets alone."

"I swear to you, kid. If I catch the Bayboys harassing anybody I'll get a meatball planted on this beach for the rest of the year." The meatball is a yellow flag with a black circle that means surfing is banned.

"Mondo, dawg."

He trots down the narrow diagonal path toward the half-mile-wide crescent bay that has an offshore deep rock formation guaranteeing some of the best surf in North America, rivaled only by North Trestles on the edge of Camp Pendleton.

"Hey there, Twitch," one of the girls calls as he walks past their encampment.

37

THE LEGEND OF BAYBOY

"Look at all the Vals," one of the other girls puts in mischievously.

As he paddles out, a real chore against the growing surf, he hears Rabbit challenging one of the Vals, ". . . Don't any of you fuckers drop in on one of our pounders. You can take the betweens."

"Next time, we'll come armed, you horse-fuckers," the Val replies. "It's a free country."

"Dude," Twitch says softly. He breaks up the confrontation and beckons over a handful of the boys into a small bobbing conference on the darkening water. "Deputy Dawg is up there." He doesn't have to remind them they're under a court order. "It's Viet Cong night. I'd suggest drawing straws, if we had straws, and we already know who's got the longest dick, so I guess it's rock-paper-scissors." One-by-one they work their way down the elimination until it's either Brandon or Ledge. The Legend, a fifty-year-old surfer who looks like he's made of nothing but rubber bands under a taut burned sheet of rubber, their last link to the earlier generations of Bayboys.

"I'll do it, Ledge," Brandon says.

"Fuck you, gremmie. I do my share. Slap hands."

The task does fall to Brandon, as Ledge's scissors cut his paper. He smiles and they all part to let him ride the next decent break in. He plants his board with the girls. They'll say he was there all night.

On top it isn't hard to avoid the dimwit deputy. Brandon knows which cars belong on Paseo and which have been driven up here by Vals. Technically the term Vals refers to anyone who lives far up in the uncool landlocked San Fernando Valley, but to them it means anyone who hasn't grown up on the west-facing slope of Palos Verdes.

He has his Swiss Army Knife open to the awl, and he grits his teeth at the screech as he drags it along the green paint of a Chevy station wagon. Then a BMW SUV gets punched in the side of a tire, and hisses down like an elephant falling to one knee.

"Who spika English?" says the guy watching the loungers at the *mosca* skeptically out the window of the full-size GMC pickup. Several day-laborers hurry forward from the driveway of the Home Depot.

"Me here, boss."

"I spik good. You take me."

"No problema, boss."

Jaime saunters up behind the others who are bobbing and clamoring at the truck window. "I'm the man you want, sir. There won't be any misunderstandings."

The man with the moustache shoves a laborer's head out of the way and looks straight at Jaime. "What's your name, kid?"

"Jamey," he says with the hard English J. "Easy to remember, easy to pronounce."

"Can you do fieldstone? It's heavy work and I want them fitted properly. Twelve dollars an hour for good work. Less if you're sloppy or slow."

"Sure, I can do it."

He's beckoned into the cab and goes around. There is no sass from the unwanted *jornaleros*. The etiquette is to accept the *patrón*'s decision gracefully. Only at a couple of city-sponsored hiring centers is there a proper dispatcher.

"I'm Mike." He doesn't offer his roughened hand. "We got us a great contract. Lady even brings out lemonade and sandwiches. Let's not F it up. Last of you guys didn't know his left from his right."

"Left," Jaime says, holding up his left hand. "Right."

They drive for a while down toward Palos Verdes. The truck has a tangled crucifix dangling from the rear-view mirror, but Jaime doesn't get his hopes up. Prudently he stays silent. He thinks instead of the look on Don Ignacio's face when he hit him unexpectedly with the stone, and the way the man's eyes rolled up to whites all at once. It was not satisfying at all. There should have been a time of begging. He has not confessed it yet, and he wonders if he will. What American priest would understand?

"It's really Jaime, ain't it?" Mike puts in eventually with a sly look, pronouncing it almost right, *hi-me*.

"It goes either way."

"Know why you guys will never run out of names? After José, you always got Hose-B, Hose-C, Hose-D, like forever."

Jaime smiles grimly. After Mike, you've got Spike, Bike and Dyke, he thinks. But he needs the money. "That's real funny, man."

"We'll get along fine. I like a guy who's not sensitive as shit."

It appears they are collecting fieldstone on the sly, driving around the back way to a dormant quarry where someone has broken the lock on a gate. He's mildly surprised to see that Mike does his share of boosting the heavy stones into the truck. Then they drive to a very large white ranch house set back from the cliffs over the ocean. There are many houses like this here, all of them big and obsessively tidy. Jaime Olivares knows it's complicated why there's so much money here and so little at home, but it doesn't mean he doesn't think about the question.

Mike backs up a driveway and then onto a ragged patch of lawn in back. They're apparently building a long retaining wall behind the house, a true retaining wall to hold back a steep slope. He hopes Mike knows what he's doing and is building it wide enough at the base. Jaime once watched the construction of a rock-fill dam outside Huépac, and they laid out the bottom of the dam amazingly wide and sturdy. This wall has just been started and still requires a lot of pick and shovel work into the slope. He can see that's going to be his job for now.

The first day, the lady seems to forget about the lemonade and sandwiches and at one o'clock Mike snaps, "Burger and Coke okay with you?" He doesn't wait for an answer before driving off.

Jaime wonders if he should keep working, but he's exhausted, and he drifts out front and then wanders across the road and along a path to the edge of the cliff where there is a delicious breeze off the glorious Pacific to dry the sweat off him. Below, a dozen surfers are bobbing on their boards behind where the waves seem to rise. He watches as one paddles fast ahead of a wave and then comes gracefully to his feet on a short board. The boy balances the oval magnificently as he scoots along just ahead of where the wave breaks. Jaime has heard of surfing, of course, but never seen it before. Like a child witnessing the grace of a backhoe being worked well for the first time, he is captivated.

He is still rapt by the amazing display of agility, reminding him of his happy days on the village soccer pitch, when Mike shows up and finds him. He's carrying a big white McDonald's bag. "I'll take $3.70 off your pay," Mike grudges as he portions out the food.

They sit on the cliff edge to eat, a good 100 feet above the green-blue ocean. Tomorrow, if there is a tomorrow, Jaime will bring something of his own to eat.

"Little surf shitheads," Mike says, watching the next lithe, suntanned boy take off on a wave. "I bet the prick that lives in our house is down there and never offers to help his mom fix anything."

"Do the rich ever work here?" Jaime says.

"Hah. You got it, *amigo*. How come your English is so good."

Jaime shrugs. "I read books."

"Good for fucking you."

Brandon is over at Condor's house playing video games when he finds the envelope in his pocket that he's completely forgotten, and it gives him a chill. "Pause it, dude."

"Hey, I'm creaming you."

"I said, pause, or I'll have to pound your ass."

He finger-slits the envelope raggedly. Some official gobbledygook he can barely make out. He tries it again slowly. Nancy Reid. He isn't sure he remembers the name but she might have been the chick he hooked up with at Rabbit's party. Has named him as a correspondent. What the fuck does that mean? He doesn't write letters to anybody.

Nancy has tested positive for HIV. Shit, too bad for her. But he had her blow him and then he fucked her, normal-like. Guys don't get it that way. Everybody knows it's a fag disease and you only get it from ass-fucking. Or sharing meth needles, like tweakers. Advisable that he be tested as soon as possible. Not probable but highly advisable to be safe.

The sound of life goes out for a moment and he doesn't hear Condor talking to him as prickly bugs run up and down his arms. This is bullshit. Why are they trying to scare him like this? He's not a queer. He doesn't even think about being a queer much. Must be a mistake.

He looks on the back of the letter, and it's his name all right where it once showed through the little celluloid window. Who told them he was a fag?

"Muévese." Technically it's his turn for the mattress, but he can see Victor is so exhausted he's unwakable. Jaime is sharing the one bedroom on 135th Street in Hawthorne with five other day-laborers. Izek is the renter of record and they each promise to pay him $134 a month. They also kick in if they need to borrow Izek's 1963 Oldsmobile, a real smoker, to get to some special job. Jaime has the right side of the bottom shelf in the old fridge for his beer and milk and the huge open can of frijoles he's bought at Smart and Final. He nudges Victor to the side and sits wearily.

"*Compa,*" Izek says, looking in. "Hang out with me Sunday. You're an educated man."

"You going to a opera?"

"Just the mall. We can watch girls and look at stuff."

Like looking at the rich man's world through three panes of bulletproof glass, Jaime thinks, but he doesn't say it. He likes Izek and it will be a change. And maybe they can make a run through the dumpsters behind the mall. He's learned you can get amazing stuff that way. *Gabachos* throw away anything if it displeases them.

"I just want the damn test. Are you going to call my mom?" He stood up as if to leave.

"Calm down, son. Is there any reason you want to be tested? Do you have any risk factors?"

"I sat on a dirty toilet seat. Man, another word from you and I'm out of here."

"Don't worry, it's all completely confidential. The law requires it that way."

"Just stick me. Jesus, how many ways can I tell you to stop treating me like a pussy. I don't suck dicks, I don't needle myself. I just want the test."

"Of course. I'll get it myself so the nurse doesn't have to know. You princelings pretty much get things the way you want, don't you?"

"You said it, doc."

They sit on a bench eating things called tacos that aren't. They are some strange U-shaped sandwich wrapped in massive sheets of wax paper. The ingredients have no flavor at all and the hard shell keeps snapping unexpectedly and letting big chunks of the food spall away in Jaime's hands. Izek empties packet after packet of what's called "super-Mex" salsa over his to give it some flavor.

"I confess. Sorry, Jaime. I made you get the Superama Taco as a trick. I knew it was *mierda*."

Jaime wraps the paper over twice and crumbles the whole mess up inside, pounding it on the bench, then he tries to scoop likely looking foodstuffs off the paper with a chunk of the shell.

"Next time the burrito. It's acceptable."

"*Claro*, pal."

"Hey, eyes up."

Two Latinas in short shorts saunter past, the closer one glancing slyly toward them and wriggling a little.

"*Qué transas, chicas?*"

The girls laugh dismissively. "Come back and see us," one says in emphatic English, "when you've got the cowshit off your boots." They think that's hilarious.

"I'm not wearing boots," Jaime calls. "But I can kick your impolite asses."

They giggle and hurry away.

"I'd like to do something else to those asses," Izek says.

"They can tell we're new, eh?" Jaime says.

"Of course. So what? Their *pocho* Spanish sucks when they even try to use it. El churcho. El trucko. Huacho out!" They dump the unmanageable remains of their meals in a barrel and stroll down the wide hallway. Jaime has been attracted for some time by a long storefront in the distance that says SURF CITY. As they near, he can hear the sound of water and squeals of delight, like boys roughhousing. Dark windows along the side of the mall allow dozens of boys in the hallway to peer into a long pool of water, painted with dolphins and starfish. At one end is what looks like the paddle wheel of an old steamship and a lot of blue plaster scooped up in the air like a wave. Two boys in neon-colored baggies wait in the water on their short boards in front of the paddle until a bell rings, and then they start paddling hard. The machine chugs ponderously to life and the pusher swings around to send a big frothy wave after them. One boy flounders but the other gets to his feet and rides along for about two-thirds the length of the pool. Before jumping off he throws out his arms and howls.

"Ay, *que padre!* I want to do that."

"You see any *carnales* in there, friend?"

Two more surf kids paddle up, the bell rings, and they're off. Both get to their feet successfully, and he sees now that the machine is designed so the wave runs at a bit of an angle and the farthest boy rides a little ahead. It isn't much of a wave compared to what he's seen at Lunada Bay, too frothy and narrow and only a half-meter high. On the next ride both boys survive to the end and kneel down successfully to slap palms as the wave peters out.

"Let's go, man. This is *gabacho* stuff. Maybe I'll get a new shirt at the Macy's."

45

On the way home, Jaime has Izek stop the car in the alley roughly behind Surf City where, with a lifting heart, he sees a familiar white oval shape poking out of the dumpster. First he notices the scars where the lid has closed on it, cutting right across a billow of flames someone has painted down one side. Then he lifts the lid and tugs it out and sees that part of the back end has snapped off. It's as if a giant knife has pared away about a hand's width of the surfboard from the middle to the rear. Beneath the shiny hard white rind, like some weird fruit, it's foamy and rough.

"Come on, man. That's all *desmadre*. It's no good no more."

Jaime bellies up on the dumpster and digs some more through the cardboard and rotting food. Miraculously, exulting, he finds the broken piece. A small shape is still missing, but it almost fits. "*Mi plancha de surf*," he says softly. "I'll be your doctor."

"You were really shredding, Twitch hon," Mavis says, touching his arm flirtatiously.

"We were all shredding," Brandon says. What he remembers, in fact, is dropping in too fast and screaming into the wind as he barely avoided wiping out.

They've had a storm ocean all day. The water feels thicker and heavier than usual, suddenly icy at times. The surge is powerful and quick when it comes, wonderful for carving and riding fancy if you're ready, lifting your heart like good dope. But now there's an offshore wind blowing it all off and they've retreated to the beach for beer and hotdogs. Fires aren't allowed but the towel girls have bought a battery-operated hotdog cooker, like a big toaster, to service their men, and it's wired up to a car battery.

"Picture this," Rabbit says. "Twitch has got himself amped and he's scuttling along like a crab from lowland car to lowland car, letting the air out of every fucking tire."

Brandon can picture very little beside some horrid cartoon pathogen, with an evil grin and big pointy teeth, multiplying itself in his bloodstream and then biting down on whatever it finds. He has a sense that he should understand something now that he has never understood before, but that sense flees and leaves the lonely silence. People around him are speaking but he doesn't hear them.

"Hooray for Twitch!"

"Mexicans, lowlanders, trolls, idiots, fags, *Vals*—our savior keeps us safe from all the dickheads."

"You can spot a Val anywhere."

"Neon trunks."

"Colored wetsuit."

"Mullet haircut." The game builds.

"Rusty old car."

"With bumper stickers!"

Rabbit shudders—"And a wimpy bungee cord safety line on his board."

They all groan and whimper and eek and roll about in the sand.

"You don't show off," Ledge announces gravely.

"You ride well," the guys all intone.

"And you don't fall off," the girls respond.

They all slap hands in the middle like some ancient ritual pledge. Brandon understands the coda and takes part, but his mind is frozen and elsewhere, in a kind of paralyzing terror. Pop, why have you gone so far away. I'm sixteen and I'm scared.

Luckily the fieldstone job with Mike has gone on and on, though Mike has not become much friendlier and usually eats alone now, or with the chubby woman who owns the house and is obviously coming on to him. Every day Jaime finds some time to walk across and watch the surfers below the cliff. He's seen the surf at Hermosa Beach now, and at Manhattan Beach, and he knows this is the very best.

Three doors up from where he lives on 135th Street is a man who is always working on his old car, and he has tools. Jaime has ingratiated himself so he can borrow the drill. At a local True Value Hardware store he has bought three long lag bolts and a bottle of Gorilla Glue. He drills the holes in his surfboard as far as the bits will reach, and then widens and deepens them with a fine rat-tail file. He makes much bigger holes for the hex-heads of the lag bolts. Then he dribbles some of the glue in each hole and tightens it together with a borrowed socket set. He is not a skilled workman and it doesn't match exactly, but all his life he has been able to correct misfits with a little sandpaper and patience.

"Ay, *que cochina!*" the car mechanic says. What a mess.

"It's strong," he insists. But as he sands it down so the edges feather neatly together, Jaime finds he abrades right through the strong outer surface. In the end he has to buy resin and fiberglass tape, and he covers the seam and the bolt holes with several layers. He doesn't know about putting pigment in the resin, so it remains transparent and the whole mess beneath shows through.

"But it's strong," he still insists. How many times in his life has he played football on a dirt pitch with a tied bundle of rags or even tied up newspaper? It's the player's skill that matters.

He keeps the repaired surfboard in the bedroom for a week, working up his nerve. Another trip to the mall with Izek teaches him that the Surf City machine costs $25 an hour and on a busy day he might not get more than a dozen rides, very little like the real ocean. He's just going to have to practice in front of God and all the *gabacho* surfers. But not in front of Izek. He cuts off a pair of jeans just above the knee, and on Sunday he carries his surfboard five-and-a-half miles under his arm to Manhattan Beach.

The surf is minimal, maybe a foot. He sits on the sand and picks out the boys who seem to ride best, watching carefully what they do. Finally he caries the board into the water.

"Mexicans stay over by the pier!" somebody calls threateningly, but he ignores it. Paddling out through the break he finds the waves a lot stronger than he thought. He can even hear sand and shells grating against the bottom. Out beyond the break he goes off by himself, where the surf is poorer, and he makes his own lineup so he can go whenever he wants. He sees a wave approaching from far out there, rising. *Uno . . . dos . . . tres.* He paddles hard and it's starting to break as he catches it. His board spits forward then turns sideways. He clings hard, still on his stomach, and straightens the board by brute arm strength, then fights to his feet. The board whips back and forth like the tail of some beached fish but he manages to stay on his feet, flailing his arms, then maybe a second or two of decent riding that makes him cry out in joy. The board flips at the end and tosses him off, but he doesn't care. He's done it.

LABORATORY REPORT Confidential

		Req No NA	Room	DOB 11/16/90	Fasting	Supv
		Date Col 11/20	Draw NG	Chart ID	Reptd	Spec No

Pat Name Brandon Dedrick	Age 16	Sex M	Provider Dr. M. Girard	Received 11/22/06	Reported 11/28/06

Test Name	Result Out of Range Reference Loc
HIV-1 AB, Elisa	Reactive

Note: This is a positive test, indicating the presence of antibodies to HIV in your blood. There are a small percentage of false positives. We recommend a retest as soon as possible, using an alternative method.

Jaime discovers that the bus along Manhattan Beach Blvd. has a rack for surfboards at the back, and he begins spending every weekend and most evenings at the beach. He knows that he is getting better when they stop yelling "Mexican" at him and stop making fun of his ugly board. He also discovers that a normal surfboard has two or three of the fin-like skegs at the rear. His has only one, off center. Something else that broke off at the mall. But already he is learning to compensate, standing with his weight to one side. One of the better surfers smiles at him toward the end of one day and nods a private acknowledgment. Jaime hopes the thumbs-up doesn't have some sinister meaning here.

Brandon sits on the edge of the cliff. The bay below is deserted, the water a slaty gray. The day is cold and rainy and the surf not worth putting on a wetsuit, and apparently everyone has a life elsewhere. Except him. He barely sees the water, can hardly keep his thoughts centered for more than a few seconds. After seeing some tearjerk movie a year or so ago, he tried to imagine being told he was going to die, and the Brandon he was then wanted to do everything fast, before it was too late. He wanted to fly to Hawaii and see the big surf at the North Shore, at Sunset, Waimea—even South Africa and Jeffreys Bay. He wanted to fly around the whole world, burn up his inheritance on exotic drinks and girls. Treat his friends. Drop his face into a big pile of blow like Pacino in *Scarface*.

But it was all wrong.

He wants nothing at all. The world is dull, gray like the sky. Empty. There is no future waiting for him. Why do anything? He hasn't told a soul, certainly not his mother. He can't bear telling his dad on the weekly call. He knows he isn't going to take some mass of drugs that will make him

sick. He won't admit to anyone that he has the fag disease.
When the time comes he will go out quick as a wink. Gun,
drugs, or off the cliff. But he can't even imagine that. Just icy
nothing.

He barely hears the car cough once and stop behind him
on Paseo del Mar, then the footsteps. One of the Bayboys
with more desire than sense. It might be Rabbit or Flea, or
even Ledge. At least someone to banter with for a few
moments and make him forget.

He looks up and is astonished to see a Mexican in cut-off
jeans carrying under his arm one of the ugliest broken
surfboards he has ever seen. It's like seeing a zebra trotting
into church. The young Mexican is ten feet down the path
before Brandon calls out.

"Hey, Mex, where the *fuck* do you think you're going?"

The Mexican stops and takes a moment before he looks
back, like Clint Eastwood in some Big Moment. "I'm going
down to surf."

"You know you don't belong here. Go home."

They stare at each other for almost thirty seconds.

"I've been working on the wall in your back yard for
almost a month."

Brandon tries to make sense of that, and slowly he recalls
seeing the young Mexican with his shirt off, wailing away
tirelessly with a pick on his mother's grand, stupid project.
Indefatigable, like all Mexicans.

"You're that Mexican. Mexicans don't surf."

"I do."

Brandon knows he should get up, challenge him physically, but he can barely lift his arm. Gravity has doubled,
trebled on him.

"Fuck it, who cares. There's no surf."

*   *   *

Jaime watches the belligerent *gabacho* boy for a few moments longer and then goes on down the narrow path, the rapid beat of his heart subsiding. What a disappointment below. The boy is right, there's almost no surf at all, just ripples, and irregular ones at that. But he's paid for the car, gassed it, and come all this way on his day off. He sits on the sand where he's seen the surfers' girls wait. If the surfers come he will stand his ground. He thinks of the sudden rolled-up whites of Don Ignacio's eyes with a mixture of anger and dread and resolve. He can do it if he must. But it is a terrible sin that he has never confessed. He wonders what they think of him in Huépac. His little brother may be proud of him. His mother and sisters ashamed. Don Ignacio always had many enemies, maybe people will think he had it coming. Jaime will have to telephone and find out if the local police or the *judiciales* are after him. If he can ever go home again.

His thoughts are interrupted by a noise, a long rumble and an even longer splashing. When he looks up he sees that a freak wave of some size has come ashore, the remnants chasing up the sand. Off on the horizon there is a gray line, seemingly rising off the surface of the sea. Is it his imagination? In a minute the swell reaches the outer edge of the bay and forms a perfect tube two meters high—a white crest foaming along from north to south, like a picture in one of the surf magazines he has read. He's never seen such a wave before and he's on his feet, rushing for the water.

Before the afternoon is out, Jaime has been treated to a personal Surf Machine, like almost no surfer before him. A freak storm is brewing far out in the Pacific. Once every three or four minutes, a swell arrives from far to the west, almost insignificant, barely noticeable until it nears the rock bay floor below him, when it rises abruptly and hurls him before it. Every time the wave rushes for twenty meters, thirty, then it tubes over. The curl is perfect, throwing foam at his heels, and his riding gets better and better with the ideal practice. He drops in and out of the tube, rides up and down the tall wave. Once he feels so anchored that he walks the nose, as he has read, almost hanging his toes off the front of the board.

Late in the afternoon, tiring, he wipes out badly, and chasing his board toward shore he looks upward and sees the silhouette of the belligerent *gabacho*, standing up against the leaden sky. He makes no gesture.

"You sucked at first, but at the end you were just incredible. I've never seen sets like that. You were shredding them, man. You must have natural skill." The boy has brought a glass of lemonade out to Jaime, who stops shoveling for a moment.

"Get him one, too, or I have trouble," Jaime says softly, indicating Mike.

"My mom's fucking him. That's plenty of goodies for him."

They exchange their Clint Eastwoods again and then Jaime walks to Mike, where he's kneeling setting stones, and hands him the glass. "The woman sends you this."

"About time."

He comes back and shovels.

"Are you afraid of him?" Brandon asks.

"He owns the job. I'm not afraid of anyone."

"Okay. I salute you, bra. Do you know you ride goofy-foot? Try it with the left in front sometime. You'll be primo."

"Thanks."

"Knock on the back door before you go." Brandon loses his upbeat expression all at once and drags himself away with tears in his eyes.

One unstable kid, Jaime thinks.

*   *   *

The gift of giving himself has been taken away. He knows he's always been selfish, self-centered, but he won't give someone death. He tells Kirsti to get lost. He walks away from Toni. He avoids the Bayboy parties and masturbates instead. It isn't just sex. He can't seem to give anything at all. Even that fucking Mexican won't take his old surfboard. He offered it and the Mexican backed away like it was a trick, like he was scalded. Brandon didn't have the energy to insist. After all, why would anyone want something from the plague fag? It was bound to be spoiled and wrecked, worse than a smashed and mended surfboard with one off-center skeg.

He almost told his dad, but he couldn't seem to claim that intimacy either, and his dad didn't really want to know, anyway. He was breezy, talking through Brandon's sullen comments.

"I'll be in Tokyo for three weeks. I'll try to call."

"Don't bother if it's a trial."

"It's no trial. Just they'll be running me ragged making presentations."

"Have fun with the Japs, dad."

Word has spread about the amazing long-period sets of the previous Sunday. Not even sets—singlets dispatched shoreward by some sea god, perfect tubes, waves to die for. But even before the Bayboys and their girls gather, the Mexican is there, wearing a loose warmup jacket with a mended tear that looks like it came from the trash. Brandon hurries across Paseo to catch him up.

"Hey, Mexican . . ."

"My name is Jaime, Gringo. Jaime Olivares Garza."

"I don't get all the names."

"The last one belongs to my mother. We honor our mothers."

"That's rad. My mom's a dork. How come you wouldn't take my surfboard? It's lots better than that piece of shit."

Jaime smiles. "I'm used to my own board. I don't want to be accused of stealing a valuable surfboard from a rich boy."

"I'm no Indian giver."

His dark eyes are puzzled. "I don't know those words."

"It means somebody who gives things and then takes them back."

Jaime laughs. "I see. The way the Indians took back all their land. You have a wonderful language."

"Uh-huh, sure." Brandon is starting to fume a little. He's stooped all the way down to offer something valuable to this Mexican who doesn't even belong here and the guy only laughs. Still, Brandon respects the skill he saw. You have to respect that. "Where did you learn to surf so well?"

Jaime is beginning to look impatient, but Brandon is blocking his path now.

"Manhattan Beach. Watching. On a wave I pretend I am the wing of an airplane."

"Primo." Just then three cars drive up that Brandon knows, then another one full of girls. The Bayboys must have convoyed here, and some of their girlfriends. He knows this changes everything to do with the Mexican, utterly. If he's seen being friendly, he's dead. And then he remembers like a giant slap across his cheek: he *is* dead. There is no future, no matter what he does. His shoulders sink visibly. "Jaime, I'm sorry, you can't surf here now," he says dully. "Those guys will kill you and then wreck your car just to make sure you *get* it. Please."

Jaime glances around as a half-dozen tanned young men in black and khaki shorts tug boards out of the back, and off the roof of their vehicles. Amazing how many of them are *guëros*. Blonds.

Brandon watches him do his Eastwood again, setting his feet. "I've killed before," Jaime says evenly. "Don't do this. You're children."

As the first boy comes down the path, Brandon sets his arms on his hips and calls loudly: "This beach is reserved for locals only!"

Jaime smiles again at this public change of sides. *Así es la vida*, he thinks. The rich. The owners. Those who give the orders. They stick with one another.

The new boy steps off the path and makes a circuit around the Mexican to stand beside Brandon. "Hey, Brand. Is this greaser giving you trouble?"

"Not yet."

Two more boys arrive and stand aside to watch the scene, then a group of the girls in their bikinis, towels over their shoulders. An older man, sinewy and fierce, plants an absolutely plain surfboard in the earth and glares at Jaime.

An ingenious idea grows in Brandon's tormented mind. If not now, when? He can go out a Bayboy hero, even become the greatest Lunada legend of all time. He can stand up to the Mexican and fight him, even though the Mexican is much bigger and obviously stronger. He can force the Mexican to push him off the cliff. The perfect death, defending the Bay! With the perfect audience.

"Go home, man!" Brandon shouts, trying to work himself up. His fear is that Jaime will say something to reveal their relationship.

"*No seas gacho, tu está de pelos,*" Jaime says. It means, Don't be such a drag, you're a cool guy, but he knows perfectly well that none of them, even if they speak a little high school Spanish, understand the slang. It is his gift to the boy.

"This is America, Mex!" Brandon shouts.

"I think Don Ignacio is dead," Jaime says softly. In practiced and habitual Spanish, he adds, "Bless me, Father, for I have sinned. It has been three months since my last Confession and my great sin is killing a man, in pride and in family shame. I am truly sorry for my sins, I repent of my sins, and I intend to try to lead a new life."

Strange noises issue from the audience, a kind of *hoo* and *eeee* and *ummm*. This toneless music strikes Brandon as intolerable, just as raw on his hearing as the incomprehensible Spanish from the other direction. He is friendless and alone, in a dying universe.

"Speak English!" Brandon cries in a kind of twisted, artificially amped-up rage. All at once Brandon is no longer in control of himself. Self-pity has taken him over like an illness, and he charges at Jaime, flailing his fists.

Jaime drops his broken surfboard to fend him off easily, sending the boy stumbling away. "Stop this, please," he says.

Brandon whirls around and comes at him again, driving the two of them toward the edge of the cliff. The entire group of surfers leans, almost imperceptibly, as if wishing to intervene but thwarted by some higher power.

"Only English! Only English!"

Jaime braces and pushes Brandon off himself again. He slips a little as his back foot breaks away a small clod of earth, only an arm's length from the edge of the cliff. He can feel the chill of the updraft and hear the crash of the surf too close behind him.

"That's enough!" Anger enters Jaime's voice for the first time. This boy's madness is actually endangering him.

They stand, hunched a little, facing one another, the American boy panting. *Como toro y torero*, Jaime thinks, and smiles to himself.

The smile enrages Brandon further. When he charges again, only he and Jaime realize what is happening from the torques and forces between them as they grapple on the very cliff edge. It is the boy who is trying to whirl them about, so Jaime is away from danger.

Extraordinary! Jaime thinks. The boy is trying to kill himself and make it look like he has done it.

"*Chingadera!*"

But Jaime is the stronger and he yanks the boy back and hurls him to the ground, where Brandon kicks upward with both feet.

A gasp rips from every throat as the Mexican cries out and disappears abruptly over the edge. This, they all understand, has just become a terrible tragedy. What they never figure out is why their friend howls in the most inconsolable of animal bawls and throws himself off the same cliff a moment later.

Over time the story of this fight slowly evolves in the hills overlooking Lunada Bay. The Bayboys and their girls do their best to tell the sheriff's deputies what they have seen, just as they saw it, but the story has a life of its own, and like every story it slowly normalizes itself over the years. What remains when the unusual and incomprehensible is filtered out is a Mexican interloper and a younger local boy who went too far defending his turf. They grappled and accidentally, as they fought, they went over the cliff together.

The lie that becomes history has its advantages. It has no irony or pointlessness. It has no random deadly diseases. And it proposes a useful lesson that the truth often does not: race is the quicksand that entraps and destroys all who come to live by it.

PORK

Pete Hautman

Ingmar Johnson was not exactly a giant in the field of architecture, but he did have the heavy black-framed eyeglasses, the cravat, the outsized ego, and me, Buddy Svenquist, his son-in-law, a state senator with aspirations to higher office. In recent years, with my invaluable help, he had landed commissions for several state-funded projects including one dozen rest stops, a four-acre warehouse near Forest Lake, and most recently the new Highway Patrol Regional Headquarters in Maple Grove.

We were sitting in a Starbucks—Ingmar and I—just across the highway from the nearly completed building.

"The problem, Ingmar, is that they're saying it looks like a penitentiary," I said.

"Who's saying?"

"The neighbors. My constituents."

"It's a fucking masterpiece," said Ingmar, sipping his coffee.

"If you say so," I said, looking away from the gray, forbidding walls. "But it could maybe have used a few windows." The concrete of the exterior wall had been cast to resemble rough-hewn stone blocks. The neighbors were right. It looked like a prison facility plunked down in a residential neighborhood of McMansions.

"People don't understand what beauty is," Ingmar said.

"People don't understand what *is* is," I said, misquoting one of my heroes.

"Form follows function," said Ingmar, quoting one of his. "*That* is what beauty is. It is about making do. Making do with a pathetic budget and a crappy site. You spend tens of millions on schools to teach idiot children to read, and then they don't. You spend billions on roads that see maybe ten, fifteen cars a day. Buildings? Pfah! You expect the Taj Mahal for three point five mil? You want *windows?*"

"I told them we'd plant some trees."

"Trees?" His impressive architect eyebrows snapped together with a nearly audible click. "Fucking trees."

"Some of the local residents were asking if we could paint it, too. They find the color a bit oppressive."

"Fucking idiots," he said. "They build a half-million-dollar piece-a-crap Hummer house on a quarter-acre lot across the street from a fucking cop shop and complain about the fucking view. What about the fucking cops? How do you think they feel about looking at those houses they can't fucking afford?"

"It landed you a nice little fucking commission," I pointed out.

Ingmar scowled and looked out the window.

"I don't need the money," he said, pretending to sip from his empty coffee cup.

It was true. Ingmar was well-fixed, largely due to money inherited from his father, who had owned most of downtown Minneapolis back in the Fifties. Ingmar was not only a lousy architect, he was a lousy dilettante architect who treated me like his pet dog. By saying "I don't need the money," he was saying "I don't need *you.*"

"So where's the granite pig going?" he said after several uncomfortable seconds.

"It's not a pig, it's an egg."

According to state law, all new public buildings were required to spend 1 percent of their construction budget on public works of art. This noble-sounding mandate dated back to the 1960s, before it became clear just how damaging and divisive works of art could be. In the case of State Patrol HQ, we were required to spend $35,000 on such. An ad hoc "arts committee" was formed, composed of one Highway Patrol bureaucrat, one local community activist, one state arts board representative, one member of the Anoka County Chamber of Commerce, one art historian from the U. of M., one art instructor from North Hennepin Community College, and the manager of the local Krispy Kreme Donuts. Ingmar had refused to participate, much to everyone's relief.

After considerable wrangling—nine meetings, two months, eighteen boxes of Krispy Kreme donuts, forty-four artist's proposals, and, finally, $7,000 in bribes—the committee settled unhappily but decidedly on Milos Mosovos, a temperamental Serbian sculptor and the husband of Governor Patch's nymphomaniac niece, Velma. Mosovos had proposed an unadorned seven-foot-long rose-colored granite egg resting on its side atop a black marble plinth.

"It's only an egg until some fucking anomic graffiti artist paints nostrils on one end and a corkscrew tail on the other," Ingmar said.

"I wish you wouldn't use words like that."

"What—'fucking'?"

" 'Anomic.' "

"Fucking illiterate. How you think Minnesota's Finest are going to like seeing a twenty-ton pig every time they go out on patrol?"

"It's not a pig. It's an egg."

"Where's it going to go?"

"Ingmar, the sculpture can go wherever you want it. You're the architect."

"Okay then. We bury it. A five-ton egg. Maybe it'll hatch."

You might think that because I am a politician, professionally conversant with the needs, desires, and fears of my fellow citizens, an individual so transparent and small-minded as my father-in-law Ingmar would be easy for me to handle.

You would be wrong.

If Ingmar Johnson's bullshit detector were not purely metaphorical, it would have looked like one of those microwave transmitter towers sprouting from the top of his oversize head. Its range was so broad, so finely tuned, and so sensitive that he was able to detect untruths even where none existed. To make matters worse, Ingmar was himself a compulsive truth-teller, incapable of the everyday lies, omissions, and oversights that fall under the categories of Tact, Diplomacy, and Common Decency.

So when I told Ingmar that interring the giant egg was not an option, he called my bluff. Later that afternoon he faxed me the pertinent paragraphs in his contract. It seemed that the architect had the final say on the ". . . placement of permanent artworks within and surrounding said structure."

Normally it would be no skin off my tender ass if a $35,000 hunk of granite got buried, but this particular hunk of granite was nitroglycerin where I was concerned. If they buried it, they might as well just toss me in the hole with it.

*   *   *

It wasn't my fault that I slept with Velma Mosovos. You would have too, and to hell with your so-called sexual preferences or marriage vows. Velma Mosovos was loaded with enough hi-test pheromones to give a female eunuch a hard-on. What she and Milos thought they were doing by getting married, I do not know. He cannot possibly have thought he was scoring an exclusive.

I met Velma on the coldest day of the year, the day that I consumed six too many glasses of merlot and fell down a flight of stairs at the grand opening of the Delmar Johnson (a *real* architect, and no relation to Ingmar) Architecture Building on the state campus in St Paul. Fortunately—as my tuxedoed ass thumped and tumbled down the concrete steps of a back stairwell where I had retreated to sneak a smoke—there were no witnesses. I thought.

Velma Mosovos, blond of hair, long of leg, large of bosom, blue of eye, devoid of impulse control, and oozing sexuality, witnessed my fall as she aborted an act of fellatio upon Delmar Johnson's son at the bottom of the stairwell.

As I lay in a crumpled mass of merlot-hazed pain trying to figure out how badly I had damaged myself, her face filled my vision like, well, a vision. Despite my inebriated condition, my dislocated shoulder, and a mild concussion—or perhaps because of those things—I fell in love.

I will spare you the details of the weeks and months that followed. Suffice it to say that Velma and I (and, I later came to learn, Velma and others as well) enjoyed an alarmingly wide variety of intimacies in an even wider variety of locations including the governor's office, her husband's studio, the elevator in the County Courthouse, the third-hole green at Lexington Country Club, a men's room at

Crosstown Mall, and (though it shames me to say it) the $10,000 Duxiana bed I share with my wife, Francine, a goddess, the mother of my children.

Milos, during that period, was extremely busy with public commissions, many of which conveniently happened to take him to distant parts of the state—mostly to rest stops, license bureaus, information kiosks, and so forth, where he erected small assemblages of stone or steel. I called in a lot of favors and blew through a lot of clout keeping Milos busy, but getting him that commission for the granite egg was the first time I'd had to jury-rig a competition.

I would not have done it but for Velma's insistence. This was just a few weeks into our fuckfest, me still infatuated to where I would go down on her in an elevator. So I did it. I got Milos the commission, and I figured that was that. At the time, I found it amusing that Milos was planning to name his big pink granite egg after his wife.

I should describe Milos, just so you do not miss this important detail:

Fucking huge.

This was a man who lifts boulders for a living.

The fact that Milos had named his granite egg "Velma's Song" (I know, I know! It hurts me too . . .) may in and of itself be regarded as an argument for internment, but I happened to know that Milos, despite his size, and Velma, despite her unbridled cuckoldry, were both mawkishly sentimental where their relationship was concerned. The egg was maniacally important to both of them, and if it were buried with my tacit approval, there would be consequences.

*　　*　　*

I suppose it was inevitable that Milos would come to suspect that something was going on between Velma and me. Discretion was not among Velma's qualities.

So when Milos showed up at my office one day, I was not entirely surprised, but I *was* very polite. Fucking *huge*— remember?

"You been doing the dirty with my Velma," he said with tears in his eyes. I remained composed, even though I thought I was about to be torn to shreds by a weepy giant. It turned out, however, that despite his sentimentality, Milos regarded his marriage as a negotiable asset. He had his eyes set on the State Patrol Building commission. It would be the perfect setting, he declared, for his tribute to Velma. "Velma's Song" was to be his masterpiece.

Being a politician, I understood. This was business. He would refrain from breaking my skull in exchange for my efforts on his behalf with the arts committee.

Of course, my affair with Velma had to end. That was fine with me—Velma's sexual eagerness had recently begun to take on a sort of moist desperation. Also, my wife had been taking an unusual interest in how I spent my time away from home, and it was a very bad time for me to suffer scandal or divorce, as certain representatives of the GOP had recently approached me with a tempting offer: if I switched parties they would put me up as their candidate for the Fifth Congressional District, a Republican stronghold.

All of which spoke to why I could not let Ingmar bury that damned egg.

I once helped a cold-blooded teenage killer named Jimmy Jase get out of jail free.

This was long before I became a state senator, and before I

was a public prosecutor. I was fresh out of law school, idealistic and full of fire, ready to take on the system, eking out a living by handling minor lawsuits and small-time criminal complaints. Basically, I took anything that came in the door.

Jimmy Jase had been arrested and charged with the shotgun killing of his ex-girlfriend, his ex-girlfriend's boyfriend, and the ex-girlfriend's boyfriend's German shepherd, so he reached out to his "Big Brother" (from the Big Brothers and Sisters program) Harold Anderson, who happened to be my older sister's husband. Harold called me, both because he knew I had nothing else on my plate, and because he hoped I'd work on the cheap. Which was accurate on both counts. I was so delighted to be working a major murder case I would have done it *pro bono*.

Jimmy Jase was a charming and beautiful lad whose ancestors hailed from every continent. Jimmy had inherited the best from each, at least in terms of his physical appearance. Imagine if Tiger Woods and Kristin Kreuk had a son. My first thought upon meeting him was that he would be very popular in the penitentiary. My second thought, after talking to him, was that he was a stone killer and should be locked up for all of eternity. Even O.J. Simpson had shown more grief and regret over the death of his ex-wife than Jimmy did over his ex-girlfriend. As far as Jimmy was concerned, the bitch was dead, now let's move on to a more important problem, that being his freedom, or lack thereof.

Fortunately for Jimmy (and unfortunately for society) the police had made several grievous errors in his arrest and interrogation, and I was able to spring him before the case went to trial. Jimmy was pleased in a smug, sociopathic sort of way: it was, after all, no more than he deserved. Upon parting he said to me, "Yo, counselor, you ever need any-body took off, you look me up."

I had no doubt he was serious.

Occasionally, a young person will approach me to inquire about politics, as in how does one become involved. I am honest with these idealistic youngsters. I tell them it is about choosing one's friends, trading favors, choosing one's ene-mies (carefully), learning what they are afraid of, and helping them to realize their dreams and avoid their nightmares while learning to milk the resulting juice.

Actually, I tell them none of that. I tell them it's about helping people, but I don't tell them why. The smart ones will figure that out on their own. Because that's really what it boils down to: trading favors and trading threats. Tit for tat. The heart and soul of politics.

I found Jimmy Jase, ten years older but still looking like a teenager, working the bar at the 923 Club, an establishment that attracted large numbers of mixed-race young men and their well-heeled admirers. I, with my gray suit and straight vibe, stood out like a football on a golf green.

Jimmy recognized me immediately.

"Yo, counselor, what you doing here?"

"Looking for you, Jimmy."

"No shit? What you want?"

I reminded Jimmy that he owed me one, a fact which he immediately acknowledged. Even sociopathic killers under-stand the political imperative.

I never intended for my wife to meet Jimmy Jase. I had, in fact, gone to considerable trouble to avoid *anyone* seeing Jimmy and me together, which was why I arranged to meet him at the Wagon Wheel Grill-Inn in Northfield, a good sixty miles outside my district. It was one of the many places Velma and I had frequented. "Just get on I-35 and go about forty miles," I told him. "It's right on the freeway. Big wagon wheel. You can't miss it."

Jimmy showed up an hour late and mad as hell.

"The fuck," he said. "Who'd a thought *North*field was *south* of the city?"

I bought him a cheeseburger combo, which seemed to mollify him. He was making his way through the basket of trans fats when Francine walked into the restaurant.

I didn't recognize her at first. Oversize sunglasses, a silk scarf, and a big-buttoned car coat gave her that phony-anonymous Jackie Onassis look. She stopped in the entry-way and scanned the restaurant until her eyes locked onto me and Jimmy. That was when I recognized her.

"What's a matter?" Jimmy asked. "You look all funny like."

"My wife," I said. Then, quickly, "You're a college student interviewing me for a poli-sci project, okay? Just be cool."

"I'm always cool, counselor." Grinning broadly, Jimmy watched Francine approach.

Turned out I didn't have to worry about acting natural. Francine was so awkward and embarrassed herself—babbling this long, incredible story about trying to find an estate sale in Northfield and getting lost and what an amazing coincidence and what on earth are you doing here anyway—that she would not have noticed a tick on my nose. It took all of five seconds for me to realize that she had followed me into the Wagon Wheel fully expecting to catch me *in flagrante delicto* with another woman. Jimmy sussed out the situation instantly—I could tell from his shit-eating grin. To my considerable relief, he played it straight, slipping into the guise of an ambitious poli-sci student, even asking Francine if she would consent to a phone interview.

"You know, so's I can get a sense of what it's like to be the wife of a successful politician."

Francine declined my invitation to join us, and left after a few awkward minutes to search for her "estate sale."

"Fuck me," I said as the door closed behind her.

Jimmy laughed. "What? Cuz you just got caught doing nothing?"

"Cuz I don't want anybody to put you and me together."

"Oh, yeah, cuz that would be *bad*. Now, suppose you just tell me what bad ass thing you want me to do for you, counselor."

Ingmar Johnson was beaten to death in his own backyard with his own garden shovel. The first blow sliced through the heavy black frames of his eyeglasses and cut deep into his forehead. The fourteen blows that followed may have been superfluous. Fortunately, and according to plan, my mother-in-law was out of town, visiting a spa in Scottsdale with Francine—a favor arranged through a friend of mine at General Mills.

Of course, they cut their weekend short when they heard about poor Ingmar.

I should mention here, lest you think that I am so petty as to have a man killed over the placement of one pink granite egg, that my wife stood to inherit 50 percent of Ingmar's considerable fortune, money that would come in very handy in my bid for national office.

The $5,000 down payment I gave to Jimmy was untraceable: the cash had come from my shoebox. There was irony: it was the same five grand—literally, the same hundred-dollar bills—I had received from the general contractor who got the State Patrol facility job.

The fatal attack on poor Ingmar was attributed to a burglar who had been interrupted in his work, and who had left no clues behind. I got that from a certain Sergeant Royce of the Maple Grove Police, who I had once helped out by putting in a word with the judge handling his divorce case.

Francine was shattered by the sudden and violent death of her father, and who could blame her? I wished I'd asked Jimmy to leave Ingmar with a presentable face. The mortician had done his best—my mother-in-law insisted on an open casket—but a guy who's had his forehead sliced open with the edge of a shovel, well, there's only so much you can do. Ingmar's poor semblance cast a pall over the entire proceedings, which had been carefully planned right down to the venue, the music, the casket, and the hand-printed order of service by—guess who?—Ingmar himself.

Still, it was a beautiful program. I would have enjoyed every minute of it had not Jimmy Jase shown up. I saw him enter the chapel, then avoided looking at him until, as I filed out of the chapel with the other family members, he caught my eye from the back pew and gave me a smarmy wink.

I am neither naïve nor vulnerable. I know when I'm being fucked with, and I know to not let it get out of hand. Jimmy Jase had made a mistake by showing up at my father-in-law's funeral. Next would come the phone call, the requests for additional funds, and so forth.

Immediately after the service I borrowed a cell phone from one of my nitwit nephews and made a call to one Anson Grant, better known as Sudsy. It took four calls; I finally reached him at his mother's house.

"Hey Suds," I said as I watched the last of the mourners file out of the chapel.

"The fuck you phone me here?" Sudsy said.

"I'm calling in that favor."

"Christ." Sudsy said.

I waited a few seconds for him to process.

"Go where I first met you," he said. "Tomorrow. They open at eight."

"Eight o'clock," I said. But he had already hung up.

Sudsy Grant was a professional hoodlum—one of a dying breed. I'd known him even longer than I'd known Jimmy.

We had met at the Viking Bar back when I was still in law school. I'd recently been dumped by my girlfriend, and was celebrating with several shots of tequila, when a burly, black-leather-clad young man bellied up next to me. He was a bit red in the face, breathing audibly, his formidable jaw pulsing, dirty blond hair standing out from his head like a lion's mane. His hands were a mess—knuckles bleeding, cut right through his boxer's calluses.

As I mentioned, I had a belly full of José Cuervo. You might have seen the T-shirt: *One tequila, I'm brilliant. Two tequilas, I'm sexy. Three tequilas, I'm bulletproof. Four tequilas, I'm invisible.* I was on number seven, just drunk enough to initiate a conversation with a homicidal biker.

"Dude, what you do to your hands? You punch out a brick wall?"

Sudsy—I did not yet know his name—turned his leonine head and fixed me with a pair of glittery blue eyes. His lip was cut wide open. Even through my alcoholic haze, I realized that I had placed myself at serious risk.

"Whoa," I said. "Buy you a drink?"

Sudsy blinked slowly (try it sometime—not easy to do) and decided that he would take the drink instead of the opportunity to squash a citizen, even one as irritating as me.

We were on our second shot of tequila when the cops showed up. Apparently, another gentleman of the Harley-Davidson persuasion had been assaulted in the alley behind the bar, and a person closely resembling my new friend Sudsy had been observed kicking said gentleman's face in.

"Bullshit," said Sudsy. "I been sittin' right here two hours or more, right, Chuckles?" That was the name he gave me.

Now, I was pretty well toasted at that point, but I knew that Sudsy and I had been acquainted for no more than twenty minutes. But some instinct kicked in—perhaps my first intimation that I had a talent for politics—and I told the police that it was God's honest truth. My good friend Sudsy had not so much as visited the restroom. The perpetrator must have been some other six-and-a-half-foot-tall jack-booted lion-maned thug.

The cops didn't buy it, of course. They hauled him off, and then the guy in the alley died, and then the lawyer Sudsy hired—a guy named Tony Bjorklund (who now holds the office of Attorney General) showed up at my apartment and asked me to testify on Sudsy's behalf. I opened my mouth to tell the lawyer that I was pretty sure his client was guilty, and that what I'd told the cops that night was the tequila talking, but the guy was a pro—he saw it coming and shut me up and backed me into my own apartment and started talking. I know talent when I see it, so I shut up and started listening.

They say a good attorney can talk a pit bull out of a death grip. It took Tony Bjorklund no time at all to convince me to revisit my memory of that night at the Viking Bar. And the more I thought about it, the more it seemed like a good idea to make a friend out of Anson "Sudsy" Grant.

A few months later, Sudsy was exonerated by a jury of his peers.

*   *   *

The Viking Bar at eight a.m. had that special wet-ashtray-sour-beer smell—it had not changed by so much as a barstool in twenty years. Sudsy was similarly timeless. Maybe just a touch of gray deep in his mane, and a few fine lines intersecting the scars on his forehead. He was sitting at one of the back tables with a bloody mary.

"Dude," he said. "What the fuck? I thought you were pure suit and tie these days. I been seeing your name in the papers."

"I thought if I wore a suit here I might get remembered."

I was dressed in my yard work outfit: jeans, flannel shirt, and a vintage North Stars cap. I'd told Francine I had to run out to get oil for the weed whacker. She didn't ask why I was doing yard work, something I hadn't done since we'd been getting free lawn service from a guy I helped out with some permits a few years back. Francine was enjoying a selection of anti-stress meds—a doctor I'd helped out with an insurance billing issue had loaded her up with samples the day after Ingmar's death. I could have told her I was going elephant hunting.

"This is the Viking," he said. "Nobody remembers nothing."

I said, "You know a guy named Jimmy Jase?"

Sudsy nodded.

I said, "You have a relationship with him?"

Sudsy shook his head very slowly.

I stared at him, using my ability to project unspoken thoughts.

Sudsy laughed. "Oh for shit," he said. "Why don't you just fucking say it?"

"You know what I want," I said.

"Fucking suits." He shook his head. "How 'bout a shot of Cuervo? For old times sake."

*   *   *

You may find it strange that I, a respectable politician with no criminal record, no history of violence or insanity, a generous, loving disposition, and no connection with organized crime would, in the space of a week, contract for two murders. All I can say is, drastic situations require drastic solutions.

You might also wonder why I first employed an instable, unreliable loser like Jimmy Jase, instead of going with a solid pro like Suds Grant the first time around. The truth is, I knew Jimmy would work cheap. I guess you get what you pay for.

The other reason was that Sudsy scared me.

The killing of Jimmy Jase occurred on a Wednesday afternoon at an Ingmar Johnson-designed rest stop on I-35. Jimmy was there to meet a man who owed him another $5,000. That would be me. Unfortunately, I was unable to tear myself away from a meeting with a lobbyist representing the Wild Rice Harvesters Association. Jimmy was instead greeted by a large leonine man with a baseball bat.

Coincidentally, all of the security cameras at the rest stop had been vandalized the night before by (according to the last few seconds of tape) a slim, attractive young man of indeterminate ethnicity. Consequently, no record of the attack existed.

The 5K I had promised Jimmy was instead delivered by Spee-Dee Messenger to Anson Grant, care of Mrs. Herbert Grant, along with an additional $35,000 that represented most of my personal cash slush fund. I hated to let all that money go, but there would soon be plenty of cheese flowing from Ingmar's estate.

You see? Sometimes these things wrap up neat as can be, and everyone lives happily ever after.

*　　　*　　　*

So I was feeling pretty good about things. I was done with Velma, and even though I missed all the crazy fucking, it was a considerable relief to not be constantly worrying about getting caught with my pants down. "Velma's Song" was proudly displayed at the entrance to the State Patrol HQ, we moved my mother-in-law into a senior high-rise, I called in a few favors to accelerate the passage of Ingmar's money through probate, and the Republicans firmed up their offer: I was all but guaranteed that congressional seat.

Francine and I were celebrating with dinner at La Belle Vie when my cell phone rang.

"I can't believe you didn't turn that thing off," Francine said.

I looked at the number. Velma's cell.

"I have to take this," I said. I don't quite know why I did that. Maybe it was because I was irritated by Francine's disapproval. I stood up from the table and made my way across the restaurant toward the restrooms.

"Hey," I said into the phone.

That was how I ended up at the home of Jerry Blue Andersen, Republican uber-wonk and the very man who had recently offered to make me a congressman.

Jerry was dead. Naked and dead on his living room floor.

Velma, wearing a maroon bathrobe with the initials JBA embroidered on the chest, was sitting on the white leather sofa smoking a cigarette.

Milos, looking contrite, sat hunched forward on the sofa arm.

"Jesus Christ," I said, staring down at the ruins of Jerry Blue Andersen's head. "I thought he was gay."

Velma gave me a look, reminding me that where Velma Mosovos was concerned, all men were heterosexual.

"What did you hit him with?" I asked Milos.

Milos pointed to an egg-shaped, toaster-sized object on the floor, which I recognized as his original artist's maquette for "Velma's Song." Milos had gifted it to me when I got him the commission. I had regifted it to Jerry Blue Andersen last week, when he saw it displayed in my office and expressed his appreciation for "fine art."

Milos had then re-regifted the granite egg to Jerry in a whole 'nother spirit.

I knew that the cops would find out about Velma. She had been spending a lot of time with Jerry. Her fingerprints and DNA would be smeared all over the place. So we came up with a story. I made Velma rehearse it several times over. He was big. He was black. Jerry tried to stop him. Jerry died. Not a very good story, but a tried and true one.

"Just remember," I said. "Big, black, and Jerry was a hero. And whatever you do, no matter how many mug shots they show you, the attacker was bigger, uglier, and blacker."

I cleaned up everything Milos could remember touching and got him out of the house. As soon as we were gone, Velma called the cops. If she stuck to her story, and if I provided Milos with a solid alibi, there was a chance we could all walk away from this thing.

The police bought Velma's story about the big black guy breaking into the house—for about twenty minutes. Then they discovered Jerry's hidden video apparatus. He had an impressive collection of home movies, several of them featuring Velma—and one featuring me and Milos as well.

In looking for the silver lining to this whole sorry mess, I can only point out that I have been helping people for the better part of my adult life, and I am owed many, many favors. For example, when the police showed up at my home the next morning, the officer in charge—a guy I'd helped out with a domestic abuse issue a few years back—agreed to let me walk from the house to the squad car without the formality of putting me in handcuffs. I, my wife, my children, and my constituents all appreciated that.

One of the many small perks I get while awaiting trial is daily delivery of both local papers. One day I opened the metro section to see a half-page color photo of "Velma's Song." I smiled. Someone had painted the small end of the granite egg with a snout. The ass end, I was certain, featured a twisted corkscrew tail.

STRANGE BEDFELLOWS

Twist Phelan

Lulu Phelps had gone through four husbands. Two were hers, and two belonged to other women. She didn't recommend the borrowed husband route.

Other than being tall and terrific in bed, Borrowed Husband Number One wasn't much of a long-term prospect. Young kids and religion put divorce out of the question, and the Secret Service detail really put a damper on romance. The latter came with the territory when you were the love-bunny of the Vice President of the United States.

After three years with the Veep, Lulu moved on to the Secretary of Agriculture, her second borrowed husband. The Secretary had a lot of experience in being borrowed. By the time Lulu got to him, he'd already had dalliances too numerous to count. It wouldn't have surprised her if there were spreadsheets somewhere.

After the Secretary, Lulu stuck to single guys—the Congressman, the analyst from OMB, the lobbyist . . . She slept her way down the political hierarchy to Dougie, the state senator who became her second husband. The first had been in Lulu's life just long enough to get her pregnant, married, and divorced, all before Tiffie was born.

Now Lulu wasn't so sure that owning was better than

borrowing. Maybe lease with an option to purchase was the way to go—most women seemed happiest as fiancées.

At least this time, she'd be the one leaving. And she wasn't going away empty-handed.

The Grand Old Party was having a grand old party in town. Well, almost grand—it was the gathering held every two years to go over committee assignments. The party chair had put Dougie in charge of convention center logistics. That had to be worth a seat on the podium the first night. Maybe even in the second row, with Lulu beside him. He hoped she would wear the red dress, the one she'd had on the night they met at the Days Inn, in front of the cigarette machine after the Elks banquet.

He still remembered her first words: "Got a light?" Her blond hair had gleamed like a trout's underbelly. Dougie could smell her perfume as he fumbled for his Zippo, as sweet as the air freshener the carwash guy spritzed into his Taurus every week.

After the cancer took Ruth and his sixtieth birthday came and went, Dougie had pretty much given up on falling in love again. That was before Lulu. He loved her. And he knew she loved him. It was in her eyes every time she opened the jeweler's boxes he gave her.

So what if the diamonds were really CZ? Things had been a little tight in the insurance business lately. And he'd make it up to her down the road. This convention could be the start of big things for him. A plum committee assignment, maybe the party's backing for a run at Congress . . . who knew how far he'd go? JFK introduced himself as the man who escorted Jacqueline Kennedy to Paris; Dougie wanted to be the man who brought Lulu Phelps back to Washington.

When Lulu met Dougie, she had been ready to try marriage again. A girl can hover around forty for only so long. And he was in politics. Too bad it turned out that Senator Douglas Phelps was really only Dougie P.

To Lulu, married didn't mean dead. Monogamous, either. Three months after "I do," she was doing Ben Chan one night a week. Ben owned a chain of drycleaners, and laughed at the Chinese laundry jokes all the way to the bank. He was the party's biggest contributor, mostly under the table. Lulu liked what Ben could do under a table, too.

But her hopes that Ben would contribute to her party had quickly faded. Damn fiscal conservative. That left hocking Dougie's jewelry and tapping the stash in his desk as the only ways to fund her getaway. There was at least half a mil in the box. Lulu figured forty thou wouldn't be missed before she was gone. After the incident with the lobbyist—calling the DA when it was clearly a loan! She didn't want any more misunderstandings with law enforcement.

Tiffie put on a red leather skirt and a sheer white shirt that revealed the black bra underneath, then stood in front of the mirror. The skirt was short and showed off the tan she sprayed on her legs every other day.

Wait until Rios saw her in the skirt. She felt his brown hand cupping her small breast and shivered. Too funny that he thought she was a virgin.

Rios was a hunk. Not like Lester, the loser from school who kept bugging her. So what if Dougie said his dad was a party chair, or whatever. He still owned a gas station.

Saying she'd meet him at the mall had shut him up. But go out with Lester for real? Not.

Dougie unlocked his desk drawer. He opened the box, counted the bills and bearer bonds, then counted them again. His body sagged against the chair-back like an inflatable doll with the plug pulled. Forty grand light.

Dougie hadn't yet met the guy he was supposed to deliver the money to. He was new to the local, worked his way up the ranks. But Dougie had heard rumors about his enforcement work in the Midwest, what he'd done to people who'd crossed the union. They'd end up missing bank accounts, fingers, sometimes their whole selves.

Maybe the guy wouldn't notice. Maybe he would believe one of the fundraisers had miscounted.

Four hundred sixty thousand dollars took up a fair bit of space. Dougie stuffed the money and bearer bonds into a brown paper bag, then glanced at the photograph of the teenager on his desk.

Dougie loved Tiffie like she was his own. She was a good girl—polite, solid Bs at school, no boyfriends or drugs. And she had the most adorable lisp.

"Tiffie?"

Tiffie unzipped the skirt and reached for her jeans. She never wanted to ruin Dougie's little princess image of her. At least he didn't totally suck as a stepfather. Decent allowance, no hugs that creeped her out, like the ones from Amy's dad.

Tiffie picked up her Blackberry and texted Rios. *c u 2nite?* Last time he'd talked about proving that she loved him. Why did guys make such a big deal out of BJs?

She pulled on a sweater and checked the mirror to make sure she'd wiped off all her lip gloss.

"Yeth, Dougie?"

Rios was small and athletic-looking, with long black hair pulled into a ponytail and a gold stud in one ear. His business card read *Event Coordinator*.

His cell phone vibrated. Rios unclipped it from his waist and read the message on the screen.

Pik u up @ 8, he texted back.

Rios grinned. Tiffie was ripe. Even though he would have liked to pick that fruit himself, Rios didn't put pleasure ahead of profit. Without make-up, Tiffie could pass for twelve. That, plus the lisp, meant he'd get top dollar for her cherry to get popped.

The cell phone vibrated again. Rios checked the Caller ID and answered.

"Eight girls? Fine." He listened. "I told you—no discounts."

He snapped the phone shut and got behind the wheel of the midnight-blue Escalade.

Fuckin' politicians. Cheap unless they were spending tax dollars. No wonder the country was going to hell.

Dougie handed Tiffie the brown paper bag. It was folded over at the top, like the lunches she used to carry to school. He'd written *Tiffie* on one side.

"You know what to do, sweetie?"

Tiffie had made deliveries for her stepfather before. She played with a curl of hair and recited the drop-off address. "A man will be waiting in the office. I give the bag to him."

"That's my girl." Dougie waggled a finger at her. "Remember, don't open the bag."

Lulu's kitten heels clopped across the wood floor. She wore low-cut jeans with rhinestones splashed around the hips and a pale green T-shirt with more rhinestones.

"You're going to the movies tonight with Lester and Amy?"

"Yeth, Mommy." Tiffie hitched her purse higher on her shoulder. Stuffed into the fake Prada were the red leather skirt and black bra. She'd change in the mall bathroom, before Rios picked her up. And she'd get Amy to deal with Lester.

"I've got a party meeting at the club tonight. Might run late," Dougie said after Tiffie had left.

Lulu shrugged. "You know Thursday is my Chinese cooking class."

Tiffie caught the bus at the corner, rode it to the stop before the mall, and found the right building. The headquarters of Local 742 were on the third floor. Waiting for the elevator, she looked in the bag. She always did.

Holy shit! Tiffie didn't know what a bearer bond was, but the sight of all those Benjamins set her atingle.

The elevator doors opened. They closed five seconds later. Tiffie still stood in the lobby.

Lulu put away Tiffie's laundry. White briefs, plain white bras. What normal teenager wore this stuff?

The matchbook was under a stack of T-shirts. Lulu knew the club. Her daughter threw a fit whenever Lulu snuck a cigarette. So what was she doing at the best place in town for scoring drugs and paid-for sex?

It took Lulu a half hour to toss Tiffie's room. She surveyed the leopard print bras, cropped tops, and micro minis. Like mother, like daughter, after all.

Lulu trusted teenagers about as much as she trusted men. Tiffie better not be into something that was gonna screw up her mother's exit strategy.

Rios spotted Tiffie next to the mall entrance. While the Escalade was still moving, he leaned across the seat, pulled on the door handle, then abruptly braked, letting the car's momentum snap open the door. He'd seen the maneuver in a movie once.

"Hop in, baby." The line was from the movie, too.

Tiffie slid into the seat, clutching the paper bag to her chest. She had it all worked out. They would take the money and fly to Mexico. Even though it was a foreign country, Tiffie was pretty sure they had to let you in if you were part-Mexican. Or were engaged to a part-Mexican.

"Put down your stuff. Let me see what you're wearing," Rios said.

Tiffie didn't let go of the bag. "You're never gonna believe what—"

"I'm on the clock, babe. Toss that crap into the back seat and lemme look at you."

Something in his tone made Tiffie do what he said. It also made her decide to keep quiet about the money.

As Rios surveyed her outfit, his mouth turned down with distaste. She looked like a ho. No way would his buyer believe he was getting cherry.

"Where's that white shirt, plaid skirt thing you do for school, babe?"

Fred Powers paced in his office at Local 742 headquarters.

The buzz was in his head again, the low-level whine that had begun after his first killing. It had gotten louder and longer with every job, even though each of the victims had it coming.

Powers began humming to himself. He often did. Woody's words were especially comforting.

"Oh you can't scare me, I'm sticking to the union, I'm sticking to the union, I'm sticking to the union. Oh, you can't scare me, I'm sticking to the union, I'm sticking to the union till the day I die . . ."

Powers had hoped when he was moved up from enforcement that the droning would stop. It hadn't. Hands pressed to his ears, he kept pacing and humming.

The noise would have to come back just when he was gonna make a score he could retire on. A former cellmate had tipped him that the fix was in. A company, not a horse. Its stock would be pumped and dumped, and Powers could get in on the ground floor if he bought by tomorrow. Hold the stock for a week while it went up, his cellmate had said. After Powers cashed out, he'd turn over the original five hundred K to the union and bank the profit overseas.

So where the hell was the delivery? The drop-off was supposed to be at seven p.m. It was almost nine.

The buzzing in Powers' head intensified. This Dougie better not be playing games. Bad enough if he'd jacked union dough, but he was screwing with Powers' money, too.

He couldn't stand it any longer. There was a bash for Ben Chan at the club tonight, a thank-you for all the dough he'd contributed to party coffers. Dougie never missed one of those things.

Powers put on his coat. He'd drop by the club, do a little fundraising of his own. As always, the gun was in his pocket. The thrum was still in his head.

Lulu plunged the wand into the tube of mascara, then swiped it over her lashes. She didn't want to be late. Usually Ben confirmed time and place, but her call had gone straight to voicemail.

She'd go to his condo. Two weeks ago, she'd discovered where he kept the hideaway key.

Rios and Tiffie lay across the Escalade's front seats, entwined so closely that if Rios breathed deeply, Tiffie's cherry would be plucked.

"Don't stop," she moaned. Her leather skirt was pushed up around her hips and her lace bra hung from the rearview mirror.

Rios forced himself to imagine fifty hundred-dollar bills, the price he'd negotiated for Tiffie's virginity. He pushed himself off her and took a breath.

"I've got something else in mind for your first time, babe." He tucked in his shirt and started the Escalade. The engine throbbed under him. The big car was his as long as he wanted it. He had photos of the married john who owned it with one of his girls.

Ten minutes later Rios saw the sign—Deer Creek Country Club. He yanked the wheel right. The paper bag slid across the back seat. Kickbacks from political consultants, under-the-table campaign donations, bribes for the privilege of running illicit drugs, women, and bets—some paid by Rios himself—slid across the seat and into the capacious door pocket.

Lulu prowled through the lavish condo. Low furniture, muted colors, silk hangings on the walls, every room empty.

Ben hated smoking. Lulu lit a cigarette, took a few puffs, crushed it out in the lacquer bowl on the granite coffee table. This is what she got after nine months of weekly "cooking classes"?

Lulu snatched up her evening bag. She'd find Dougie at the club, take him home, do that thing with the scarves he liked. Should be worth another pair of diamond earrings. Every contribution to her bon voyage fund helped.

A thought struck Lulu.

Dougie treated Tiffie okay. The money would last a lot longer if Lulu was on her own.

Deer Creek Country Club was built in the Southern tradition; the main building was a gracious two-story fronted by a portico and flanked by white-columned wings. In the back were smaller buildings that could be rented for private parties and business meetings. Each of these "cabins" had a main room with a fireplace, a separate dining area, a kitchen, and three bedroom suites. In the late Forties officials from the Truman administration had convened in Cabin One to iron out problems with the Marshall Plan. A plaque commemorating the event was posted beside the front door. Whenever Dougie was in charge of making reservations for party events, he requested Cabin One. Truman was his idol.

Now he leaned against the bar and checked his phone. No calls. Maybe the guy hadn't noticed the delivery was short.

Dougie put away the phone and signaled for another scotch. He was a little nervous, but not about the drop-off. Tonight's gathering was in honor of the party's chief fundraiser. Procuring girls was part of the job, but Dougie had outdone himself tonight. Maybe enough to get himself moved up to the front row on the podium.

Lulu pulled her Miata into the club parking lot, narrowly missing the black Escalade that hogged two spaces. Some people were just asking to be keyed.

She was about to pull into an empty slot at the end when she saw it, the frog-like headlights in the next row. There weren't that many Porsches in town, and only one with a *Zen Mstr* personalized plate.

Well, Lulu would show Ben some Zen. She slammed the Miata's door hard enough to set off the car alarm. Accompanied by the klaxon of bells, she stalked across the asphalt, waved off the doorman, and pushed through the club's main doors.

"I hate these clothes." Tiffie started to tie her shirttails to bare her abs but Rios stopped her.

"You look fine, babe." He clamped a hand onto her upper arm and started for Cabin One.

Tiffie dragged her feet. "Ish too quiet. I wanna go to a party." Her lisp was more pronounced than usual.

Rios jerked her arm. "Shut up."

"Don't tell me—" Tiffie stumbled and nearly fell. She and Rios had popped some X in the parking lot, but it wasn't kicking in like it usually did. Tiffie was having trouble walking, and her brain felt like it was wrapped in wet wool.

Rios smiled in anticipation. Five thousand big ones . . .

"The party's here, babe. And you're the guest of honor." He led Tiffie through the back entrance to Cabin One.

Having bullied Ben Chan's whereabouts from the maitre d', Lulu marched through the cabin's front door and scanned the room. Zen Master was nowhere to be seen, but Dougie was standing at the bar.

What was her husband doing here? He usually did his drinking in the main building.

Lulu took another look around the room, more carefully this time. Definitely no Ben. Well, she'd deal with him later. Right now she was gonna earn that last pair of diamond earrings.

She undid another button on her blouse, put on a smile, and plowed through the crowd toward her husband.

Dougie checked his watch. Time to make sure the party's reward for its chief moneyman had arrived. He was heading for the hallway that led to the private bedrooms when someone called his name.

"Dougie! Wait!" The familiar voice screeched in his ears. Lulu?

Overcome with panic, Dougie bolted down the corridor.

Usually the thief was on the first plane out of town with the stolen delivery. Or he hid the cash and came up with a story how he was jumped, Powers reflected. Dougie had done neither. Instead, here he was at the club, lumbering down the cabin hallway with a busty older blonde in pursuit. Neither noticed Powers watching through one of the cabin's bedroom windows.

Maybe this old pol was smarter than he seemed. Powers doubted it, but he couldn't take a chance. He hoisted himself through the window. The buzz still droned in his ears, messing up his balance. He landed awkwardly and grimaced at the twinge in his knee.

Powers took the gun from his pocket. Hardware had a way of scaring the truth from people. He limped down the corridor after the Senator and the blonde.

Lulu had it figured out in a flash. The wolfish look on Ben's face as he stared at her daughter, the pimp who gripped Tiffie's arm, Dougie's face going pale as he took in the political payback he'd set up.

"You son of a bitch!" she screamed as she leaped for the closest of the three men—Dougie—and started scratching.

Dougie raised his arms to shield his face from his wife's talon-like nails. Lulu curled her hands into fists and switched to pummeling. Her exertions jarred loose a diamond earring.

Out of the corner of her eye, Lulu saw a man slip into the room. The maitre d'? She circled to Dougie's other side, wanting to get in some last licks before the man intervened.

Something crunched beneath her foot. Her earring. Lulu stopped hitting Dougie as the realization hit her. Real diamonds didn't crumble when stepped on.

Her shriek was operatic. "Cheap bastard!"

Lulu resumed her pounding. Borrowed husbands, single guys, the ones you married—they all deserved to burn in Hell. The maitre d' had moved within range, and Lulu took a swipe at him, too. He dodged the blow, then yelped and grabbed his knee.

The gunshot wasn't that loud, but Lulu knew what it was. Horrified, she stared at Ben, crumpled against the back of the sofa, a patch of red blooming like a rose on his shirt front.

The maitre d' stared at Ben, too. His hands, one still holding the gun, were pressed against his ears. Lulu realized he didn't work at the club. She had never seen him before.

With a moan, Dougie collapsed. His face went from white to gray as he clawed at his tie. Sweat beaded his scalp. His breathing rasped against the silence in the room.

Lulu grabbed Tiffie's hand.

The teenager twisted free. "Rios! Wait!"

Ignoring Tiffie, Rios darted for the exit. The one now blocked by the man who wasn't the maitre d'.

Rios groped in his pocket and withdrew a sliver of metal. Light caught the blade.

The man raised his gun and fired. Rios went down.

Tiffie started screaming.

"Shut up!" the man with the gun yelled.

Tiffie didn't shut up.

The man's expression went curiously serene. This terrified Lulu more than his scowl had. She tried to clamp her hand over her daughter's mouth. Tiffie fought back and they both crashed to the floor. Tiffie kept screaming.

Still appearing calm, the man with the gun bent over Dougie and spoke into his ear.

Lulu didn't catch her husband's response. She watched him raise a quavering hand and point at Tiffie.

The man with the gun straightened and walked toward them. Lulu heard low singing.

"Oh, you can't scare me . . ."

Powers joined the panicked crowd pouring out of the building. He couldn't believe the girl wouldn't give up where the money was. Even after her mother told her to. Kids these days had no respect.

Out of sympathy, he'd shot the blonde first. No one should have to watch their kid die, even a little bitch like that.

He got into his car, slipped the gun under the seat. His sure thing—and retirement—would have to wait for another day. At least the buzz in his head had stopped.

But there was still politics to deal with. He took out his cell phone.

The party chair answered on the first ring.

"You've got a problem," Powers said.

Lester's dad slammed down the phone receiver.

"Fuck!"

He should never have put Dougie in charge. He'd thought the guy was old-school, knew how things were supposed to be done.

Without the union's cooperation, the convention would be a disaster. Lester's dad had a day, maybe two, to come up with half a mil. Otherwise, he'd be out of politics and back to pumping gas and peddling brake jobs at his service station full-time.

He dropped his head into his hands and moaned.

Lester looped the tow chain around the Escalade's rear axle.

No one had claimed the SUV after last night's shootings. Picky about its parking lot being used by nonmembers, the club had called Lester's dad and asked him to tow the vehicle.

His dad had sent Lester out on the call. It was the first time Lester had ever seen him hung-over.

Lester tugged on the chain to make sure it was secure. If he'd owned a ride like this, maybe Tiffie would have gone out with him. Not that he cared about that stuck-up bitch anymore. He loved Amy now. Still, it was weird to think about a whole family wiped out, if you counted the step dad dying of a heart attack.

Lester peered through the tinted glass. Was that an iPod in the dash holder?

At ten in the morning, the lot was deserted, save for the parked cars of early golfers. After a look around to make sure he was alone, Lester took the Slim Jim from the tow truck.

The Escalade's door lock popped open in half a minute. The iPod disappeared into Lester's pocket in even less time.

Maybe there was a car charger. Lester searched the interior of the SUV. He pulled the brown bag out of the rear door pocket, opened it, and did a double take.

After he'd stashed the money into his backpack, Lester let himself think about what he'd buy Amy.

Girls were hot for diamond earrings, right?

THE ART OF AVARICE

Darrell James

In the back seat of his limo, behind the abandoned textile mill, North Carolina Governor Berk Cabot watched as the young woman finished buttoning her blouse. Rain had left a wet sheen on the pavement. Beyond the tinted windows, he could see lights across the river. The Raleigh skyline was lit up like a Christmas tree against the black sky.

"There's something I want to give you," Berk said, slipping a hand into his overcoat pocket. He came out with a small jewel case, opened it, and withdrew a thin silver chain. The setting held a small pink diamond chip. He let it dangle before the girl. "Something to show my appreciation for all your support and hard work."

"Oh, my God," came the girl's reply.

"It's just a bauble, really," Berk said, stringing it around the girl's neck and latching it. "But I'd like you to have it."

"It's beautiful."

The girl adjusted the setting so that it nestled amid her cleavage. She leaned in and gave Berk a quick peck on the cheek.

"So, perhaps I'll see you around campaign headquarters again?" Berk said.

"Governor Cabot, yes sir, if I know you're gonna be there."

Minutes ago this young woman had been going down on him. Lynette or Leanne, something like that, a political science major from UNC. One of the volunteers. Now she was addressing him the way she did at campaign headquarters. His driver had seen it all in the rearview mirror. *Jesus, what was this,* Berk considered, *his fifth term?*

Berk thought of his wife now. Margaret Ann Davis Cabot, First Lady of North Carolina. He pictured her back at the Governor's mansion, beneath the covers as she would likely be this time of night. Dressed in flannel pajamas, a Breathe-Right strip on her nose. He regarded this perky little volunteer as she opened the limo door and slid out. Caught a glimpse of smooth bare thigh before she smoothed her pleated skirt and closed the door. Watched her cross in midnight drizzle to her late-model Honda, do a cute little twirl, and give him a wave before slipping inside and starting the engine.

Berk let his gaze move to the darkened textile mill, the rust stains that colored the corrugated siding, the busted window panes. He thought of the tobacco lobbyists that would be in his office, 10 a.m. tomorrow morning. Drab creatures. Thought of the press conference later that day. And wondered, as the girl drove away, just how far down the polls he might slip before sunrise.

From where she was parked down the gravel road that ran perpendicular to the highway, Charlise Upton could see the front of the garage where Donnie Ray came on Wednesday nights to be with friends. It was this part of his old life he couldn't give up.

Beyond the high chain-link perimeter, light spilled from the open roll-up door and onto the parking area, where a handful of cars were parked. There were Cameros, Firebirds,

Dodge Challengers, and the like, all of them with wide tires and racing stripes. Inside, a bunch of good ol' boys. Donnie's racing buddies. Some of them his age, left over from the old days. A few of them younger. Turning camshafts, drinking beer, and listening to Donnie Ray tell stories of the glory days. Another hour passed as Charlise flipped pages in a fashion magazine before Donnie Ray came out. Appearing in the glow of light, he carried a beer bottle to the car with him. Some of the older guys were following, still bullshitting. Donnie Ray a little tipsy on his feet. Charlise waited until he was behind the wheel of his Firebird before picking up her cell phone and punching a number.

"Berk, baby?" she said to the tentative voice on the phone. "You want to win the election, don't you, lover?"

"What?" came the reply.

"You're trailing the stockcar boy by a six-point margin. I believe you could use a little help. What do you think, sugar?"

"Who is this?"

"Just think of me as the Tooth Fairy. Check the morning papers. This first one is free."

Charlise ended the call.

By now, Donnie Ray had finished his high-fiving and was backing his Pontiac around. She watched him point it toward the opening in the fenceline, spin the tires on the wet pavement, and lurch out onto the highway heading west. This time Charlise dialed nine-one-one.

"*What's your emergency?*"

"There's a black Firebird, with orange and yellow flames, heading south on Pritchert Road," she said into the phone. "It's weaving something terrible."

Berk Cabot was still studying the cell phone in his hand, thinking about the cool, seductive, female voice, trying to picture the mystery woman behind it. She was no one he recognized, seemingly. But a southern girl, a voice like that.

"Governor Cabot, sir?" The baritone voice that nudged him belonged to Lyle, his driver. They were passing shop fronts, curving south on Capitol Drive. Lyle was anticipating new instructions.

"Keep going," Berk said into the intercom. "Take me on home."

Berk eased back in his seat as Lyle nudged the gas pedal. He laid his head back on the seat rest and closed his eyes. The woman had asked: Did he want to win the election? *Of course he did.* Told him to watch the morning papers. What did she mean by that? Told him this one was free. Who was this woman? And, moreover, how did she get his private number?

With the occasional waft of passing traffic, Berk thought about the upcoming election. He thought of the governor's mansion. The limo. The bodyguards. His full-time driver, Lyle. He considered the money. The celebrity. The glad-hands that greased his palm and lined his pockets with campaign funds. The party working day and night to secure his re-election. The volunteers, all of them enthusiastically chanting his name. Some of them, like Lynette or Leanne, eager to please. Why then was he behind in the polls?

That was easy, Berk reminded himself.

Donnie Ray Banner running on nothing but his name.

If you had lived in Wake County for any length of time—hell, if you'd just parachuted in the day before—you'd know Donnie Ray Banner on a first-name basis. He'd been North Carolina's native son for the past twenty years. Six-time NASCAR champion. A sandy-haired sonofabitch with Robert Redford charm. Now making his bid for the governorship. Rumor had it that he'd squandered his fortune made from prize money and endorsements. And that he was only running to make a financial comeback. Still the public and the media loved him. He looked good on camera. Came across as a regular guy. And where the female demographic weighed in . . . well, there were the tar-heel mothers with their racing souvenirs who could still remember the days of spotting their panties whenever Donnie Ray revved his engine.

Whenever his numbers sagged a bit, all it took was for Donnie Ray to pop a toothpick in his mouth, make a fast lap around the capitol building, and give a wave to the camera. And, sure enough, a day later his lead would jump another point. The fast-track golden boy from Fayetteville was running on a platform of hero worship and making Berk Cabot, the reigning governor for more than a decade now, look like a schoolgirl.

When the *Charlotte Register* hit the streets, six a.m. Saturday morning, some of the shine had been taken off Donnie Ray's lead.

It was seven that evening before Julian Fadder, Berk's campaign manager, caught up with the Governor to talk about it. He found him at the Argyle Room, an exclusive, private smoking club for industry execs and politicians.

"I've been trying to reach you all fucking day, Berk. You see this?" Julian waved a folded section of the *Register* as he sunk into the sofa next to him.

Berk was looking off, only halfway listening. His mind was on the telephone call of the night before. *This first one is free,* he heard the girl say in the silky voice that caused things to stir low inside. Now he shifted his eyes to his campaign manager—a fidgety little guy with his tie loosened, his

97

sleeves rolled above the elbow, still working hard into the evening hours.

"I've read it," Berk said.

"Well, you should be jumping up and down, my friend. I knew this tire jockey couldn't get through an entire campaign without screwing up. This is fan-fucking-tastic, Berk. You listening?" Julian began to read. "Gubernatorial challenger Donnie Ray Banner was pulled over by Wake County Sheriff's Deputies at two-fifteen this morning and charged with driving with an open container of alcohol in the car. The candidate was fined and released. When asked if Banner had been under the influence, a spokesperson for the department said that the matter was still under investigation." Julian looked up. "They're letting him off. DUI, and they're giving the sonofabitch a celebrity free pass."

Berk was off in his head again, his gaze out across the smoky room toward the bar where a couple of appellate court judges were entertaining a pair of female flight attendants they'd brought in with them. Could this actually be the event the woman on the phone had predicted? If so, how would she have known? It was intriguing, Berk thought. It was also damn disturbing.

"I got a call last night," he said, keeping his voice low. They were in a sequestered seating area in the corner, dim lamplight creating a mood. "A woman who said we should watch the papers this morning, there would be a surprise."

Julian cocked his head. "A call? Do you know who she was?"

"No. Just that we could expect news to break regarding the election . . . uh, hold on . . ." His cell phone was ringing. Berk answered. "Yes?"

"I assume you've seen the polls?" the silky voice said.

Berk locked Julian with his eyes. "*It's her,*" he mimed with his lips. Julian sat forward in his seat.

"Why, yes, darlin', I certainly have," Berk said into the phone. "The pundits have Banner slipping a couple of notches following his lapse of judgment. They tell me I'm now just four points off his heels. Should I believe this was your doing?"

"If you want this race, Governor, you'd better believe it."

"Then you have my eternal gratitude. Now, to what do I owe the pleasure of this call?"

"Just stay tuned, sugar," the silky voice said. "See what comes next."

The line went dead. Berk studied the call-screen, the number blocked, then flipped the phone shut and tossed it on the table.

Julian was waiting, a crease lining his brow.

Berk said, "She wants us to believe she has the power to throw this thing our way."

"Well, there's no . . . I mean . . . how could she? Did she say what she wants?"

Berk un-sleeved a fresh cigar, snipped the end of it, struck fire and huffed it to life. He blew smoke toward the ceiling, then turned his face to his campaign manager. "Not yet. She's going to toy with us some more."

A dark-haired waitress appeared wearing a short cocktail outfit and heels. Her narrow waist was tightly belted. Berk offered his empty glass to her. "Darlin', would you be so kind? Bring me another daiquiri, please? And bring my friend here a beer."

When the girl went off to fill the order, Julian said, "I don't know, Berk." He was shaking his head.

"It's not to worry, my friend. It's part of politics here in the south. We have our own special ways. We sip our coffee from a saucer. We chain our dogs to the porch, then send the cat to lay down with them. We see unbridled greed over-pouring its bounds, and it brings to mind Jack Daniel's over ice. Why do you suppose that is?"

Julian shrugged his brow.

"No, see, I can respect this woman's avarice," Berk said. "But what bothers me most is how damned confident she is."

"You want to know if she can pull it off," Julian said. It was more of a statement than a question.

"What I want to know," Berk said, drawing on his cigar and letting the smoke curl skyward, "is how she knows so damn much about Donnie Ray Banner."

Donnie Ray was on the bed in his boxers, his back against the headboard, his legs crossed at the ankles. "You know, you could have at least given me some warning," he called to the open bathroom doorway.

Calling back from inside, Charlise said, "I thought we agreed you weren't to know what comes next. It keeps it spontaneous, unrehearsed."

"Yeah, but drunk driving? I could have lost my license. Jesus, Charlise. A racecar driver without a license. It's just a damn good thing I knew the cop who pulled me over. He went to school with us. Jeff Reagan. You remember him? Yeah, you must. Played on the football team. Probably one of the guys you did beneath the bleachers."

Charlise appeared outside the doorway with a towel wrapped about her. She was still as sexy as she'd been back then. More so, now that she'd matured. A crisp blonde bob had replaced the ponytail she used to wear. Her hips had taken on a seductive, womanly curve.

"You see?" Charlise said, her hip cocked. "Everyone still thinks 'cause I was a cheerleader, I must have been a slut. I never did anyone those days. I was holding out for a better offer." Not giving him the opportunity to respond, she turned back inside the bathroom.

Donnie Ray picked up the TV remote, clicked it a couple of times, but nothing happened. He tossed it. Let his gaze wander about the motel room. It was nice enough this time. Even if the TV didn't work. Discreet. Seven miles outside of town, on the old state route highway leading toward Durham. Way the hell the other direction from where his wife, Mayleen, would be at home alone. His three boys, older now, were off on their own. It was funny how things turned out.

He'd had the hots for Charlise all the way since junior high. Every guy at Jefferson Davis did. But then he began dating Mayleen. That was their senior year, and soon after she was pregnant with their first child. Two years out of high school, Donnie Ray learned that Charlise had married a salesman who'd come through town selling farm tractors, and had moved across the state to Greenville. The marriage lasted six months, the last news he had of her.

He'd been retired from racing for seven years when Charlise suddenly appeared behind him in the grocery checkout line. She'd goosed him once, saying, *Hey, good-looking.* That chance encounter had led to drinks at a local bar. The first two walked them down memory lane. The third one had them touching hands across the table. The fourth had Donnie Ray's pants around his ankles and Charlise's legs across both the front and back seats of her Mercedes. That was more than a year and a half ago. Since that time, they'd been carrying on a crossroads affair, catching love on the run at one motel or another around Wake county. It was Charlise who suggested they do something unbelievable together.

The plan, as Charlise had laid it out for him that night six months ago, was to put him in the run-off as a gubernatorial candidate.

"You kidding me?" was Donnie Ray's response.

Sitting up in bed with the covers pulled to their chins and passing a joint back and forth between them, Charlise had told him, no. It was something she'd been thinking about for a while. He'd be a natural to gain the lead. Good looks, built-in popularity. Look at the others who'd done it. At least two movie stars and a professional wrestler. "But in this case, we do something different," Charlise said. "As you don't actually have any interest in being the governor, once we're ahead in the polls, we sell the election off to Berk Cabot, the incumbent."

"You mean, take a fall?" Donnie Ray said.

"Like a fighter that gets paid to lay down. Yeah."

"Okaay . . ."

The marijuana had Donnie considering. He could use the money, that was for sure. Dress up for a change. Put on a nice set of clothes. And what the hell, it could be a hoot. Get his face in the camera again. He asked, "But what do I know about running for governor?"

"You just let me handle the politics."

Donnie Ray had to ask then. "Yeah? And what would an ex-stripper know about politics?"

The question drew him a hard look.

"Don't knock stripping, Donnie Ray," Charlise had said, her chin out. "You can learn a lot about life in a nudie club. The way I see it, running for office is not much different than doing a lap dance. You only have to show them the promise of what's to come. You don't actually have to give it to them."

That had been then. Now, here he was, a little over a week away from election day with Charlise working the Governor for a payday.

In the bathroom, Charlise slipped out of the towel and into a terry bathrobe. She took time to study her face in the mirror, touch at the lines around her eyes. So many years wasted. You set out in life with a dream. Her dream was to have it good. Be married to someone with money. Someone famous maybe. Someone like Donnie Ray Banner. But then life has a way of slipping away from you. And things don't always turn out the way you imagine. Donnie Ray had already squandered his first fortune. And . . . well, there was Mayleen.

From the room outside, she heard Donnie Ray say, "You know, sometimes I think about what it might be like to actually be the governor."

Charlise didn't respond right away. Instead, she cinched the robe tighter and went out to join him.

He said, "I kind of like the picture of being sworn into office."

"Is that right? And is Mayleen by your side in this picture? What about me? This was my idea—my plan that brought us this far. You think Mayleen should get the glory?"

"I'm just dreaming, Charlise. Don't get uptight about it." Donnie Ray rolled off the bed and started pulling on his slacks.

"You're not staying?"

"I'm sorry, Char. I have to go tonight."

"You're going home to her."

Donnie Ray gave her a look beneath his brow. "I've got an image to uphold so it doesn't look like I'm throwing this thing. You said so yourself."

Charlise watched him pull his shirt on and begin working the buttons. He was still trim for his age. And did look good. Gubernatorial, actually, in a suit and tie.

"You know," Charlise said. "I could still give you the governorship. It's not too late. But I'm not exactly picturing Mayleen at your side when you place your hand on the Bible."

Donnie Ray finished his buttons. "What? You? Come on, Charlise. How would that look thirty days after the election. The governor-elect of North Carolina divorces wife and marries . . ." He hesitated.

"An ex-stripper?"

"Come on. She's my wife and the mother of my kids. Let's just play this out the way we planned it."

"Then what, Donnie?"

"Then you take your half and spend it, I guess. What do you want from me?"

Charlise watched as Donnie Ray finished tucking his shirt tail in. He wrapped his tie about his neck, and threw his jacket across his shoulder. Then he crossed to her and tried to give her a peck on the lips. She gave him the cold side of her cheek instead.

"I'll see you mid-week," he said. "Just put that little head of yours to work and think about how next to sabotage me. Okay? Just don't let me lose my license." Donnie Ray gave her a friendly poke in the ribs and was out the door and gone.

Charlise waited until the door had closed in Donnie's wake, then crossed to the phone that sat on the nightstand. When the sleepy female voice came on the line, she said, "Mayleen, honey. Do you have any naked pictures of your husband? . . . No? Well, I do. I'll send you one by email."

*   *   *

By mid-week, rumors of Donnie Ray Banner's indiscretion had found root in Fayetteville and reverberated across the state. The polls showed Berk Cabot closing the gap, and the media were now calling the governor's race a dead heat.

Back in the hotel, Wednesday night, Charlise waited for Donnie Ray on the bed, dressed in a filmy negligee, silk panties underneath. He came in the way she expected, gunning for a fight.

"You've gone too far this time, Charlise."

"Relax, honey. You want the money or not?"

Charlise busied herself with applying red lacquer to her toenails, while Donnie Ray paced at the foot of the bed.

"Yeah, but my wife, Charlise? Goddamn it!"

"Don't tell me you never took any of those twisty little racecar groupies behind the pit van for a quickie. And don't tell me Mayleen didn't know about it."

"Those times were discreet. Jesus Christ, she's too embarrassed to answer the phone. The whole damn state is talking about it."

"Well, come on, sugar. The scam doesn't work unless the voters know about it." Charlise inspected her toes, wiggled them to speed the drying process, then sealed the bottle of nail polish and set it aside on the nightstand. "It takes negative press to affect the polls. Mayleen will get over it. She will. And so will you when you see your half of the payoff. Now, come on over here and join me." She patted the bed beside her.

Donnie Ray didn't move. "I had a long talk with Mayleen last night," he said. "I told her all about you and me. I told her everything."

"Wait. You told her about the scam?"

Donnie Ray nodded. "She remembers you from high school. We talked about the race, and Mayleen asked a lot of questions about what it would be like to be the First Lady. Mayleen told me she would stick by me."

"Well, see, there you go. All it takes is a little sweet talk." Charlise touched at the enamel on her toenails.

"And," Donnie Ray said, "I told her I was going to win the election."

Charlise looked up.

Donnie Ray was staring back at her, his eyes level, his jaw set.

"It's just what you told her," Charlise said, something of a question in her voice. "To placate her."

"It's what I intend to do. I've decided to win."

Momentarily Charlise had nothing to say. Then the words came. "Sure. You go ahead, Donnie Ray. I can just see Mayleen at your side. Hayseed mother of three. Tell her to lose a couple of pounds before she gets on camera. You can't win this without me. I'm the one controlling the vote."

"We'll see."

"We'll see? Then what? You think you've got the brain-power to run an entire state?"

Charlise knew she'd gone a step too far. Donnie Ray's eyes leveled on her, the affable blue in them turned a darker shade of gray. "Like you said, Charlise. It's a lot like giving a lap dance. Any lowlife can do it."

Donnie Ray turned for the door.

Charlise sprang from the bed and caught up with him before he could turn the knob. "I'm sorry, Donnie. Really. I'm just worried about you, baby."

Donnie Ray hesitated, a weary slump entering his shoulders. He let his head drop to the cool metal surface of the jamb.

Charlise lifted his hand from the knob and slid her body between him and the door. He tried to turn away, but she pulled him back. He turned his face from her, but she pressed her lips to the curve of his neck. "Don't go." She drew herself closer, letting perfume and the warmth of her body go to work.

"I have to go, Charlise."

He made another attempt at the door and Charlise blocked his way again. This time she put her lips to the lobe of his ear.

"Stay."

"I can't. Mayleen is waiting. She needs me."

"So do I," Charlise said, bringing one of Donnie Ray's hands to the warm place between her thighs. "Can't you feel how much I need you?"

He tried to pull away, but Charlise held him there, moving against him, and letting her tongue slip inside his ear. She could feel his resistance faltering, and said with all confidence, "You want me, don't you, baby?"

Donnie Ray gave in. He grabbed a handful of silky fabric and tore, and took her there against the door in an angry, heated rush.

Charlise paid it out until Donnie Ray had spent his shame inside her.

Breathless and weak, Donnie pulled away from her.

"You want to be governor, baby," Charlise said, taking his face in her hands and bringing his eyes to look into hers. "We can do that. I just want to know that it's me who'll be by your side. Can you promise me that?"

Charlise saw the light go out of Donnie's eyes. He zipped his pants, brushed her roughly aside and, in an instant, was out the door and gone.

Charlise remained with her back against the wall, listening to the sound of Donnie Ray's Firebird starting up. The sound of tires squealing on pavement.

THE ART OF AVARICE

Slowly, she eased the door closed, then crossed to the phone on the desk and punched in a number. When the voice came on, she said, "Berk, sugar, I've given you a horse race. Now, let's talk about a landslide."

In the study at the governor's mansion, Berk Cabot stood with his back to the desk, his gaze out across the lawn to where security lights ringed the garden perimeter. It was the call he'd been waiting for.

"A landslide? Well, now, that's a pretty big swing in public opinion, wouldn't you say? Just how do you plan to manage that, darling?"

"You can leave the how to me," the silky voice told him. "But, let's just say, by tomorrow night, a serious tragedy will befall the Banner family."

"You must be psychic to know such things," Berk said.

"I just know one thing, sugar. You can't win a race if you're not around to run it."

Berk found his plush leather desk chair and eased into it. He settled back, crossing his legs at the knee. Beyond the window, near the perimeter wall, a security guard made his rounds. Berk said, "Well, darling, why don't you just tell me what you want and we'll see if I can accommodate."

The silky voice on the phone said, "One million dollars, lover. Cash. Small bills."

Berk gave a whistle into the phone. "And, just where do you suppose I might get that kind of money?"

"Do we need a discussion on illegal campaign contributions? Bring the money in a suitcase to the top floor of the 440 Building on Hargett Street, midnight tomorrow. Take the elevator to the top floor and wait with your cell phone until you hear from me. That simple."

Berk was trying to picture the woman, bring some recognition to the voice. "And what guarantee do I have you'll deliver the election. I don't even know your name."

"Think back, Berk, baby. VIP room. After hours. Private party. The Gold Club. You told me you'd never seen a girl with dollar signs tattooed above her coochie. I know it's been a while, lover. But I'd be hurt if you'd forgotten."

Berk began nodding to himself. "Short blonde hair," he said. "I recall you had no need for surgical enhancement."

"And that's your guarantee. You know who I am. And I know you have people who could find me if I don't come through. You see how it is, lover?"

Berk saw. The girl was smart. "I do admire ambition," he said.

"Just be sure to come alone, sugar."

The following night—four days to the election—Berk Cabot entered the lobby of the 440 Building with the suitcase. He was expecting to find a security guard on duty, but saw no one behind the desk. The lights of Raleigh were beyond the glass. The building was eerily silent.

Berk found the elevators in an alcove off the lobby, tested them, and found them operable. He boarded one and punched the number for the fourteenth floor. Exactly as he'd been instructed.

The doors opened into another small alcove at the top. To his right, behind glass, were the offices of Ryson, Brogan, and Merit, a law firm. To his left was an investment brokerage. Both offices were sealed tight. The lights were out. The hallways were dark and lifeless. Berk checked his watch and waited.

At the stroke of midnight his cell phone rang.

"Set the suitcase in the elevator and send it down alone," Charlise said. "Don't try to come with it, sugar. I can see you on the security monitor."

Berk glanced around the alcove but saw nothing in the way of cameras. The woman could be bluffing. No matter. Yes, it was a lot of money to risk, but then again, it wasn't his to worry about. Wouldn't the campaign supporters want it this way? After all, they had given it freely and generously to secure his re-election. And as the woman had said, he knew exactly how to find her.

Berk thought of her the way he remembered her from the Gold Club. He would love to get another look at the tattoo. Another touch. But that likely wouldn't happen. This woman was in control. And there was a lot more at stake than a gratuitous feel. Berk pressed the button for the elevator and the nearest doors opened. He set the suitcase inside. Then, as an after thought, he drew from his coat pocket a small jewelry case. One of his baubles. A pendant with a thin silver chain and a tiny pink diamond chip as its setting. Why not? Put a cherry on top. A way of saying thanks to the lady who was saving his campaign.

Berk threaded the chain through the handle of the suit-case and wrapped it so the diamond chip found its perch on top. He then pressed the button for the lobby and stepped off. He waited as the doors closed and the whir of the elevator whistled through the cracks.

Berk pictured the money on the ride down. Pictured the cool seductive beauty as he'd remembered her in his mind. There were all kinds of women in this world, Berk thought. But there was something especially stimulating about the ones who had balls.

*   *   *

Charlise snatched up the suitcase almost before the doors could open. She noticed the tiny pendant necklace wound through the handle, and had to smile. The southern governor had style. Without taking time to remove it, Charlise found the door leading to the parking garage and took the stairs two at a time going down.

She crossed quickly through the darkened subterrain, hearing her own footfalls echoing through the hollow space. She ducked between cars, throwing furtive glances over her shoulder, sprinting the last several feet to her Mercedes, parked in the corner. Only then did she see the figure lurking in the shadows, and froze with her hand on the door handle.

"Who's there?"

The figure said nothing, but stepped into the light.

"What are *you* doing here?" Charlise said.

In answer, a hand came up to reveal a gun. Charlise caught her breath as the figure pointed the muzzle at her and squeezed the trigger.

January rolled around, and Donnie Ray Banner placed his hand on the Bible and swore to do his duty and to uphold the laws of the State. By his side was his wife, Mayleen, a frumpy, but now lavishly dressed hometown girl, who was moments away from becoming the First Lady of North Carolina.

Berk Cabot still couldn't figure out what happened.

On the Saturday prior to the election, news of a murder had shared time in the media with the final countdown to the vote. The body of an attractive, forty-three-year-old woman, a Fayetteville native, had been found dumped alongside the road, half a state away. A former stripper named Charlise Upton. A *Re-elect Berk Cabot* campaign brochure had been discovered stuffed down the front of her jeans. There was no mention of money, Berk reminded himself. No leads. And no apparent motive. Nothing truly incriminating.

Still, the insinuations were damning.

The whisper campaign that followed was enough to sink Berk in the polls. It was fueled mostly by the Banner camp, and, surprisingly, by Mayleen Banner herself, who had suddenly taken a frontline interest in her husband's campaign.

Berk watched the swearing-in ceremony from a place at the back of the dais, working hard to keep the knot in his throat from rising to the top. A rare skiff of winter snow had dusted the Capitol steps and lawn. On the podium, Mayleen Banner smiled demurely as her husband, the newly sworn governor, gave a wave to the crowd, much the way Berk remembered seeing him do some years ago at the speedway in Charlotte. Now the fair-haired boy was his successor. What exactly had gone wrong?

Cameras flashed, streamers streamed, and confetti danced on the cool winter air. And in one single glint of light, former Governor Berk Cabot had his answer.

There, around the neck of the new First Lady, Mayleen Banner, was a pendant. A thin silver chain with a tiny pink diamond chip as its setting—a bauble really.

Berk Cabot nodded his appreciation, then stepped down from the dais and made his way off through the crowd. It was nothing to make an issue of, the way he saw it. It was the way politics were done here in the south. It was dogs and cats living together. It was avarice as a form of art.

It brought to mind Jack Daniel's over ice.

AMBITION

Michele Martinez

June

"Miss . . . ?" Dick Maslin glanced down at her résumé, which sat between them on his desk. "*Ortega.*"

"Ashley."

"Ashley. Tell me about yourself."

"I was vice-president of the College Democrats. I majored in Government—"

"No, no. Assume I've read this," he said, tapping the page.

The résumé was upside-down to her, but she could read the B+/A- he'd written next to her name. That wasn't her GPA, it was his assessment of her, right there in black and white.

"I spent all my free time working on campaigns," Ashley said. "I don't have any hobbies, if that's what you're getting at. I'm all politics, all the time."

She flashed a smile high-wattage enough to defuse the tension in any room, but it didn't work on him. He was a bear of a man. His bulk and his bushy blond hair promised a jolly guy, an easy interview, but they lied. He was on Master-of-the-Universe pills like everybody else in this company town. In her brand new interview suit, Ashley felt confident that she could handle him.

"I mean your bio," he said. "Bio is everything these days."

She glanced at the résumé again. He'd double-underlined her last name. *Oh, that bio. He wants me to dance,* she thought.

"Well, I'm from Reading, Pennsylvania, which is almost fifty percent Hispanic. More like seventy-five percent in my age group. We're the wave of the future. We're the new voters, we're the next labor market, you name it."

"You're right about that. You speak Spanish?"

"Fluently. My family are humble people. I was the first to go to college."

From the way he nodded, she saw that she was hitting all the right notes. He was that predictable. She relaxed.

"My father's Puerto Rican, my mother's from Ecuador," she continued. "She immigrated when she was fifteen. She cleans houses. My dad drives a bus. I'm the oldest of five kids. I worked nights at Burger King to pay for college. When I go back home now and see my classmates, some have kids of their own. Some are in jail."

Mostly true, she thought. *Stop me any time, Dick.*

"Your parents must be very proud of you."

She noticed the photograph on his desk, nearly overlooked among the avalanche of handshake photos lining the walls. His kids were about her age.

"I love my parents so much," she said. "You should've seen the looks on their faces at my commencement. The tears in their eyes. I'll never forget."

The phone on the desk started to ring. He checked the caller ID but decided not to answer.

"Where do you see yourself in ten years?" he asked.

"In a job like yours. An A.A. for a high-profile Congressman or Senator."

Ten? she thought. *Shoot me.*

She'd learned the Hill jargon in a job interview that she'd flubbed three days ago, and she tossed it around like a pro now. A.A., Administrative Assistant, the guy who ran the office, like Maslin himself. L.C., legislative correspondent, answers constituent mail. L.A., legislative assistant, higher on the totem pole, more access to the member. She'd studied up. Never make the same mistake twice, that was her motto.

"Are you considering other offers?" Maslin asked.

"One."

"Oh? What's that?"

What the hell had possessed her to say such a thing?

"From Senator Romer's office. I have to give them an answer by tomorrow."

She crossed her fingers that he wouldn't check, that he wasn't lunch buddies with Romer's A.A.

"So if I offered you the position . . . ?"

"Oh, I'd accept on the spot. Definitely. The Congressman is a charismatic up-and-comer with a big future ahead of him. I'd consider myself so lucky to work for him. Besides, my other offer is for an L.C. job, and I'd rather be an L.A. More responsibility. More input into policy."

"What we do here is not about policy in the grand sense, you realize, Ashley," Maslin said. "It's more like trench warfare. We get re-elected. We celebrate. The next morning we start thinking about the next campaign."

"Dick, I live for campaigns."

"We need team players."

"You're looking at one."

Maslin studied her résumé again. He didn't appear entirely convinced. She fixed her eyes on him like she'd die if she didn't get this job. That wasn't so far from the truth. She could only afford to stay in D.C. for a few more days, then it was back home to live with her parents.

His phone rang. He checked the caller ID. She could tell he wanted to take this one. She watched him hesitate, then reach for the receiver.

"Hold on a second," he said into the phone.

Maslin extended his hand across the desk and shook hers. "Welcome aboard, Ashley. Be a team player, and you'll do all right around here."

February

"These are excellent talking points," Maslin said, scanning the page, his reading glasses threatening to fall off the end of his nose as he nodded.

"You sound surprised."

Ashley crossed her legs. Involuntarily, he glanced at them.

"No. It's just, you haven't been here that long, and the work is very polished. I'll barely need to edit them before I give them to the Congressman."

"Edit? What are you planning to edit?"

"You shouldn't take it personally, you know. I edit everybody, including staffers who've been here a helluva lot longer than you."

"I'm not offended. I try to learn from my mistakes, that's all," she said.

"I wouldn't call this a mistake. It's more a difference of opinion. The position you staked out on the civil liberties thing is a little aggressive, don't you think? I may need to tone it down."

Ashley leaned forward. "Dick, remember at the staff meeting on Friday, the Congressman complained his press has been trending negative lately?"

MICHELE MARTINEZ

"Yes?"

"Well, I've been analyzing the views of the opinion makers at the network affiliates—"

"I think he was talking about the newspaper."

"Nobody reads anymore. One positive story on TV and you wipe out the effects of ten editorials. Trust me. Do this my way, you'll get some very respectful coverage, at least from Channel 9."

"That's a very interesting suggestion. What makes you think Channel 9 agrees with you on this one?"

"Like I said, I've been analyzing. I go on their website every morning and watch the podcast from the night before."

He frowned. "I didn't know you could do that. Since when?"

"Just recently. You should try it. Much more informative than those boring news summaries we get from the district office."

"I may do that."

"Time to enter the twenty-first century." She laughed, the sound warm enough to take the sting out of her words.

"This is very good work," he said. "I'm going to give serious consideration to what you're proposing here."

"Thank you."

"You know, we should talk. Lisa Aronoff was just in here. Did you realize she's planning to start law school at night this summer?"

"No, I didn't know that. Lisa doesn't exactly confide in me."

"Me neither, apparently. It was the first I'd heard. She claims she can handle the workload, but I'm skeptical. I'm

117

thinking about giving you responsibility for some of her issue areas."

"Whatever I can do to help, Dick."

December

Ashley looked up from the phone call to find Dick Maslin standing over her desk.

"Hang up. I need to talk to you. Now."

He looked seriously pissed. Luckily it was after seven on a snowy night, and all the other cubicles in the L.A.s' room were empty. This might get ugly, and she hated getting dressed down in front of the crew. Bad for the image. They'd all sensed that a battle was brewing, and Ashley wanted them to believe she'd emerge the winner.

"Let me call you back," she said into the phone.

"Who invited *you* to this thing with the gaming industry people tonight?" he demanded after she'd hung up.

"The Congressman did," she replied, eyes wide.

"Don't give me that innocent look. You and I both know he doesn't go around inviting junior staffers to sensitive, high-level meetings without running it by me first."

"I'm not so junior anymore, Dick. Two years is a long time on the Hill."

"It hasn't been two years. Besides, it never would have occurred to him to bring you unless somebody planted the suggestion in his mind. That somebody wouldn't happen to be you, would it?"

"The casinos bill is in my portfolio."

"How do you figure that?"

"I handle judicial issues. It's a judicial issue."

"A judicial issue? What, because it has legal implications? Under that definition, everything's in your portfolio, Ashley. Oh, wait a minute, what am I saying? That *is* your position, isn't it?"

"The only other place it could go is under Native Amer-·ican affairs. But I spoke to Rod and he assured me he wasn't handling it, so I figured it was fair game."

"Did you ever think of asking me, since I run this office? Rod *isn't* handling it. *I'm* handling it. The thing's a mine-field. I need to deal with it personally."

"With all due respect, Dick, how was I supposed to know? I didn't see you in the committee room when the bill got marked up."

"You went to the mark-up on a bill you were never assigned?" he asked.

"I attend mark-up on all significant legislation in my issue areas. If I waited for a specific instruction, nothing would ever get done. Listen, when you hired me, you said you wanted self-starters, and that's what you got. Dick, I know this bill inside out. I've already briefed the Congressman. I should be the one at the meet-and-greet tonight. I'm the only person in the office who's up to speed."

"I said I wanted team players, not self-starters. In your case, Ashley, there's a helluva difference between those two things. In fact, I'd say there's a gaping chasm."

Her big brown eyes went moist. "I'm sorry you feel that way. Maybe I messed up this one. Just so you know, it's only because I care about doing a good job. I was trying to advance the Congressman's interests."

"Look, it's obvious that you care about the job," he said, sighing. "I see that you work harder than anybody else, but—"

"*But* I should have communicated better. Granted. It won't happen again. I never make the same mistake twice. You know that about me. Can you forgive me?"

"It's not about forgiveness. I need to handle this bill personally. You back off, and stay backed off. Are we clear?"

"Dick, you're the boss," she said. "If that's what you want me to do, that's what I'll do."

Ashley's gaze wandered to the display on the bottom of her computer screen, which read 7:15 p.m., the time she'd told the Congressman that she'd swing by to pick him up for the meet-and-greet. The display changed to 7:16, and, right on cue, her phone lit up.

"Oh," she said, sounding surprised, "it's the Congressman's inside line."

Dick cast her a suspicious look. "I'll speak to him myself."

She picked up the phone and handed it to him.

"No, Mike, it's Dick. I was sitting here with Ashley getting briefed on the casinos bill. I'll be the one coming along with you to meet the gaming industry people. She says—uh, yes, she did, but I . . . Mike, I really feel I should be there personally . . . Because . . . Look, the downsides are greater than the upsides on this thing, and it could come back to bite us in the ass. It could end up looking like we . . . I understand, but this is a complex matter. Between the Native Americans on the one hand and the State Gaming Commission on the other . . . Yes, she is, I agree completely. She's also still relatively inexperienced . . . I've made my position clear . . . Right. All right. You're the boss."

Dick hung up. "He'll meet you at the front door."

August

"So your objection is to the timing?" Ashley asked, leaning forward, her elbows on the snowy white tablecloth.

"You could say that," Dick replied. "I understand that the relationship pre-exists, and that it has to be maintained. But now is not the moment for the Congressman to get his picture taken with this guy."

"In my view, now is *exactly* the moment, precisely because of the election bearing down on us. Dick, the campaign needs the money. And Mike's cool with it. I talked to him already."

"Keep your voice down," he said, glancing around. "Here's the real problem. What if somebody draws the connection between this contribution and what we did on the casinos bill last year?"

The waiter arrived with their food, and Dick fell silent.

"Oh, you got the brook trout," Ashley said. "I love how they make it here."

"How often have you been to this place?" he asked, glancing up from salting his food.

She shrugged.

"Seriously. Does Mike take you?"

"When we have something important to discuss. Look, I'm prepared to be the bad guy and say no to a photo op. Bad hair day, whatever. Hell, Pugliese is savvy enough. He should understand the need to fly under the radar. But we can't call off the dinner. That would make bad waves right when we're about to get to the handshake on this contribution. And you're being paranoid about the casinos bill. Nobody's even thinking about it these days, and the contribution is being made through another entity entirely. I've got everything under control, don't worry."

He shook his head. "I'm going to have to overrule you on this one, Ash, sorry. Too risky."

"You can't."

"What do you mean?"

"Didn't Mike tell you?"

His fork stopped halfway to his mouth. "What now?"

"Brianne's pregnant. She's taking a leave of absence. I'm moving over to the campaign."

"As *deputy director?*"

"Don't act so shocked. Brianne's been relying on my ideas for the past six months anyway, and Mike knows it. I'm good, Dick. When are you gonna get that through your thick skull and stop fighting the inevitable?"

"What's the inevitable? That you steal my job?"

You said it, I didn't, she thought.

"Of course not. That I'll be playing an important role in the campaign. That's all."

"How is it that I'm just hearing about this now? You went behind my back, didn't you?"

"Don't get melodramatic. The decision was only made last night, and here I am telling you about it already. Nobody's keeping anything from you."

"You're telling me *after* the fact. I run the office. I should've been party to these discussions all along. How long have you been discussing this with Mike?"

"Not long."

"How long?"

"You're really making this lunch unpleasant. I'm running the campaign, okay? Get over it. Enjoy your food."

"Running it? Sandy may have something to say about that."

"Please. Sandy's a figurehead."

"You know, I've always believed that people are born with a certain amount of guile and sneakiness in them, and you really prove my theory, Ashley. I see it in my children, too. One is honest as the day is long. The other knows how to spin. I saw from the moment you walked in the door that you were trouble, and yet I hired you anyway."

Your phone was ringing, you lazy ox. You got what you deserved.

"Politics is spin. You should be glad I'm a good spinner, Dick. I'm keeping us both in clover."

"Jesus God, I've created a monster."

She flashed her million-dollar smile. It only made him worry more.

"Hey, if you can't beat 'em, join 'em. Trust me, that's the best advice you'll ever get when it comes to dealing with me. Would you pass the salt?"

June

"You don't appear to be taking this very seriously," Dick said, leaning back in the guest chair in Ashley's office.

After the campaign, the Congressman's scheduling aide had quit suddenly for unexplained reasons, and Ashley had wound up with his job, giving her both this office and control over the Congressman's daily schedule. Dick had to go through Ashley now whenever he wanted Mike to show up someplace.

"Would you get your shoe off my desk, please?" she said.

Dick sat up. "I'm just saying, Alan Butterworth is a very savvy lawyer. He did excellent work for Potter's A.A. when he was being investigated by the Ethics Committee, and he even cut his fee in recognition of all the free publicity he got on the matter."

"There isn't going to be any publicity. This is just a subpoena for information. It's Pugliese they're investigating, not me. All I have to do is say I don't know anything."

"Your contacts in the Justice Department think that'll work?"

She eyed him warily. He had better contacts in the Justice Department than she did. She hadn't been able to find out a thing.

"Don't yours?" Ashley forced herself to ask. She hated to appear weak—or poorly informed, which amounted to the same thing—but these were unusual circumstances.

"No, that's what I've been trying to tell you," Dick replied. "My guy says the gaming industry investigation is gonna be huge, that these subpoenas are only the first wave, the tip of the iceberg. The Attorney General needs to look like he's tough on corruption after the scandal last year, and this is his ticket."

"I don't see how that affects me," Ashley said, but there were dark shadows around her eyes.

"How can you *not* see? You need a lawyer, Ash. And, painful as it is, I think you should consider stepping back on some of your duties while the investigation plays out. I'm sure you'll come out fine in the end, but the publicity could get hairy for a while. And after everything you went through, everything we all went through, to get him re-elected, you don't want to be responsible for screwing things up for Mike."

"Duh, now I understand. This is a power play. I must be off my game, not seeing it sooner."

"Power play?"

"Oh, come on. You've resented me ever since I took over scheduling. No, wait—since I went over to the campaign, even before that. You're jealous of how close I am to Mike. Now you're going all alarmist so you can create momentum to force me out. Admit it, Dick. I won't be mad. I'll admire your chutzpah, even."

"I wish you wouldn't get defensive on me. I'm only trying to help, and you need all the friends you can get right now."

"What did you say to Mike?"

"I haven't said a word to Mike. I'm not convinced he would listen if I did. I'm trying to be as supportive of you as I can, Ashley. Maybe you forget that I hired you, I trained you. Your actions reflect on me. Mike's concerns need to be front and center, and I would hope, after everything we've been through over the years, that you understand that. I shouldn't be the only one in this room looking out for his reputation. I know if our positions were reversed, protecting the seat would be your biggest concern."

Our positions reversed, she thought. *That can still be arranged. Never too late. That special prosecutor is gonna get an earful.*

"Don't worry," she said. "I have a plan. The seat will be protected. Everything is under control. I appreciate your support, Dick. I really do."

"It's times like this that you find out who your friends are," he said. And his gaze bored in on her in a strange way, a way she couldn't quite read.

September

"How the hell did they find us?" Ashley blurted into her cell phone. "You were the only one who knew we were here."

"Maybe you were followed," Dick said calmly.

He could afford to be calm. He was a mile away, in the quiet of the office on the Hill, not barricaded in this miserable hotel room looking out the window at the swarm of reporters on the street below. Normally Ashley was clear-headed in a crisis, but now she struggled to keep her breathing under control. She refused to let Dick hear the panic in her voice.

"You're big news now, kiddo. Some lowly wire service stringer thought it was worth his time to tail you," he said.

Why don't I believe that, Dick? she wanted to say, but decided not to risk alienating him. The fact was, she didn't know how they'd found her. Maybe Dick was right; maybe she had been followed. On second thought, it didn't seem likely that he'd sic the press on them when Mike was here, too. He wouldn't, would he?

"You must be right," she said. "I'll have to be more careful."

"The question now is how to sneak Mike past them. God, can you imagine the fallout?"

"It's perfectly innocent. You must know that. We just needed a private place to disc—"

"If you want my help, Ashley, don't insult my intelligence."

"You don't know—"

"I *do* know. I've known for a long time. I have proof."

"Proof? You've been spying on us?"

"I didn't have to. There are security cameras all over the office. You've been caught on tape. More than once. Naturally, since I'm still the A.A., at least in name, the Capitol police came to me with the problem."

"And you kept it to yourself?"

"You'd rather I make it public?"

"You could've told Mike."

"I did. I talked to him. He didn't listen."

"He never mentioned anything to me about it."

"What can I say? He's a gentleman. Although I bet his wife doesn't think so."

"Oh, now you're getting all moralistic on me?"

There was a pause on the other end of the line. "Dick?"

"It's over, Ashley. You lost."

"What's that supposed to mean?"

"Would you put Mike on, please? There's something I need to say to him."

"What? You can tell me."

"Just put him on."

"He's not here. He went down to the basement a few minutes ago to see if he could find a back exit."

"I'll call his cell."

"Dick—"

She looked at her phone. The display read, "Call Ended."

"You'll regret that," Ashley said under her breath.

She threw her phone down on the bed, then tumbled after it, collapsing, her arm draped over her face. She wouldn't cry and she certainly couldn't sleep, but squeezing her eyes shut would help her think.

Dick must've found out somehow about what she'd told the grand jury. That was the explanation. He was pissed off, he was bluffing. She'd be doing the same thing in his shoes, but there couldn't be any doubt of the outcome. She'd taken care of things, played her cards right. It had been her word against Dick's in the beginning, but then she'd approached Pugliese and won him over to her side. Pugliese had testified, too, and backed up everything Ashley said. She knew he had, because they'd sat down together and gotten their stories straight. They'd gone over what he'd say word for word, how the campaign contribution had been Dick's baby from the get-go. Ashley had never seen the transcript of Pugliese's testimony, but that didn't worry her. Every idiot knew grand jury proceedings were secret.

Although it did give her pause that Dick hadn't been hauled away in cuffs by now. Shouldn't that have happened already?

Ashley got up and went over to the window, tugging aside the ugly floral drapes and peering out. *Jesus!* Mike was down there, surrounded by cameras. She ran to the television and flipped it on, channel-surfing until she found him. The banner on the bottom of the screen read "Breaking News—Rep. Mike Esposito Indicted in Gaming Scandal and Resigns."

"—completely innocent of all charges," Mike was saying. Tears stood out in his eyes. "The charges are serious, however, and it will take all my time and energy to fight them. I do not feel that I can continue to serve my constituents responsibly during the pendency of this investigation. For that reason, I have tendered my resignation to the Speaker effective immediately. Governor Wilson will be calling a special election to fill the vacancy. I am confident that my name will be cleared, and I am deeply grateful for the support of my wife and the prayers of my friends and constituents at this difficult time. Thank you and God bless."

Mike strode away, head bowed, but the cameras followed. Reporters were running backwards, shouting questions at him.

"Is it true that Raymond Pugliese funneled cash payments through a Cayman Islands shell corporation at the direction of your aide Ashley Ortega?"

"Congressman, were you and Miss Ortega having an affair?"

"Your chief of staff, Richard Maslin, has announced his intention to run for your seat? Will you be supporting him?"

"No comment."

As she watched, the camera jerked suddenly and spun around. After a second of vertigo, it righted itself, and the cameraman and reporter began running in the opposite direction. Mike was gone, and in his place was the image of the front of the hotel. *This* hotel. She saw several unmarked cars, haphazardly parked, that hadn't been there when she'd arrived earlier, and the broad retreating backs of a number of men in navy blue FBI jackets.

Confused, Ashley ran back to the window, but there was little to see from this angle. The action had all moved inside the hotel now.

Shit.

Ashley grabbed her handbag and ran for the door, but before she could get to it, fists started pounding on the outside. She'd keep her head. That's who she was. She wouldn't lose her grip because of a temporary setback.

"Ashley Ortega?" a man's voice called.

Ashley put her eye to the peephole. There were at least five of them out there. "Who is it?"

"FBI, ma'am. We have a warrant for your arrest on charges of bribery, perjury and obstruction of justice. Open the door, please."

As she reached for the doorknob, Ashley was already thinking about how to spin this for the cameras.

MADAME SECRETARY'S LOVER MAN

Jake Lamar

I

Dear Colleagues,

Ain't nobody gonna believe this shit, I know that already. That's why I'm leaving this document with y'all. Just you two. I shall hereafter refer to you fellas, in this document, as Colleague A and Colleague B. Do with this document what you will. I figure whatever happens to me, at least there'll be two brothers out there who know the truth. But I'm also writing this with the idea it might be read by other folks as well. Someday. Maybe when all three of us are dead and buried.

Now, y'all know Dante Fuller ain't no wordsmith. I'm a artist, a painter. I've struggled to survive while making my art. And thanks largely to the efforts of you two, Colleagues A and B, I've been able to hold down a job in the fine arts department of this here institute of higher learning for goin' on three years now.

All my recent troubles began with a conversation with you two about three months ago. We were in one of those steak and ale joints not far from campus, just offa the highway. We'd finished the steaks and were on our fourth or fifth pitcher of ale when I posed the question.

"So—would you do Condi?"

Colleague A, you just about spat out your beer. "You mean fuck her?"

Colleague B, you mighta been the drunkest of us all cuz you said, "You mean Condoleezza Rice?"

As I recall, the rest of the conversation went something like this:

ME: Who the fuck else do you know goes by the name of Condi?

A: Oh, man, I've never even thought about it. I mean, you just don't think of her that way.

ME: I do. I gotta jones for Condi.

A: Get out.

ME: I'm serious. You wouldn't fuck her?

A: Aw, man, with those buck teeth?

ME: What about you?

B: She's a lesbian.

ME: That's not the question.

B: Well, that's my answer.

A: Why you say she's a dyke?

B: I didn't say "dyke." You did. I say she's a lesbian because she's been in the public eye nearly twenty years and she's never been seriously linked with any love interest. And whenever you have a case like that, when a well-known person is not known to have been dating anybody, that well-known person, be they male or female, is inevitably gay.

A: But wasn't she with that old football player?

B: He was the beard. A decoy. Whoever her real lover is, it's a woman.

ME: Well, I think she's fine as shit.

A: You're serious?

ME: Hell, yes.

A: You think she'd be interested in you, some drea-dlocked, paint-splattered nigga who makes twenty grand a year? She's fucking the President!

ME: You think so?

A: Isn't it obvious? She accidentally called him her husband in an interview.

B: That doesn't mean she's fucking him.

A: Well, she ain't no lesbian!

B: Yo, man, I don't mean it as an insult. She's gay and she's very discreet about it, that's all. What's insulting is to say she's only got where she is 'cause she's fucking the boss man.

ME: Any way you look at it, the sista is hot—and I think she needs some good lovin'.

A: From the likes of you?

ME: Why you keep sayin' it like that? She's a woman and I'm a man and that's all that's gonna matter. I ain't talkin' about marryin' her.

A: There *is* something about her, I gotta admit it.

ME: Those long legs, that juicy butt.

A: And that power thing. The hyperintelligence. The dominatrix attitude. Yeah, I could dig it.

ME: If Condi walked in here right now, which one of us do you think she would choose?

B: The waitress.

A: You.

ME: Me.

Now here's the part where y'all will say Dante was hallu-cinatin': "I knew he was one of them drugged-out Jimi-era acid-trippin' hippie-dippie niggas." Don't think I don't know that's what you buppie PhD's thinka me. All I'm sayin' is this really happened.

I know y'all didn't make it to that group show I was in—at that gallery in Georgetown. It's about an hour's trip from campus and I understand that both of you, A and B, are family men, wifey and kiddies and the whole nine yards.

Anyway, I've actually sold some paintings in the past few years. Made a nice piece a change for each one, too. And my work's been gettin' seriously shown—displayed in elite galleries and shit, not just on the multikulti circuit, but in white folks' galleries in NYC as well as D.C. This is to say: I was just starting to attract collectors. Serious art fucks. People who write big checks.

I went to the opening of the Georgetown gallery show. And I saw how people gawked at my portrait of Condi. She hadn't posed for it—of course not. The painting was Condi as Xena the Warrior Goddess—or Athena or Artemis, whoever the hell you consider a supernatural, primordial, ass-kickin' female icon. It was Condi, fierce and glowering, in silver headdress, leather bra and short buckskin skirt, brandishing a blood-streaked sword, bathed in a golden light; her bare midriff, her naked, muscular, dark brown thighs, glistening with sweat.

I stood there in the corner, sipping my wine and nibbling my cheese, observing how the Washington yuppie and buppie elite regarded my Condi canvas, not knowing whether to love it or loathe it; to respect it as homage; scorn it as propaganda; or laugh ironically at the apparent satire. They didn't know what the fuck to think. Cuz none of them saw it the way I did—as explicitly erotic art.

I returned to campus late that night, having failed to make a sale, figuring that I would only truly be understood posthumously.

Three nights later, my telephone rang, 'round about midnight. I'd just gone to sleep, and it was only the nasal harshness of that white man's voice on the other end that told me I wasn't dreaming.

"Dante Fuller?"

"Yeah?"

"Be dressed and ready to leave your apartment in ten minutes. By order of the United States government."

I figured it was a drug charge, even though I had no drugs in my possession. I dragged my ass out of bed, took a piss, put on a pair of paint-splattered dungarees, a tie-dyed T-shirt, slipped into my tattered Converse hightops and weatherbeaten suede jacket. Brushed my teeth but left my dreads unbound.

I stepped outside into the chilly night air and saw a sleek black limousine glide up in front of the entry way of my apartment block. Yes, I thought, it was definitely cops. But top cops. Feds. I figured they would drag me in for questioning, find I was useless to them, then take me home before dawn. I only hoped this would not affect my job at the college.

Three white dudes in the car. Two rode up front, one rode in the back with me. Rigid, clean-cut. If they hadn't been wearing dark suits with crisp white shirts and red striped ties, I woulda thought they were military.

"Aren't you gonna read me my rights?" I asked, sounding a whole lot cooler than I felt.

"You're not under arrest, sir," the dude sitting directly in front of me said.

Somehow, the fact that he called me "sir" freaked me out even more. "Well, er, can you tell me where we're going?"

"That's a negative, sir," the dude said, managing to sound both gruff and polite.

All through the hour-long ride my mind was spinning. They said they were with the government, they seemed like military types, we were on the highway, heading to D.C. Did these motherfuckers think I was a terrorist? Or did they think I knew a terrorist and could give them some info? Or did this have something to do with my ex-wife? My second ex-wife, that is. She's Brazilian, you know, and lives in São Paulo with our daughter. I figured it had something to do with that. My stupid ex-wife had done some stupid shit that was causing some kinda international problem having to do with my daughter's dual citizenship or some shit like that. I'm tellin' you, fellas, it was hard to think coherently in this situation.

Finally we get to the northwest quadrant, drive past the facade of the Mayflower hotel, turn down a side street and pull into an alley. Two of the agents get out of the car with me. We enter the basement of the hotel, then get on the service elevator. We get off on the top floor and the dudes escort me down the hallway. You ever been to the Mayflower? Oh, man. We walked down the long hallway, the carpet thick beneath my sneakers. The walls looked like they were upholstered, the fabric decorated in a floral design. There were paintings of men in powdered wigs hanging on the walls. We stepped through a set of mahogany double doors and I found myself in a small foyer-type room. There were four other white dudes in dark suits standing there. But these dudes all had wires hanging out of their ears. While one dude frisked me, I heard another speak into a little device: "The guest has arrived."

Now I really did begin to feel like I was hallucinatin'. But I swear to you I was stone cold sober and completely alert. One of the secret service agents opened another set of mahogany doors, and gestured for me to pass through them. I stepped into the living room of what had to be the most posh suite in the hotel. The doors closed behind me. I looked around at all the fancy furniture, more paintings of stern-faced white men in powdered wigs. I would have liked to check out the view, but all the floral-patterned drapes were closed. I let out a little laugh, a chuckle of anxiety and disbelief. Then I saw her.

Secretary of State Condoleezza Rice, perhaps the most powerful woman in the world, certainly the most powerful American woman at that moment in time, and without a doubt the most powerful African-American woman in all of human history strode toward me in her forward-leaning gait, across the plush carpet. She had burst through the door of the suite's bedroom, smiling radiantly, even more beautiful in the flesh than she was on film—or in my painting. But, as in my portrait of her, she seemed to be bathed in a golden light. She wore a cream-colored pantsuit, and a reddish brown blouse with a lady-like cameo pinned at the collar.

"Good evening, Professor Fuller," she said in that clipped, oh-so-proper, schoolmarm voice we all know so well. "Glad you could make it."

I was literally dumbstruck and struck dumb, so astonished I could not speak. She stopped about three feet in front of me. It looked as if she had been about to extend her hand, but had suddenly changed her mind. She looked me up and down, no longer smiling, an expression of serious concentration on her face. Physically, she was just as I'd imagined. Perfectly coiffed, exuding charisma and self-confidence, her body taut and lithe, a tennis player's body. What I could never have imagined was how good she would smell. That mix of perfume and pheromones is indescribable. I remember worrying, as I stood there staring in awe, if my mouth was hanging open.

I swallowed hard, then managed to say, struggling to play it cool, "Uh, hi."

"Professor," she said, a wry twinkle in her eyes, "I think you need to sit down."

I eased myself onto the couch. "Thank you . . . er . . ." I couldn't think of what to call her. Then the words just tumbled out: ". . . Madame Secretary."

She smiled broadly, wowing me with that famous over-bite, obviously pleased by my respect for protocol. "What are you drinking?"

Slowly, very slowly, I was regaining my sense of reality. "Scotch and soda . . . please."

Condi Rice walked over to the bar and fixed my drink. I don't know how long it took—certainly less than a minute—but it was enough time for me to wonder what the fuck I was doing there. In my worst case scenario, she'd seen my painting and decided that it constituted an act of sedition. Maybe it was against the Patriot Act or somethin' and she was gonna lay the law down on me. In my best case scenario . . . well . . .

Condi handed me my Scotch and soda and sat down beside me on the couch. She took a sip from a glass of clear liquid and ice cubes, maybe mineral water, maybe vodka, I couldn't tell.

"Thank you," I said.

"Don't be scared."

That was enough to flip me back into traditional black male mode. "I ain't scared."

Condi flashed her toothy grin again. "I know everything about you."

"Everything?"

"Well, let's say I know the basic bio." She then rattled off my date and place of birth, the names of the schools I'd attended, including the two art schools I'd been kicked out of, the names and whereabouts of my two ex-wives and

137

my daughter, the birth and death dates of both my parents, my entire employment record, the various cities in which I'd lived in my fifty-five years on this planet . . . What can I say? I was impressed by the thoroughness of research that had been done. Astounded by her ability to recite this long list of facts. Vaguely threatened by the breadth of her knowledge of my life. But mainly, I was flattered. Beyond flattered. I was puffed up with pride, ready to burst.

"And," the Secretary of State concluded, "a friend of mine bought your painting of me."

"You've seen it?"

"Of course I've seen it. Do you think you'd be sitting here if I hadn't?"

"Uh, no, I guess not. What I mean to say is, well, presumably, you . . . you liked it?"

Condi took a long sip of her drink, stared at me appraisingly. It's hard for me to describe how I felt at that moment. I think I felt the way women must feel when men brazenly ogle them. I mean, I was still flattered . . . but I felt kinda . . . vulnerable.

"Some people I know thought it was crass and stereotypical," Condi said. "But I'm not that politically correct. The friend who bought it thought it offered an interesting insight."

"And you agree?"

"Well, let's just say I don't disagree." Condi glanced at her watch. "Professor Fuller, I have a very busy schedule. Not a lot of time for normal pursuits, such as dating, et cetera. I find you rather attractive. I think it's fair to say that the feeling is mutual."

"Um, yes, that would be fair to say."

"Good. We have thirty minutes."

Now knowing y'all as I do, my Colleagues A and B, I'm sure you're gonna want all the down and dirty details. But you ain't gonna get 'em. Suffice it to say, Madame Secretary and I repaired to the luxurious bedroom. The encounter was passionate and intense. Not a lot of foreplay. Not a lot of afterplay. Just a lot of play. And, on the subject of satisfaction, let's just say that . . . How to put it . . . ? Nobody *comes* before the Secretary of State.

One minute we were lying there, sweaty and sated. The next minute Condi was up and puttering about the bedroom. She slipped into one of the thick white hotel bathrobes. "Get dressed," she said.

I didn't particularly like the way she had abruptly ordered me but I wasn't exactly in a position to complain. I rose from the bed and started getting dressed.

"Go back out the way you came in. You'll get a ride back to your house."

"Thank you, Con—"

At that moment, before the second syllable could even leave my mouth, she shot me a glare that froze my blood. I quickly regained my senses.

"Thank you, Madame Secretary," I said.

Suddenly, I heard an electronic beep. Condi Rice picked up a cell phone from the nightstand. "Hello? . . . Yuri!"

Then she started babbling in what sounded like a madwoman's gibberish. It took a few seconds for me to realize that she was prattling away in rapid-fire Russian. I tried to wave to get Condi's attention but it was clear she had forgotten all about me.

I left the bedroom, walked through the main room of the suite, passed through the double doors and stepped back into the foyer where the six white men in dark suits were waiting, their faces utterly blank. The two dudes who'd brought me up there to the suite escorted me back down-stairs, to the alley where the limousine was still waiting. During the hour-long drive back from D.C. nobody in the car said a word. But I was replaying in my mind my brief tryst with the Warrior Goddess.

The limo pulled up to my suburban apartment block. "Thanks, guys," I said. "Good night."

No reply. Once inside my apartment, I collapsed on the bed and started laughing hysterically. I laughed and laughed until my body ached from exhaustion. Laughed myself to sleep.

Six weeks passed. I thought about that night, those thirty minutes at the Mayflower, all the time. I couldn't get Condi outta my head. I wanted to tell you fellas about it but I knew y'all woulda laughed in my face, then questioned my sanity. Just when I figured I would have to forget Condi, accept the fact that the Mayflower was just a one-night—or rather, a half-hour—stand, I got another phone call, the same voice, the white agent who seemed to be the head of the three-man escort team. He used the same exact words as last time.

"Be dressed and ready to leave your apartment in ten minutes. By order of the United States government."

It was Monday night—last night—about nine o'clock. This time I had a more appropriate outfit ready. My one nice suit, black with thick white pinstripes, and a navy blue satin shirt. It had been hanging in the closet, dry-cleaned and ready to be slipped into on a moment's notice, for damn near the whole six weeks. I splashed on some cologne and tied my dreads back.

"Hi guys!" I said chirpily, in a kinda male Condi voice, as I entered the limousine.

"Good evening, Professor," the head dude said.

"Where to tonight, pray tell?" I trilled.

"The less said the better, sir," the head dude said in his gruff but polite tone.

They drove me out to some Air Force base. Bizarre atmosphere. Like an airport, only no terminals, no passengers. Lots of planes. The booming noise of jets taking off, landing, and being refueled filled the air. Floodlights sweeping across the black night sky. We drove around for a long time, passing through three different security gates. The car stopped in front of a massive jet that looked like Air Force One. I was escorted up the metal staircase, entered through the back door of the plane. Another four-man security detail. This time, I noticed a dude I hadn't seen at the Mayflower. He had to be six and a half feet tall, practically bursting out of his suit, kinda swarthy, a vaguely Turkish aspect about him, with a shaved head that looked like it coulda been made of granite. While one of the other Secret Service dudes frisked me, the Turk glowered at me like he wanted to shish-kebab my black ass.

The head dude led me down a long corridor with closed doors on both sides. Felt more like a hotel than any airplane I'd ever been on. He stopped, pushed a buzzer beside a door, then said, "Please enter, sir."

I stepped through the door, into a noisy, dimly lit room; heard the door close and lock behind me. It took a moment for me to realize that the only light in the room was coming from a flat-screen TV, and the noise was the broadcast of a football game. A moment later, I saw her, bathed in the bluish glow of the TV screen. Condi was sitting up in a king-size bed, leaning back against an array of white pillows, the white sheets pulled up to her bare brown shoulders. She held a remote control in her hand. The Secretary of State was smiling at me. I felt my heart swell. There was something so sweet and girlish about her at that moment. And something so intimate about the whole scene. Like we were a young married couple and I was just getting home from a late night at the office to find my lovely wife waiting up in bed for me.

"Good evening, Professor Fuller."

"Good evening, Madame Secretary."

"Half-time is about to start. Get your clothes off and get over here."

Once again, the action was fast and intense. Afterward, I lay on my back, feeling drained and euphoric.

"Wow," Condi said, "that's the ultimate aerobic workout."

"You know what?" I said, unable to censor myself. "A friend of mine thinks you're gay."

I looked up at Condi. She was leaning over me, propped up on her elbow, smiling enigmatically in the glow of the TV.

"Hey, baby," she said, in a tone of voice, an accent, I had never heard come out of her before, "I likes da meat . . . and da fish."

I burst into hysterical laughter. Condi continued to smile her cryptic little smile. Suddenly, she turned and picked up the remote, raised the volume on the TV. "Second half just started. You follow the NFL?"

My laughter died down. "Naw," I said, trying to sound as if I had more important things to do with my time.

Condi was totally focused on the game now. Me, I didn't know what the fuck was going on. Only football game I ever watch is the Super Bowl, and I don't really watch it. I just go to whatever Super Bowl party I'm invited to and get drunk.

"Aw, shoot!" Condi said in exasperation. "These chumps couldn't get a first down if their lives depended on it."

"Yeah," I said, revealing an ignorance that must have disappointed her.

"You should get dressed," she said as a commercial appeared on the screen.

"Okay," I said, without moving an inch.

A cell phone beeped. Condi quickly scooped it up from the nightstand, then raised a finger to her lips. A common enough gesture; but there was something particularly violent and forbidding in the way she signaled me to keep my mouth shut.

"Hello, Mr President," Condi said in her most chirpy sing-song. "Of course, I'm watching the game . . . I'm flying to Tel Aviv in a couple of hours . . . Yes, I know . . . Mmm-hmm . . . Well, you know my feelings on the question . . ."

I lay there, wondering what grave matters of state were being discussed. Then, I heard Condi say:

"Never bet against a ten-point spread . . . Yes, Mr President. Talk to you tomorrow."

She clicked off the phone and sighed. "Last of the river-boat gamblers," she said, shaking her head.

"Madame Secretary?" I asked.

"You still here?" Condi snapped.

I sat up in the bed. I had to know if she was fucking Dubya. I just had to know. "Can I ask you a personal question?"

"You already asked one," she said coldly. The game was back on and Condi was staring straight ahead at the screen. "One is all you're allowed. Now get dressed and get out of here. You'll get a ride home, just like the last time."

I rose from the bed, got dressed. Then I sat back down, beside Condi, on the edge of the bed, to lace up my shoes. I heard another commercial come on.

"Madame Secretary," I said. Condi looked straight into my eyes now, her expression deadly serious. She pulled the sheets a little more snugly around her naked body. I sat inches away from her, fully clothed. "When will I see you again?"

"I don't know, Professor Fuller."

"I think that maybe . . ."

It was weird, fellas—I felt emotions bubbling up inside me that I could not control, words just forming in my mouth, spilling out, beyond my will . . .

". . . maybe I'm in love with you."

The Secretary of State tilted her head and squinted meanly at me. "Are you drunk?"

"No, ma'am."

"Are you on drugs, then? I know you have a record."

"Please, Madame Secretary . . ."

I'm tellin' you, my Colleagues A and B, the words were just coming out of me, uncontrollably. I felt like, for the first time, I was speaking, expressing myself verbally, in the way I had only ever been able to express myself before through my art, through paint on a canvas. I continued, knowing I was speaking too intensely, feeling my emotions galloping away, out of my grasp.

". . . Madame Secretary, I want to be with you. To cherish you. Always and forever."

"Professor Fuller, you know that just isn't possible."

Condi's voice had changed. Or, rather, it had reverted to her usual condescending public tone.

"You think I'm not good enough for you?" I didn't want to say it, but I did, my voice sounding like somebody else's. There was an anger, a righteous indignation, that I did not recognize in my own voice. "I offer you my love . . . Madame Secretary . . . and you throw it back in my face."

It barely registered with me at the time, but now I remember, I see it clearly, that at that moment, she reached over to the nightstand and pushed a button.

"Professor Fuller, I really think you should go now."

"Is it cuz you're fuckin' that cracker?"

"Excuse me?"

"What if I tell the world?" I said, my voice rising. "Huh, what about that? What if I hold a press conference and tell everybody about our little thing?"

"Are you threatening me? Have you really got the balls to try to blackmail me? Who would ever believe you?"

"I love you, Condi."

I heard the door burst open behind me. Just as I turned around, I saw the head dude and the granite-headed Turk rushing toward me. I leapt from the bed, ready to fight them.

Pointless.

The two of them had me in some sort of torture hold. One of them had my arms twisted behind my back; the other held my legs splayed wide. I saw a white-haired man carrying a syringe race into the room. I screamed in agony as he jammed the needle into my neck.

So: my dear Colleagues, A and B, I woke up this morning, fully clothed in my black pinstriped suit and navy blue satin shirt, on top of my own bed, in my tiny apartment. I have no idea how I got here. I only know that last night I was on the Secretary of State's plane. I just turned on CNN and saw that she has arrived safely in Tel Aviv.

I think I am supposed to be dead. I think they gave me . . . What to call it . . . ? An *under*dose.

They shot me up, brought me back to my apartment. And I was supposed to be found dead, probably by the landlord or the superintendent, one of these days.

Anyway: I'm alive. But I don't know for how much longer. So I write this testimony. And I will put it in the mail to you today. The muthafuckas missed on the first try. They'll get it right the second time. Whenever that may be.

In any event, my life insurance, my will and all that shit is in order. My daughter in Brazil will get everything. Not much of an inheritance, today anyway. Who knows how it will be in the future, if my works begin to sell for higher and higher prices? Funny how people always prefer their artists dead.

Call me when you get this letter. See if I'm still alive.
Your Friend,
Dante Fuller

II

When Clifford Alton, a professor of American history at Madison Colonial College in Virginia, received Dante Fuller's letter that frigid Wednesday afternoon in December, he considered it a perverse practical joke. He could only wonder what the punchline, the prankster's payoff, was going to be. He called Dante to tell him he didn't find it funny. But when he got the painter's answering machine, he decided not to leave a message.

When Randall Baxter, a professor of American literature at the same college, received the same letter that same afternoon, he thought that Dante Fuller had lost his mind. He'd always found Dante a bit strange, but he'd never taken him for a delusional schizophrenic. He called Dante to tell him that he should seek psychiatric counseling immediately. But when he got the painter's answering machine, he, too, decided not to leave a message.

Dante Fuller did not know that his colleagues Alton and Baxter had recently had a falling-out. The source of their conflict was Condoleezza Rice, or, more accurately, Professor Alton's publishing a scholarly article in late November, supporting the Secretary of State on everything from the Iraq war policy to her defense of the Bush Administration's response to Hurricane Katrina. Baxter was furious. He believed Alton had only published the piece to please the white conservative establishment at Madison, in the hopes that he might be named the new Assistant Dean of the Faculty.

Alton and Baxter did not phone each other upon receiving Dante Fuller's letter. But the following evening, they saw each other at the faculty Christmas party.

"Hello, Colleague A," Baxter said.

"Greetings, Colleague B," Alton replied with a nervous laugh.

They carried their glasses of eggnog to a quiet corner of the faculty dining room, so that they would be able to talk out of the earshot of other drinking, chattering professors.

"What the fuck, Cliff?"

"I don't know, Randy. I was hoping Dante would show up here tonight and we'd have a big laugh over it."

"Laugh? You think this is a joke?"

"What, you think it's serious?"

"I think Dante is seriously disturbed and should probably be in a psychiatric hospital, under heavy medication."

"Whew! I thought you believed what he'd written. Given the Left's demonization of Condi."

"Yeah, whatever."

At that moment, Howard Pendergast, the Dean of the Faculty, walked up to Alton and Baxter. "Have you guys heard the news? Dante Fuller's body was found in an alley in south-east Washington early this morning. He'd been shot three times in the head. The police think it was a drug deal gone wrong."

"Good Lord," Randall Baxter said.

"We were just wondering where he was tonight," Clifford Alton said.

"I thought about making an announcement," Dean Pendergast said, "but I don't want to spoil the party. Most people here didn't even know who Fuller was. And we're probably going to abolish the fine arts program next year. Anyway, there'll be an item in the newspaper tomorrow. Fuller's ex-wife is coming up from Brazil to claim the body. Sorry to be the bearer of bad news. All the same, Merry Christmas."

The following Monday afternoon, Baxter got an urgent phone call from Alton.

"Could you come over to my place, right away, please?"

Half an hour later, Baxter showed up at his colleague's suburban home, about a mile from the heart of campus. Alton led Baxter into the living room, explaining that his wife and two children had left town Saturday to visit her parents in California. Alton was going to join them on Christmas Eve. Since first semester classes had already ended, he had planned to catch up on administrative paperwork. But he couldn't concentrate.

"I'm really rattled, man," Alton said.

"So I see," Baxter replied.

"Aren't you a little freaked out by what happened to Dante?"

"Not really. I think he was just in the last throes of a death spiral drug addiction when he wrote that fucked-up letter."

"Okay, maybe you're right. But I'm not a fucked-up drug addict and ever since Saturday morning, when I drove my wife and kids to the airport, I've had the feeling that I'm being followed."

"What?"

"Watched. Like, under surveillance. I keep seeing this black limousine."

Baxter chuckled softly and shook his head. "You're over-worked, my man. Go join your family in California."

"Randy, you know damn well, even if we don't always see eye-to-eye when it comes to politics, that I'm a sane, level-headed person."

Baxter rose from his chair, clearly eager to leave. "I know that, man. That's why I say I think you are more than ready for Christmas vacation."

Alton walked his colleague to the front door. "By the way, what did you do with Dante's letter?"

"After I found out he was dead, I burned it. What did you do with your copy?"

Alton hesitated, just long enough for Baxter to know that whatever response he gave would be a lie: "I shredded it."

"All right, man. Anyway, don't worry. Nobody's out to get you. Since that flattering article you published last month, everybody knows you're Condi's biggest fan."

Alton shrugged, forced a laugh. "Well, maybe her second biggest."

It was after midnight. The football game had just ended. Alton turned off the TV, brushed his teeth and slipped into his pajamas. He was about to snap off the bedside lamp when the phone rang.

"Hello?"

"Clifford Alton?" Though Alton had never heard this harsh and nasal male voice before, he recognized it imme-diately.

"Yes?"

"Be dressed and ready to leave your house in ten minutes. By order of the United States government."

Alton got out of bed, put on a crisp, sky-blue shirt with a button-down collar, a Madison Colonial College necktie, a pair of khaki pants, penny loafers and his best tweed jacket. He stood by the window, waiting for the black limo to appear. His hands were trembling, though more out of eager anticipation than fear. Whatever Madame Secretary might expect from him, he hoped he would be up to the task.

COLLATERAL DAMAGE

Robert Greer

It wasn't that she was ugly; she was simply unattractive. You couldn't call her uncoordinated or ungainly, although she wasn't at all athletic. And in spite of what her political detractors were fond of saying, she wasn't mean, spiteful, or hateful. What Hannah Rossmore Stenton was—if the essence of a human being could be summarized so tersely—was self-centered and uncaring.

She'd always been smart, insecure, and ambitious. She'd also been needy, calculating, and clever—and unnervingly cold when you came right down to it. But you couldn't describe her as cruel, the way some of those occupying the reactionary halls of the American political right often did—simply heartless.

Hannah was used to others' assessments of her, and although those appraisals occasionally grated on her, when it was all "netted out," as her long-dead alcoholic father had been so fond of saying—when she was president of the United States—she'd have no reason to concern herself with other people's evaluations of her. Others' opinions be damned. But at the moment, she had a larger, more pressing problem to attend to. A problem that superseded any possible concerns about denunciations. Right now she needed to talk to a man about dealing with the one person who could derail her fast-moving train to the presidency. A man who would kill her chief rival for the Democratic Party's presidential nomination, Broderick Losomma.

She had watched Losomma's stock rise ever since the snows of New Hampshire, where he'd finished second in that state's primary and come within a whisker of upsetting her front-running applecart. She'd been riding in that jet-powered applecart ever since she'd filled her husband's California senate seat eight years earlier, after the popular, womanizing and corrupt Will Stenton had committed suicide in Florida. Stenton had blown out the roof of his mouth and the top of his head two days after being caught by DEA agents in a hotel in Coral Gables, Florida, with three nude, coked-out female aides and a satchelful of suspected Colombian drug money.

Losomma hadn't sneaked up on Stenton (who'd stopped using the name Rossmore-Stenton six months earlier, after she and her handlers had reasoned that in the eyes of voters she had distanced herself enough from her husband's tragic, life-ending faux pas). No, Losomma had chopped away at Hannah's once considerable pre-New Hampshire lead bit by bit, piece by piece, whittling away at her press popularity, her grassroots support, and finally her insider party loyalty—until now, two days before Denver's 2008 Democratic national convention, her once seemingly insurmountable 20 lead in the polls had all but evaporated, and she and Losomma found themselves in a virtual dead heat.

Hannah looked more agitated than nervous as, pacing the floor of her penthouse suite in Denver's recently refurbished Marriott City Center Hotel, she prepared to attend a hastily convened evening press conference. She stopped momentarily, glanced out the western wall of windows that gave her a perfect eight o'clock sunset view of some of the highest peaks in the Rockies, and then turned toward her campaign manager, Tucker Doleman, who was sitting across the room from her. Doleman's thinning salt-and-pepper hair and deep dimples gave him an impish *aw, shucks* look. Aware that Hannah's pacing normally preceded an outburst, he wasn't at all surprised when it came.

"I don't care what that big-eared, pin-striped-suit-wearing Yale elitist claims he is, he's anything but black," Hannah bellowed. "His father's white."

"And his mother's black, Hannah," came Doleman's response. "White father, black mother: any way you slice it, Losomma's still a black man in America in spite of our Rainbow Coalition times."

Hannah shook her head in disgust. "Just like him, lucking out when it comes to race. Too bad it's not 1930. The elephant-eared jerk. He's played all the odds, Tucker, and won. Yale undergrad, Stanford Law, U.S. Senate—a black man who claims to have pulled himself up by his bootstraps. What a snow job." Hannah let out a sigh. "You know what I see when I look at him and that high yellow, pixyish little wife of his and their two charming, fat-cheeked, all-American children? I see a white man, Tucker. A white man in blackface who's out to steal my job. His kids go to a private country day school, for Christ's sake, and his wife's not some maid, she's a doctor. The SOB's feeding the voters a line. If he's a black man, then so's the Pope."

Doleman shook his head. "He's feeding voters what they want, Hannah. You should understand that better than anyone. He's playing every angle, just like us. It's no different than your being the long-grieving widow or the ultimate twenty-first-century working woman. All Losomma's doing is moving the merchandise. And so should we."

Hannah looked exasperated. "Oh, come off it, Tucker. You can stuff the political correctness. There's no one in this room but us chickens. Losomma's a black man who's comfortable being a white man, wishing he were born an oil-rich Texan and hoping he can pass himself off as a New York City Jew. He's a chameleon, Tucker. And a light-weight one at that. And he's standing in the way of my date with the presidency. We need to do something about him."

Doleman smiled. "He'll do it to himself, Hannah. Just give him enough time. He's unseasoned, untested, unorthodox, and naïve. He'll stumble."

"He hasn't so far, and we're on the eve of the convention."

Doleman walked over to Hannah and draped a reassuring arm over her shoulder. "He'll put his foot in his mouth while we're here in Denver. Trust me."

Tucker's singsong, know-it-all tone tended to grate on Hannah, but his last delivery hit home, and she trusted his insight. During the past four years, he'd been able to slip past her protective armor and see what made the daughter of a barmaid and disabled postal worker tick. And she'd done the same when it came to him. He'd first impressed her with his shrewdness, then with his infinite political knowledge, and finally with his uncanny ability to always make the right decision at the most opportune time. He had directed her initial Senate run after her husband's death, charting her course through rough political waters. He'd guided her overwhelmingly successful second Senate run, and he had drawn up her blueprint for a run at the presidency.

After years of strategizing and squeezing every ounce of advantage out of her demographics, Tucker and Hannah had melded into a team. Not a lustful, loving, or heart-strings-tweaking kind of team, but a precise, eyes-on-the-prize tandem. Oh, they had slept together, no question, and on occasion they'd both even enjoyed the sex, but their bond wasn't the kind that united them like lovers or man and wife or even friends. What they had become over the years was as close as two people could come to being symbiotic—and why not? They had shared the same kind of hurtful, personality-shaping youthful experiences. They both understood what it was to be laughed at and made fun of; what it was like to be called Fat Ankles and Bubble Butt, Freakface and Geek. They both understood that one day they would shout above the voices of every playground bully and homecoming queen, every football-team captain and cheerleader, "Look at me now, you bastards—look at me now!"

What they each had learned before sprouting their first pubescent genital hairs was that they had skills they could use to overcome all obstacles: the power to manipulate; the capacity to get other people to do their bidding; the ability to make sense out of nonsense; the strength to entice and orchestrate and make fools believe in them—link them to their own hopes and dreams. In all the years since they'd had to face down schoolyard bullying and put-downs and taunting and in-crowd lockouts, Hannah Stenton and Tucker Doleman had become the very essence of deception: twenty-first-century American politicians of the highest order.

Looking up at her campaign chief, sometime lover, confidant, and friend, and thinking about how she could ensure that Losomma would stumble, Hannah said, "No need to humor me, Tucker. Losomma's breathing down our necks, and we can't count on him making a big enough mistake to save us—the stakes are too high. We've got to do something."

Doleman had the urge to say, "No, Hannah, *you're* breathing down *his* neck," but he knew better than to burst her bubble. She was the kind of person who performed best as a front-runner. If she had the slightest hint that she might be looking at Broderick Losomma from behind, she'd collapse in ways that could cost them the nomination. His job was to keep Hannah focused, keep her from thinking about the fact that she was just an uncomely little fat-ankled girl with the unique ability to manipulate. Eyeing his watch, he said, "Almost showtime. We'd better go. Never pays to keep the press waiting. As for strategy, when it comes to Losomma, we stay the course. It's gotten us this far, and it'll get us to the White House. No last-minute deviations, Hannah, okay?"

Hannah offered Tucker an insincere smile. "I've followed your lead so far, haven't I?"

"Yes. And it's put us on the threshold of this nomination, Hannah. Trust me. All we need to do now is continue to sell your program. *Hannah Stenton, Crucial to America's Needs.* Six powerful words that'll carry you into the White House. We stick with them, okay?"

"Okay," Hannah said softly. She had no intention of rewriting slogans, scuttling strategies, or altering any of Tucker's long-thought-out plans. She'd go with the flow. Yin and yang, push and pull. It was all part of their symbiosis. Part of the reason things had always worked for them. He could do his job. She would do hers.

Pinkie Niedemeyer had lost all of his front teeth, top and bottom, eyetooth to eyetooth, and the pinkie finger of his left hand during a New Year's Eve firefight outside the village of Song Ve three days before he'd been scheduled to come home from a year-long tour of duty in Vietnam. He'd received a Purple Heart for doing his duty that day—and earned himself a nickname.

Now, almost four decades later, Pinkie, the Rocky Mountain region's top settlement agent—a name he much preferred to "hit man"—found himself standing on the earthen shoulder of Denver's High Line Canal, a sixty-six-mile-long artificial waterway that wove through the Mile High City. Pinkie was rocking from side to side and talking in hushed tones to Senator Hannah Rossmore-Stenton, a woman who would likely be the next president of the United States.

It hadn't been easy for Hannah to slip away from her hotel—and from Tucker Doleman, the press, aides, bodyguards, well-wishers, and hangers-on—but she had, just as decades earlier she'd outsmarted the losers who had taunted her with cries of, "There goes Fat Ankles." She glanced self-consciously toward her feet, barely able to make out her shoes in the one a.m. darkness.

Wondering whether Rossmore-Stenton, or whatever she was calling herself nowadays, was the kind of woman who would have second thoughts about sending men to war, experience fear when facing down some Third World despot, or sweat over unleashing a nuclear weapon, Pinkie stopped rocking and looked Hannah squarely in the eyes. "How'd you get my name?"

"I have my sources, Mr Niedemeyer. As I suspect you have yours. Now, what's your position on my offer? I'd prefer not to stand here talking all night."

The skinny, six-foot-two, pockmark-faced hit man's answer came slowly. "I'll tell you what, Senator." There was a hint of formality in Pinkie's voice. "Normally I wouldn't give your proposition a second thought. I don't take political assignments. Too many unwarranted egos, and too much wishy-washiness involved. No disrespect, Senator, but in my experience, politicians tend to lack backbone. But since you're here, which I know took guts, I'll take your offer under advisement. I'll have an answer for you by tomorrow. Now, if you don't mind me asking, considering the risk, why didn't you send some lackey to talk to me?"

Hannah forced a smile. "Because, Mr Niedemeyer, by doing things this way, face to face, we develop a certain kind of symbiosis. I offer you a proposition. You respond to my offer. No middlemen involved. No liars or double dealers. No would-be extortionists or lingering bloodsuckers lurking to one day demand their due. The very essence of our relationship, Mr Niedemeyer, is you and I. I prefer things that way in everything I do."

Pinkie nodded understandingly. "And what if I turn down the job?"

"Then, Mr Niedemeyer, I'll get someone else."

"Logical. But suppose I go off the deep end—run to the public or your political adversaries or the press—and tell them about your offer?"

"You wouldn't do that, Mr Niedemeyer. I've checked you out, stem to stern. But if for some unfathomable reason you did do one of those things you just mentioned, it would be your word against mine. No middlemen, remember? And after I protested your accusations as the babblings of a deranged hit man and hung you out to dry, I'd have you killed."

Not one bit surprised by Hannah's answer, Pinkie said, "And you're certain you could do that?"

"In the blink of an eye, Mr Niedemeyer. I found you, didn't I? I can dispense with you just as easily." Hannah stared Pinkie directly in the eye. "I'd like your answer by tomorrow morning. Eight a.m. at the latest."

"And the pay for eliminating Mr Losomma? Mind running that figure by me once again?"

Hannah looked Pinkie up and down and said, with a hint of suspicion in her tone, "You're not wearing a wire, are you,

Mr Niedemeyer? And you're not trolling for more money, I hope. The pay's two hundred thousand. The same as what I quoted you earlier." Hannah slipped her hand into her jacket pocket and fumbled with the 9mm she'd brought along.

Pinkie smiled, aware that the would-be president was armed. "No wires, Senator. I asked you the question again because I love to hear the sound of someone offering me money. It's what I live for. I'll have an answer for you by eight. How do I get in touch?"

"You don't. I'll contact you." Hannah reached into the pocket of her sweats and slipped out a matchbook-sized cell phone. Pinkie's reaction to the sudden move was to pull his .44. Calmly eyeing the gun barrel, Hannah said, "It's not a gun, Mr. Niedemeyer. It's a phone. A very special kind of phone." She handed the phone to Pinkie. "I have one to match. You can make four calls on it before the operational chip inside self-destructs."

"Kinda James Bond-ish," Pinkie said, slipping the phone into his pocket.

"I'd say it's a lot more *Mission Impossible*. I'll talk to you tomorrow morning. And remember, you can only make four calls." Hannah turned, stepped quickly up onto the canal's equestrian path, and walked off into the darkness, leaving Pinkie fingering the cell phone and wondering if Hannah Rossmore-Stenton had been a mirage.

Broderick Losomma was less about substance than appearance, and more about orchestrating opportunity for himself than for others. He'd begun his presidential campaign with a relatively small donor base concentrated in his home state of Michigan. He'd been an early opponent of the Iraq War, and it was that polarizing issue—one that, considering the polls, he could now claim he'd been on the right side of from the start—and his quest to be America's first black president that had been the fuel behind an amazingly robust fundraising machine.

Kennedyesque in "blackface," the forty-six-year-old Losomma, on his way to the nomination, had mugged with Detroit auto workers, backslapped steel workers in Gary, Indiana, hugged up with Teamster truckers in Cleveland, and glad-handed his way into the purses of Hollywood and Wall Street. Nineteen months prior to the election, he had raised $25 million against Hannah Stenton's $26 million, and it had been that inflow of cash and his showing in New Hampshire that had caused Hannah Stenton and Tucker Doleman to finally sit up and take notice.

Dapper, glib, photogenic, and articulate, Losomma was jokingly referred to by some in the Stenton camp as white America's *Great Black Hope*. And despite the fact that he'd once found it difficult to identify Iraq on the globe, he'd become many Americans' first choice for president.

Dressed in a fashionable black pinstripe suit and sporting a silver-and-blue-striped tie, Losomma, with an ever-present American flag pinned to his left lapel, sat lunching with his press secretary, Joey Maloof, in a private dining room in Denver's famed Brown Palace Hotel. The opening bell of the Democratic convention was less than seventy hours away.

Maloof, a moon-faced, fifth-generation Bostonian, one-time Massachusetts congressman, and Irish to the core, stroked his chin thoughtfully in response to the proposal Losomma had just offered. "It's a good idea, I have to admit that, and it'll give us a healthy dose of positive press before the opening gavel. But following a trail that Eisenhower blazed? In case you've forgotten, Broderick, Ike was a Republican."

"So?" Losomma shook his head in protest. "Sometimes your thinking's way too narrow, Joey. We're here in the hotel Ike bedded down in whenever he came to Denver, and in case you've missed it, there seem to be more photos around Denver of Ike fly-fishing up in the Colorado mountains than there are of the man on D-day. What better photo op could we ask for than to go fly-fishing up on the Fraser River—Ike's river, just like America's favorite grandfather? I can play the outdoorsman, just like Ike. Fly-fish on Ike's personal stream. We'll show people I'm part of the West. Even give Ike a plug, play at being bipartisan. When you come right down to it, we'll out-Ike Ike. Tell me this, Joey: What could be better than a trip to the pristine Colorado mountains to fish for our supper? It's quintessentially American. Besides, it'll give Westerners a feel for my love and appreciation of their land, and maybe even grab us a few fishing and hunting votes along the way. It's a cinch the Fraser River's not a place Miss Fat Ankles will be going."

"Have you fly-fished before?" It was a question Maloof had never before thought of asking Losomma. "If you haven't, forget the trip. And if you have, we'll need documentation. We sure don't want some staged photo op coming back to bite us in the ass. Remember what happened to Dukakis and Kerry."

"No problem. We're golden," said Losomma, smiling as he recalled the utter fool Democratic hopeful Michael Dukakis had made of himself by posing in a tank turret during the 1992 presidential election, and the absolute phoniness that had emanated from Senator John Kerry as, barely able to hold a shotgun properly, he had stalked through backwoods brush on a staged quail hunt during the 2004 election. "I learned to fly-fish in college, knowing it might someday come in handy. Just like I learned to fence.

Hated them both. But I can dredge up a half-dozen photo verifications, and that's what's important. We've got ourselves a win–win here, Joey. Sportsman, team player, outdoorsman, bipartisan reverence to Ike. The press will eat it up. I'll make a pitch for keeping our western streams clear and pristine, and talk about the need for pure water for generations of unborn Americans. What more could we ask for, Joey?"

"A win," said the always pragmatic Maloof. "Pure and simple—a win and the nomination. But you've sold me. I think we just might gain ourselves a few delegates and some voters with your plan. Gonna take the family?"

"No," Losomma said, shaking his head. "Like James Brown used to say, God rest his soul, 'It's a man's world.' We sell the piece as me getting away—with, of course, the wife and kids' blessing—to fly-fish on the great General Eisenhower's favorite river in order to ponder and reflect. And on the very eve of the convention, much as Ike did on the cusp of D-day." Losomma broke into an ear-to-ear grin.

Maloof offered a dutiful nod. "How far away is Fraser, anyway?"

"Eighty-five miles north-west, I'm told. It's a perfect little place in a perfect little valley surrounded by 12,000 mountains. America the Beautiful, Joey. Just waiting there for me to arrive."

Maloof looked puzzled. "You've been there before?"

"Nope. Only seen pictures of the place."

"Who'll go with you?"

Losomma flashed his campaign chairman a coy smile. "You, me, and Benny Wilkins."

"Me? You know I hate the outdoors. It makes me sneeze. And only one bodyguard? We'll need two at least."

"I said it's a man's world, Joey. I don't want to look like a pansy. Benny will do just fine." Losomma took a sip of tepid coffee and frowned at the bitterness. "Think you can round me up major press coverage in less than 24 hours? I want this to hit like a ton of bricks before the opening gavel."

"That's what you pay me for," said Maloof.

"And handsomely, I might add. Don't forget to bring along your Claritan, Joey-boy. I don't want you sneezing your head off all day while we're up there in the mountains. You might scare off the little fishies."

Maloof had nailed down the print and TV coverage for what he and campaign insiders were jokingly calling *Losomma's Romp in the Rockies* by late evening. As Broderick Losomma stood in a bathroom doorway of the Brown Palace Hotel's presidential suite, brushing his teeth and watching his wife's chest rise and fall as she slept peacefully several feet away, he couldn't help but smile and think that he was at the top of his game. Plans for his fly-fishing trip had moved ahead without a hitch, and he'd even had time to practice his casting. Thinking that he was on the fast track to become president of the United States, he nonetheless understood that he'd need to orchestrate a lot more than some hastily staged photo opportunity and backwoods press conference if he expected to win his party's nomination. What he needed was to dispense with Hannah Stenton and Tucker Doleman—effectively grind them into the dirt. As he saw it, Doleman could do him the most harm, not Stenton. It was Doleman, a seasoned manipulator, backslapper, and last-minute twister of arms, who could buttonhole the uncommitted delegates he was counting on and swing their allegiance Stenton's way. It was Doleman who told Hannah what to do and when to do it. She couldn't function without him—every pol in America and even the public knew it.

What he needed was to somehow pull Tucker Doleman and Hannah Stenton apart. Snip the strings between puppet and puppeteer, and assure himself the half-dozen or so votes he still needed to nail down the nomination. He had to come up with something that would destroy their symbiosis, and he was pretty certain he had that something.

For months he'd had his people working on an angle that would force Hannah to jettison Doleman—an angle that would cause uncommitted delegates who were leaning Hannah's way to question her judgment, wring their hands in disbelief, scream, "Oh, no!" and drop her like a hot potato. Two days before, after months of slogging through the political dungheaps, he'd stumbled across what he needed. Now he only had to wait for the right time to spring the trapdoor that would swallow Tucker Doleman.

Stepping back into the bathroom and thinking that his timing was absolutely right, he put away his toothbrush, glanced at himself in the mirror, grinned, and whispered, "Time for a fastball, Tucker. Let's see if you can hit it."

Hannah had little difficulty learning about Broderick Losomma's planned fly-fishing trip on the Fraser River. She had people whose job it was to snoop out every move Losomma made. Besides, the press was integral to his little photo op junket, and that meant there could be no secrets.

An hour before Losomma left for Fraser, fully rested after a peaceful night's sleep, to talk to the press and make pretty pictures, Hannah and a surprisingly chagrined-looking Tucker knew not only where he was headed but the exact location of the remote mountain cabin where he'd be staying for the night. They also knew the name of the well-heeled political supporter who'd offered Losomma the use of the cabin and the approximate time Losomma was expected to return to the Mile High City the following morning. More importantly, Hannah had shared the information with Pinkie Niedemeyer, who'd called her just before daybreak to say he'd take the job.

An hour and twenty minutes out of Denver, Broderick Losomma's rented sports utility vehicle crested the 11,000-foot Berthoud Pass, and began its midmorning descent into the Fraser River valley. Losomma, Maloof, and bodyguard Benny Wilkins, men who'd been prisoners of the East Coast and Midwest for most of their lives, found themselves a bit taken aback by the grandeur of the drive across the valley.

The seven-mile trip from the village of Fraser, the nation's unofficial icebox, to their remote fishing-cabin destination turned out to be a bone-crushing, kidney-jarring ride along a washboard road that was barely more than a cowpath. The drive so upset Joey Maloof's stomach that after it was over, as he stood, with three antacid tablets in his hand, in the kitchen of the rustic three-bedroom cabin that smelled of linseed oil and mildew, he had the feeling that their plan to portray Losomma as a man of the West might turn out to be a mistake.

"I sure hope the media boys have the kind of stomachs that can handle that ride." Shaking his head, Maloof popped the antacids into his mouth and rolled his eyes.

Losomma laughed. "They're the press, Joey. They get paid to cover wars. A little buckboard ride won't stop 'em."

"Buckboard! Damn! Next thing I know you'll be talking about *hombres*, gully washes, ten-gallon hats, and six-guns."

"When in Rome," Losomma said with a grin.

Benny Wilkins, an ebony-skinned, six-foot-four-inch, 255-pound onetime Tennessee State University linebacker, who planned to enter training that fall to become a Secret Service agent, snickered.

"How about a few less snickers and a little more recon, Benny," Maloof said curtly. "Head outside and check out the surroundings for the senator. And make sure that country-yokel sheriff in charge of local security set up at least a one-mile perimeter."

Wilkins' response was a near salute. "Okay." He was out the front door in seconds.

Losomma listened to his heavy-footed bodyguard thump down the front steps before turning to Maloof. "What time are we on, Joey?" His question had the ring of a game-show host.

Maloof checked his watch. "It's eleven o'clock now. I told everyone to be here by one."

"Good." Losomma knelt and picked up his fly-rod case. Unscrewing the top and slipping out the unassembled rod, he glanced toward the back door of the cabin, which led to the river. "Gives me plenty of time to get familiar with my props." Slipping the two halves of the fly rod together, he rose and walked toward the back door. "I'll be outside practicing," he said to Maloof with a smile.

Three miles northwest of the fishing cabin, Pinkie Niedemeyer stood on a cutbank above the meandering Fraser River, staring down at a pool of slow-moving pocket water. Every few seconds the nose of a lunker rainbow broke the water's surface. As if auditioning for Pinkie with each rise, the huge trout slurped a mouthful of emerging caddis-fly nymphs before quickly disappearing.

Familiar with the Fraser, a river he'd fly-fished scores of times, and attuned to the surrounding landscape, Pinkie had reached the abandoned-looking cabin Hannah had told him about well ahead of Losomma and his crew. He'd scoped it out, picked out several possible shooting spots, and cased the front- and back-door entries before hiking upstream to where he now stood.

Glancing skyward toward the noonday sun, he dropped to one knee and unrolled a five-by-five-foot piece of oiled canvas. A fly-rod case and a Luger 9mm automatic, its barrel tooled to take a silencer, rested in the middle of the canvas. His plan, currently in flux, was to get close enough to Losomma to get the kind of confirmatory kill shot that Hannah Stenton had requested in her phone call to him just as he'd crested Berthoud Pass early that morning. He didn't like the idea of getting that close to his target—he'd planned all along to take Losomma out with a long-range shot from a 30.06. But the extra $25,000 Stenton had offered for the up-close-and-personal confirmatory kill had been enticement enough to make him pull out the Luger and at least think about it.

For now he'd stay where he was and fish, maybe even roast a hot dog or two until it was almost dusk. By then Losomma's rendezvous with the press would be history, and the Grand County sheriff and his security entourage would be home for the evening, patting themselves on the back over a job well done. The bend in the river just north of where Pinkie stood was so thick with willows, so difficult to access, and so marshy that it was unlikely any fisherman would stop there to offer the river a second look. Pinkie had the river to himself, and he knew he could linger where he was all day without encountering another person.

Hannah had told him that Losomma would have two other people with him—a bodyguard and his press secretary. How he'd eventually separate Losomma from the other two men was a concern, since he didn't want to have to kill all three. But business was business, and he would if he had to. His assignment was to make the kill look like a failed robbery or the random act of some backwoods *Deliverance* kind of nutcase. Hannah's final instructions to him had been *Whatever you do, don't let things get traced back to me.* He thought about starting a fire in the woods in order to smoke Losomma out and pick off the senator when his inquisitiveness got the better of him. But that would probably force him to kill three men. He wasn't certain how things would play out in the end, but they would. They always did. Once he finished his assignment, he'd head back upriver to where his four-by-four was parked, just off an old logging trail a half-mile upstream from where he now stood. He'd then head north along that trail until it intersected a county road that would take him north to Wyoming.

Mosquitoes buzzed around his head, and the hungry lunker trout in the pool below had stopped feeding, when Pinkie packed up his things twenty minutes later and disappeared into a thicket of willows to think through the options he'd settled on for killing Losomma, and to wait for dusk.

Broderick Losomma's fly-fishing photo op and streamside press conference had gone pretty much as he'd intended— his way, always his way. Charming, debonair, and ingratiating, he'd left the close-to-twenty members of the Colorado and national media as he always expected to leave them— begging for more.

What he hadn't counted on was Tucker Doleman's appearance at the cabin's front door just as dusk approached. After a heated shouting match and standoff in the doorway—during which Joey Maloof, smelling political blood, and Benny Wilkins, 9mm drawn and aimed squarely at Doleman's head, had refused to leave—Losomma had finally convinced both men to take a brief after-dinner stroll so he could talk to Doleman in private. After patting Tucker down for weapons, finding none, and being told in no uncertain terms by Losomma to *take a walk*, Wilkins had walked away from the cabin with a reluctant Joey Maloof in tow.

Pinkie Niedemeyer had worked his way to within thirty yards of the cabin's streamside back door when Maloof and Wilkins walked out the front door. Shaking their heads in protest, the two men headed toward the access road they had driven in on earlier. They were twenty yards away from the cabin when Pinkie, staring up at them from an erosion gully, made his move toward the cabin. He watched the big black man slip a pack of cigarettes out of his pocket, tap out a smoke, and light up as his smaller, nervous-looking white companion struggled to keep up.

Pinkie had been watching the cabin for over an hour when the mysterious fourth man had arrived at the front door. Hannah Stenton had told him more about Losomma and his two companions than he cared to know, but the new arrival, a man boiling with rage, had him baffled. The newcomer had provided him with an unexpected advantage, however. He now had only two people to deal with inside the cabin.

Looking around to make certain that he could make it back down to the river before Losomma's bodyguard and campaign manager returned, Pinkie smiled knowingly. Four decades earlier he'd spent a year running through the muddy jungles of Vietnam carrying an M16 and with forty pounds of weight on his back. Racing up a riverbed carrying a rifle case would be a snap.

Maloof and Wilkins, who'd stopped to talk, were out of earshot and nearly forty yards away when the voices inside the cabin escalated to accusatory shouts.

Distraught and misty-eyed, Tucker Doleman stood a few feet from Losomma, who was seated in an antique pressed-back chair, a bottle of Budweiser in hand. Eyeing Doleman smugly and taking a sip of beer, Losomma said, "You reap what you sow, Tucker."

"You're bilge, Losomma—the high-grade, unadulterated, garbage-scow kind. Where the hell did you get these pictures, anyway?" He slammed an opened eight-by-ten manila envelope down on a nearby table. Several glossy photographs nosed their way out of that envelope.

Losomma smiled. It was the smile of a man who knew he was about to be the winner in a high-stakes poker game. "From your friendly corner kiddie-porn store, Tucker. It's 2008; there're scores of them in every city. But you know that better than me, don't you? You're the one all hugged up, bare-assed, to half-naked boys in those pictures. Never knew you were into little boys, Tuck. I always thought you preferred girls with fat ankles. Shame, shame, shame. I can see the headlines now. *Brains Behind Stenton Bangs Boys and Gets Busted.*"

Doleman's face turned pale, and his upper lip began to quiver. "So use it, you fuckin' half-breed. We'll win the nomination anyway."

"There's no need for name-calling, Tucker. And just for the record, no, you won't. You might still be able to pull a win out of your ass if all you had to do was convince our sweet, wholesome Democratic delegates that you weren't a womanizer or a drunk or maybe even just a flat-out crook. But a child molester? Nope! You can't come back from that. And neither can Hannah."

"Horseshit. No one's voting for me. They're voting for Hannah."

Losomma shook his head. "Oh, Tucker, please. A vote for Hannah is a vote for you. The whole damn country knows that. The woman couldn't find the little girls' room without you taking her there. And we know for certain that you couldn't zip your fly without her standing there to help. The two of you are clingier than the stink on shit. You know it, I know it, and every delegate who'll be voting up here in these beautiful Rockies of ours knows it."

Looking wounded and suddenly defenseless, Doleman said, "Those photos are from a long, long time ago, Broderick."

"I know. I was told the whole skinny." Going for the jugular and enjoying it, Losomma continued to smile. "Should've learned to keep your wiener in the bun, Tuck. You and Miss Fat Ankles bought the farm the day you took those pictures."

Seething with anger, Doleman suddenly imagined himself back on a schoolyard playground, being taunted and made fun of. As the taunts escalated, echoing in his head, he found himself hand in hand with Hannah Stenton as, racing away from their tormenters, they yelled back, "We'll show you. We'll show you." His thoughts had turned to killing Losomma barehanded when the back door to the cabin flew open and banged into a wall.

Dressed in black and sporting a ski mask, Pinkie Niedemeyer stood less than ten feet away from the two startled men. When Doleman opened his mouth to scream, two muffled pops erupted from Pinkie's 9mm. Doleman slumped to the floor without so much as a moan.

Losomma turned to run, but a third bullet from Pinkie's Luger slammed into his neck, severing his carotid artery.

There was another soft pop, and a fourth bullet spiraled between Losomma's first and second ribs, penetrating the would-be president's pulmonary artery. He dropped on top of Doleman with a grunt. Both men were dead by the time Pinkie slipped out the cabin's back door.

Pinkie had been told by Stenton to use any means necessary to solve her Losomma problem. He'd have no trouble telling her that in order to carry out her directive, he'd had to kill a second man. Her instructions, after all, had been explicit: *No dangling participles, Mr. Niedemeyer. Steal something. Ransack the place. Do whatever you have to, even if you have to take out Maloof. Make it look like a madman might've been on the loose. Just make certain my opponent is dead when you leave and that nothing can be traced to me.*

He hadn't filled Hannah Stenton's prescription perfectly. But Losomma was dead, and there had been no witnesses, and that was what counted. He hadn't had time to make his work look like that of a madman or a robber. But what did that really matter in the end? His job was done.

As he raced up the rocky riverbed, gulping air, never looking back, he was certain that the woman who'd hired him would understand that, in his business, things didn't always work out perfectly. What could it matter to her anyway? He'd completed his assignment and, as she'd requested, there were no dangling participles. What did it matter that some unlucky visitor who'd appeared out of nowhere was also dead? The visitor was a nobody to her, after all. His job had been to handle Losomma, and he had. It was no different from Vietnam, when you came right down to it. He'd carried out his mission, and there'd been some minor collateral damage. So what? It happens. Bottom line was, his job was done, and now he was headed safely back to base camp and home.

SLINGIN'

Black Artemis

"Yo, only thing I want to know is what you got on this bitch," Hightower says. "If you want my name and money, y'all need to get something on her. Nelida Montoya need to be got but good."

I warned Kenneth to stay away from this guy, no matter how much money he has or how famous he is. Shit, Jackson "Hi-Jack" Hightower is not famous. He's infamous. Scandalous. So notorious he makes Biggie Smalls look like Will Smith. All the qualities a candidate wants to avoid in a supporter. Unless you're in his line of business—which according to the authorities includes everything from drug trafficking to gun running—you don't get into bed with a guy like Hightower.

My warnings continued from the first moment Kenneth conjured up this ridiculous idea right until the elevator doors opened to the basement of the Explicit Content loft in SoHo. Christ, Hightower didn't have enough sense to distance himself from the biggest scandal to hit the rap music scene since the rise and fall of Suge Knight and Death Row Records. Who advises this man? First thing I would I have had him do was shut down Explicit Content once his boss skipped bail and went into hiding while facing countless charges, ranging from murder to kidnapping and every felony in between. Instead he assumed the position of CEO of the label. Hightower should have sold this loft, liquidated the label's assets, gotten rid of all those thug rappers—starting with the ghetto idiots who named themselves after a movie about snuff films—and made restitution to those "models" they bamboozled into prostitution. Then I would have instructed him to invest whatever remained and lay low for a while. Two years, at minimum, I would have insisted. Then I would have orchestrated a comeback so sweet, Hollywood would have turned it into an Oscar winner.

But I don't work for Jackson "Hi-Jack" Hightower, and lately I find myself regretting coming to work for Kenneth Payne. Had I known sooner that he was such a fame-monger, I would be sitting beside Nelida Montoya at her fundraising luncheon at Victor's Café. But I grew tired of running campaigns for dark horses with no war chests, and I truly believe—I still believe—that Kenneth can beat Montoya. I don't like rap, and I never did, but even I remember K-Pain's 1998 summer anthem "King of Bling", with that brilliant sampling of Coltrane's "Lush Life." Kenneth only had one hit, but he managed his money well, which meant he had the resources to manage a viable campaign. However, it never occurred to me that his bid for state assembly was just his latest grasp for celebrity.

Kenneth wanted to host a fundraiser at Diddy's restaurant. I had no problem with that. Accept Jay-Z's check? Fine, since I no longer work cheap. After arguing about it for over a week, I even relented to Kenneth's insistence that we seek an endorsement from Russell Simmons. I had speculated that Simmons had lost credibility with anyone conscientious enough to vote when he defended the diamond industry in Africa, but I'd seriously underestimated his continued appeal among voters aged eighteen to twenty-five. So I was wrong about Rush Simmons, and I am man enough to admit that.

But I'm not wrong about Hightower. He proves it when five minutes into this meeting he wants to know what dirt we have on Nelida Montoya. Honestly, it floored me that he even knew her name and recognized that she was Kenneth's only threat in the primary. Eighty-two percent of registered voters in the 56th district are Democrats; whoever wins this primary is guaranteed the seat.

Kenneth grins at me and pats me on the shoulder before turning back to Hightower. "My boy Cruz here got our oppo guy all over that."

"Oppo guy?" Hightower fidgets. "You got retired po-po working on your campaign."

"Aw, hell, nah," says Kenneth.

"He a P.I. or what?"

"Oppo as in opposition research," I explain. "He searches for information on Nelida Montoya that we can use to discredit her."

"Now that's what I'm talking about." Hightower relaxes into his massive leather chair. "Like what?"

"Things like extreme or even conflicting statements on political issues, suspicious financial records, questionable personal relations or . . ." I remember who I'm speaking to and stop before saying *business ties*. "Our man on this is highly qualified. He worked for six years at the Democratic National Committee, then as research director for . . ."

"Fuck alla that." Hightower waves dismissively at me. "Just tell me what he's got on that Montoya bitch."

Not much, I think. After attending the Dalton School, she went to Wesleyan where she graduated *magna cum laude*. I would have given ten years of my life to attend Dalton, but I had to settle for the Bronx High School of Science because my father—instead of starting a successful import business so he could afford to send me to a decent college—decided to leave my mother, return to the island and start another family. Unlike Montoya, who never worked a single day until she graduated from Wesleyan, I had to hold three jobs to afford Yale. Three jobs and a rigorous curriculum equals no social life, ergo excellent preparation for life on the campaign trail.

Anyway, Montoya is so clean she probably squeaks when she exhales. I cannot grasp how she came to be such a hip hop "head," as they refer to themselves. If she were a rapper, she would pen corny jingles for McDonald's and Target. My guess is that Montoya did not have a penchant for the artistic life (since talent rarely matters) because she chose to carve out a niche for herself as a one-woman crusade. Quite the cinch to form a charitable organization, appoint yourself as the executive director and publicly flout the law in the name of social change when Papi pays your bills. Montoya's rap sheet consists of three arrests—all for civil disobedience. In fact, she brags about them in her campaign brochures.

Back in 2000, she was among those arrested at the United Nations with actress Rosie Perez protesting U.S. naval bombings on the island of Vieques, Puerto Rico. Montoya was also charged with disorderly conduct at a rally after the fatal police shooting of the unarmed Sean Bell on the eve of his wedding.

Her most recent arrest took place at a sit-in at radio station Hot 97. Slick Montoya arranged for a professional videographer to record her leading the other protestors in their chant, chaining herself to the door of the station manager's office, and getting carried out by security. The video is all over YouTube and plays automatically once her

MySpace page loads. All this long before she officially announced her intention to run and hired my rival, Gunn, to run her campaign.

Although Montoya always manages to rally the troops to her battle of choice, at its essence her so-called Cipher 4 Change is a one-woman show. Kenneth told to me that in hip hop parlance a cipher is a circle in which like minds commune, usually over artistic expression or philosophical matters. I explained to him that, in the precise world of mathematics, cipher equals zero. Or in the simple terms of Merriam-Webster, cipher has no weight, worth or influence. His opponent's Cipher 4 Change consists of no one besides herself, and yet she has succeeded in catapulting herself into the public sphere as a "hip hop activist" who must be reckoned with.

And that is the paradox of Nelida Montoya, and why she is such a formidable threat to Kenneth. She's not only attractive, clean and rich. She's also gutsy and smart. No wonder she made a strategic move to Bedford-Stuyvesant to wage her campaign—which reminds me of the one measly thing we have on her.

"To start," I say with as much enthusiasm as I can muster, "we can make a strong case that Montoya is a carpetbagger."

"For real." Hightower's eyes widen. "That dime's a dyke?" Then his signature sneer reappears on his face. "Man, that ain't shit. Nowa-fuckin'-days, that don't mean squat, especially since that bitch is fine. You broadcast that a hottie like that eats pussy, you might as well throw in the towel on this here election right now." He actually laughs at the thought.

Kenneth struggles to not laugh, too—whether along with Hightower or at him, I'm unsure—while I stuff the untouched campaign material I had placed on his desk back into my briefcase.

"Nah, that's carpet*bagger* not carpet-*muncher*, bro. That means her ass is fake, son. She ain't true blue Bed-Stuy, do or die, like me. Montoya only moved there to run because she thinks she has a better chance of winning *my* seat than the one wherever the fuck she's from in Queens."

"Jackson Heights," I say.

Hightower gives a slight nod. "You mean like when Hillary Clinton moved her ass to New York to run instead of running in Illinois or Arkansas for senate."

"Exactly." Perhaps, like Simmons, I underestimated him, too.

Hightower muses. "Now why would that bitch bring her ass all the way from Jackson Heights to Bed-Stuy to run for office if she ain't hiding nothing? What do folks in her parts know about her?"

"I'm telling you, Jack, if Montoya got any bones, my boy Cruz is gonna excavate every last one of them motherfuckers," says Kenneth. "But I don't gotta tell you that takes loot, right, son?"

I grin at Kenneth for reminding me what I saw in him. Nelida may be polished, but she also comes off cold and righteous. Kenneth is charismatic. He knows how to read his audience and play to it. Why he turned out to be a one-hit wonder will always be a mystery to me.

Hightower, however, seems unconvinced. He says, "I pride myself on being a straight-shootin' nigga, so let me be real with y'all." Then he reaches across his desk for a binder and slides it across the desk toward me. "A few days ago Montoya was sitting right where you are now asking me to write a check and endorse her candidacy, too. And the truth, kid? She looks better for me than you do right now."

I flip through the binder which is a tidy compilation of Montoya's campaign material. It includes a briefing booklet that bullets her positions on all the relevant political issues facing the district. All the press clippings of her activist outbursts. Kenneth had a brief stint as an activist, but that was back in college and the yellowing newsprint of *The Kingsmen*, Brooklyn College's student weekly, is laughable compared to Montoya's byline on a *New York Daily News* editorial or a color photograph of her brandishing a bullhorn on the cover of *El Diario–La Prensa*. Gunn even included both a CD and DVD of all her candidate's radio and television appearances. I barely hear Hightower as I look through the binder. The sound of me kicking myself is too loud.

"Folks are getting sick of all the gutter shit in hip hop, so a nigga needs to reinvent himself to stay on top," says Hightower. "That's why I don't rhyme no more, I gots to rock this mogul shit full-time and a half, ya feel me?"

All Kenneth and I can do is nod.

"Take my politicking to a whole other level, which means getting down with some candidates who are gonna have my back as a businessman."

"Then ride with me, son," Kenneth says. "I got you."

Hightower snickers. "Anybody I finance is gonna have me, dog. That's the nature of this shit." My feeble nod grows feverish, because he's absolutely right. "But I can't just ride with anyone. I gotta rock with someone who makes me look good out there," he says, as he points where Broadway would be visible if we were not in this windowless cave he calls an office. My claustrophobia kicks in. "And given the gully places I've been and the swanky places I wanna be, Montoya looks better for me." Hightower shakes his head and squints at us. "But that's also why I don't completely trust the bitch, know what I'm sayin'?"

Gesturing toward the binder in my hand, Kenneth says, "Yeah, I don't see no clips of all those fucked up things she said about Explicit Content in there."

"She copped to that before I could even call it out," says Hightower. "She told me that's precisely why I can improve my image, and therefore, my business, if I roll with her. That's why I asked you what you got on this bitch."

Perhaps it's the claustrophobia, but I'm losing patience. "Just so we can be clear, are you endorsing Nelida Montoya, are you saying you're staying out of this race, or what?"

Ignoring me, Hightower says, "Look, I want to ride with you, Kenny. We niggas in this game need to stick together, and if you ask me, I think this bitch is trying to set us all up. Me, Rush, Jigga, Diddy, all of us. She gonna take our money and our endorsements, roll up into Albany and then ram some activist accountability corporate responsibility-type shit right up our asses, and we're just going to have to grin and take it. Nah, man, I ain't the one. In the long run, who knows what that bitch is gonna do, but right now, endorsing her is good for business. Unless . . ." Kenneth and I lean forward. "Gunn is organizing a political action committee—Hip Hop for Montoya or some shit like that. Next Monday, they're holding a press conference at Borough Hall with all the famous hip hop heads who are endorsing her. I told her that I would make my decision by then, which buys y'all a week."

"To do what?" asks Kenneth.

Hightower winks. "Dig up them bones."

Ordinarily, I advise my candidates to avoid going negative first. As tempting as it may be to share some juicy morsels with the voting public, wait until your opponent strikes first, I always say. That way you can go full throttle, and no one can blame you for defending yourself. But I have to save face and prove I can rock with these dogs. No, I'm not one of the countless yes-men they encounter in the entertainment industry. I am one of *them*. A man who acquired all that he has with no resources at his disposal save ambition. And I like to win, especially against those who have had everything handed to them.

"Done," I say. One week from today, I intend to give Jackson Hightower something on Nelida Montoya even if I have to invent it myself.

When Kenneth Payne and Wilmer Cruz swagger into the 40/40 Club, it takes my all not to fly across the room and backslap those stupid smirks off their faces. I polish off my merlot and hiss into Nelida's ear, "I can't believe you agreed to meet them here."

"It's neutral territory."

"Since when is a sports bar neutral territory?"

"Back off, Monet." Nelida grabs her Angel Jackson clutch and lifts herself out of the white and gold round chair suspended from the ceiling. I bite my tongue not to crack how she looks like she just hatched from an egg. "I didn't exactly have a choice."

"Ms Montoya," Payne says as he offers her his hand. Not only does she take it, she allows the unctuous fool to press his fat lips against it. Cruz extends his hand toward me, and I give it the same look I reserve for the puny dicks of ill-chosen fuck buddies. He snatches his hand back and shoves it in his pocket.

Nelida says, "Shall we proceed to Jay's Room?"

Payne seems impressed. "Girl, what you know about Jay's Room?"

"When you insisted on meeting here, Ms Montoya asked me to reserve it," I explain. "You know, for privacy."

Payne mugs at Cruz, and I don't know what keeps me from lunging for his throat. Before turning to lead them to the VIP section, Nelida gives me a look of gratitude, recognizing and appreciating my restraint. She knows, despite this Prada pantsuit—the only one I ever owned that cost three figures, which she bought for me—I ain't like her. Not below the surface. I may keep my hair and nails tight and work with a speech coach to play this game, but at my core I'm still straight Brownsville. I don't lie to myself about it, nor am I embarrassed by it. Like Pacino says about his angst in *Heat*, I preserve my hood because I need it. It keeps me sharp, on the edge, where I gotta be.

But I have to be careful because it takes little from another hood rat like Kenneth Payne to bring it out of me, even if it doesn't belong. He must drive Cruz insane—although that anal motherfucker doesn't fool me, trying to hide behind those Kenneth Cole shoes and the King's English. Son of a bitch still reeks of pre-gentrification Washington Heights.

No sooner do we close the door to Jay's Room and take our seats in front of the sixty-inch plasma TV when I demand to know, "How did you get your filthy hands on those disgusting pictures?"

"That's not as important," says Cruz, "as what Ms Montoya is willing to do to keep them hidden."

"You mean drop out of the race?" True to the script I had mentally written, I say, "That's not possible. The primary is less than a month away, and we've amassed too much support. We will not succumb to your dirty tactics and disappoint our constituents and donors."

True to his crass nature, Payne says, "You don't think pictures of your girl slobbin' five different knobs over the course of one night won't disappoint them?" He cackles and nudges Cruz, who actually seems to have the sense to be concerned that we haven't balked. "Sweetheart, if we release those photographs, your campaign is over. Shit, you're whole fuckin' life is over."

"Release them," says Nelida as she takes the remote to mute the plasma television. "Not only will I still have a campaign, boys, you just might win me several million more votes than I need to win." Then she stands and walks over to the screen showing replays of the last baseball Subway Series. With her back to us, Nelida looks up at the screen as one might before God, raising her hands like a priest at an altar. "I know how you picture it, Kenneth. I see you with those photographs in your hands, imagining thousands of sixteen-year-old boys downloading them from the internet. You see your personal favorite strategically blurred on the cover of the *New York Post* underneath an embarrassing headline. You visualize me rushing from my office to my car, shielding my face from the news cameras and mics, too mortified to even whisper *No comment*."

Then Nelida turns, flashing that ever-present smile of confident restraint. "The problem, Kenneth, is that your picture is incomplete. Allow me to supply the missing details." She paces back toward us, the glow from the muted sixty-inch screen hanging above her head creating a silvery blue aura around her. "Less than twenty-four hours after the scandal hits, I make a single appearance to defend myself."

"On *The Tyra Banks Show*," I add. Then I improvise. "She and Tyra go way back. You know how women bond when they have a no-good man in common." Truth is, Nelida doesn't know Tyra from a pile of bricks. Neither do I. Hell, if anyone involved in the campaign did, I would have exploited that months ago. But my confidence in this bluff surges. If Payne does leak the photos, no way is scandal-loving Tyra going to pass on this. If she can give a whole hour to Supahead when she doesn't even like that trick, surely Tyra won't refuse an exclusive with Nelida.

"I appear on my friend's program, and I simply tell the truth."

Cruz scoffs. "You can point the finger at our campaign all you like. This is politics . . ."

"This shit is hip hop," interjects Payne.

". . . and if you can't prove that we leaked the photographs . . ."

". . . which y'all can't . . ."

". . . no one will believe you. All they'll believe is what they see. Another freak in Juicy Couture trying to blame a Black man for her own promiscuity." Cruz's voice is strong, but he drums those Kenneth Coles against the floor like a smack-head trying to kick. Unlike his gully-ass boss, the boy's smart enough to be nervous. "Crying victim is a waste of time."

"Oh, I won't cry victim, gentlemen," Nelida says. "I'll do what Americans crave most from their wayward public figures yet rarely receive." She takes the television remote and starts to flip through the muted channels. Paris Hilton flashes across the screen, ignoring the paparazzi while typing away on her Sidekick. "I'll prostate myself before them and beg forgiveness." Nelida clicks through the channels and stops on Lindsay Lohan as she preens on a red carpet at some L.A. premiere.

"I'll fault my pampered upbringing and apologize for my youthful indiscretions. And then I'll take the opportunity to list all the examples of my evolution since my wild-child days. My crusade to hold hip hop artists accountable for their words and images; my charitable donations to youth organizations from the Big Apple to the Bay Area; and my volunteer hours spent empowering girls who are lost, just as I was once." Nelida stops on a hip hop video of the typical shit—thugs drinking forties and tossing around money while half-naked chicks bump and grind on them.

"And that's only going to make Tyra and her audience of millions ask why would someone do such an ugly thing to such a good soul like me? Because I experimented in college just like any normal teenager?"

"Or maybe because she's trying to clean up hip hop," I say.

"Or maybe because I'm a woman." And as if these cats could forget, Nelida lowers herself on the arm of Payne's chair. I catch him eyeing her bare thighs and taking a whiff of her perfume, his nose wriggling like a rat near a scrap of cheese. "Of course, I couldn't possibly convince everyone. I have neither the hubris nor naiveté to believe that any of your hardcore fans, Kenneth, will think me a martyr."

I lean forward to give Payne a sisterly pat on his knee. "You do know what *hubris* means?"

Cruz wipes my hand off Payne's leg like a jealous lover. "For your information, Ms Montoya is not the only candidate in this race who attended college."

"That's right. He did two and half years at Brooklyn College before dropping out to manage the Clockers, who ended up suing him for embezzlement." *Yeah, motherfucker, I have the dirt on your boy, too.* "In fact, Payne used their royalties to bankroll his own album, right?"

"You really underestimated my graciousness, Kenneth. Just took it for granted," says Nelida, and damn, she genuinely sounds hurt. "Ms Gunn wanted to use that information against you in an ad campaign from the start, but I forbid her to do it."

"I just thought that voters who didn't follow the music industry should be made aware of your financial management style. I mean, if that's the way you handle money entrusted to you by close business associates, how might you handle the taxpayers' money?"

Nelida brings us back to the script. "As I said, I won't convince everyone of my radical transformation, but I don't need to. Several hundreds of thousands of Tyra's fans will."

I repeat, "Hundreds of thousands."

"Some will volunteer, others will send money, some will do both. And I'll probably get an avalanche of endorsements from national women's organizations, who ordinarily stay out of local elections. Those endorsements mean greater exposure and more money."

"White women's money."

"I can't lie to you, Kenneth. If you were to leak those photos, I would be supremely humiliated at first." Nelida places her perfectly manicured hands onto Payne's shoulders and starts to massage them. "But thanks to my campaign manager extraordinaire, I know how to spin that scandal into a win, and I'm quite willing to make that sacrifice. I almost wish you would, Kenneth."

Payne chews on his bottom lip for a few seconds, then throws a glance at Cruz. He's shook, boring footprints into the floor. Foolish motherfucker, thinking his Ivy League degree would advantage him. They said it themselves. This is hip hop meets politics. The game was grimy long before we rolled up onto it. All we're doing is putting our unique brand on shit, and Cruz's prissy little first-generation pedigree isn't worth a damn around here.

Payne finally says, "I appreciate how far you're willing to go to win this election, Nelida. You've earned my respect for that." Then he slaps her hands off his shoulders, stands up, and straightens his lapels. "By this time tomorrow, you'll know how far *I'm* willing to go to win." He motions for Cruz to follow him as he heads for the exit.

Cruz rises, the smirk inching over his face like a five o'clock shadow. "Ladies," he says as he salutes. "Believe me when I say it's been a pleasure."

I can't hold back any longer. "Fuck you!" But Payne and Cruz just laugh and give each other a pound.

"Monet!"

"I told you who you were dealing with, Nel." I jump to my feet. "I said it's only a matter of time before he goes negative so you better make the pre-emptive strike." Even though the door has closed behind them, I can still hear Payne and Cruz snickering in the corridor. "We have a truckload of shit on that shiesty bastard, and you wouldn't let me use any of it."

"We don't need to," Nelida says, noticing a miniscule chip on her French manicure. "I better stop at the Dashing Diva and hope they can squeeze me in."

I pull her hand away from her face. "You can't be serious."

"There's nothing we can do until they make a move but stay on our original course, Monet." She grabs her clutch and starts toward the door. "What's on the itinerary?"

I sigh and glance at my Blackberry. "You need to be at Hot 97 in the next forty-five minutes."

"Hot 97?" Nelida stops in mid-stride to flash me a smile. "On drive-time, no less?"

"No big deal," I say, even though we both know it was a major coup given the countless times over the past few years Nel has appeared on New York 1, Fox News and in *The Village Voice* criticizing the radio station for fueling beefs between rappers, playing offensive lyrics, and sponsoring on-air asinine stunts like the "Smackfest," where two stupid chicks take turns slapping each other until one draws blood, winning five hundred bucks. "Angie Martinez says she has mad respect for you."

"And I have great respect for *you*," says Nel. "Cruz did me a favor when he turned me down, Monet, because you are the best in the business." Her acknowledgment means so much that I'm at a loss for words. I never understood why Cruz went with Payne, but maybe he got wind of Nel's college antics and decided Payne was the lesser of two evils. His loss, my gain.

"And I apologize again for not disclosing everything," says Nelida. "But honestly, I was so drunk that night, I don't recall a thing after the threesome."

I sigh. "Well, what's done is done."

We reach the main entrance to the 40/40 Club when Nelida puts an arm around me. "Stop worrying, Monet. No matter what tricks our opponents have up their sleeves, I am going to be the next representative of New York State Assembly District 56, and you will be my chief of staff. And that's just the beginning." And I can see in Nel's eyes as clearly as I know she can see in mine the next stop: Congress. And if we can go that far, why stop there?

Nelida pushes open the door, and we walk out onto West 24th Street right in the middle of one of New York's infamously impromptu summer showers. The sky goes from baby blue to arsenic gray in seconds, and then dumps tubs of grape-sized drops of polluted rain on whoever thought they were slick enough to get from point A to point B without getting doused. It only lasts a few minutes, but it soaks you to the bone.

"Shit!" Nelida mumbles under her breath, in a rare lapse of grace. She shields her updo with her clutch as I hold open the door for her to dodge back inside the lounge. She barely turns when I hear three loud pops. She screams in pain and falls against me. We both tumble against the door. As I slink to the ground under the weight of Nelida's body, dark blood spurts from her shoulder and seeps through the front of my silk camisole.

"Somebody, help!" I yell as I scramble to dial 911 on my Blackberry. "They shot my friend!"

I thought she was playin' with me when she said that she would come to pick up the check personally and give me a ride to the press conference. Figured at the last minute she would send some staffer instead, but there she was in my reception area. When my assistant told me that she came alone, I made her send her in right away. You don't make a bitch like that wait.

Nelida walks into my office fine as all hell in this blood-red suit and matching slingbacks. The cream-colored sling around her arm is studded with red jewels like some designer got to it, and she's rocking the same Cavalli sunglasses I just bought my wifey. I can't front. I love Trudy, but the Cavallis look better on Nelida.

I point to the sling and ask, "You got one for every outfit, right?"

Nelida Montoya glides across the room and eases herself into a chair across my desk. "Now you know I have more important things on which to spend your money, Mr Hightower."

Not only do the bitch got jokes, she delivers them all proper and shit. I got to laugh. "Girl, you still gonna hit me up? You don't need my money or my endorsement. Even though the charges ain't stick, Payne's got no chance of beating you now that everyone thinks he tried to have you killed."

"Regardless, I still have bills to pay, so your contribution will come in handy."

I shrug, open a drawer, and pull out the leather binder where I keep my business checks. I grab my pen and ask,

"Who do I make it out to again?" I start to scrawl the date across the top. "Hip Hop for Montoya, right?"

"Actually, make it out to cash."

I stop writing. "To cash?"

"Please."

Now I put the motherfuckin' pen down. "I thought you had bills to pay."

"I do." Nelida slides her sunglasses to the top of her head and looks at me with them goddamn hypnotic eyes. "I'm giving your check to the man I hired to shoot me in front of 40/40."

"Say what?"

"Oh, Jackson, please don't make me repeat myself. I want to put all this ugliness behind me." Nelida eases back into the chair and crosses those perfect fuckin' legs. "And since this campaign donation is not being reported to the state election board, why don't you be chivalrous and double the amount so I can clear this debt?"

"Hell nah!" I slam the binder shut. "I ain't giving you a goddamn dime until you tell me why the fuck you would do something so gangsta." Truth be told, I never understood why a bourgie chick like Nelida would want to run for office any-goddamn-way. With her upbringing and those looks, she could marry herself a white boy. Probably not some New England blue-blood whose family is old money, being she's still a brown-skinned Dominican chick from an outer borough and shit. But Nelida could easily land some self-made motherfucker in media or some shit like that, and get paid just for marrying his ass. You know, a nigga like me.

Nelida pouts. "We have a press conference in less than an hour." She sounds all annoyed, and it's mad cute. "Or have you forgotten?"

"Nah, I ain't forget," I say. "But I ain't going unless you give me the 4-1-1." I stand up, walk around my desk and lean on the edge, striking a GQ pose.

I expect Nelida to go off on me, but instead she gives me that smile I'm sure has tripped up many a motherfucker. "As sweet as it is, you don't have to pretend to be so surprised for my sake." She slinks her way over to me, all seductive and whatnot. "I know you saw the photos, too, Jackson. Obviously, you know what I'm capable of when I embark on something."

"Don't get it twisted," I say. "I've been in this industry way too long to be surprised by the shit people do after one too many."

"But I wasn't drunk at all." Nelida reaches out and strokes my Pucci tie. "I knew what I was doing, and I loved every minute of it."

I knock her hand off me. "Lyin' ass bitch."

Nelida laughs. I wait for her either to insist that she's telling the truth or to admit that she was yanking my chain. But she don't do either. Instead she says, "Look, what happened, happened. There was evidence of it, and Kenneth Payne was going to use it to bury me. I had to take extreme measure to fight back, especially when he called my bluff."

"What bluff?"

She tells me how her campaign manager Monet Gunn told her that if he leaked the photos, she would cop to the sexcapade on Tyra Banks' talk show, trying to make Kenny think that if he put her freaky ass on blast, he'd be doing her a favor. That's some risky-ass shit, and I sure as hell wouldn't have bought it. I still don't know why this election means so much to this chick, but as far as how much she wants it? Shit, I'm mad crystal.

"Monet's a great political strategist. She has more balls than Payne and Cruz put together," says Nelida. "But I had serious doubts that they would back down, and I had to put a back-up plan into place. One that I had to keep to myself." Now she's twiddling with my pocket square and shit. This time I don't stop her. "Until now." Nelida leans closer to me, and I can smell cinnamon on her breath. "It feels so good, Jackson, to unburden myself this way. To confide in a man who understands a thing or two about ambition."

Yo, you know what? Fuck Bey and Jigga. And fuck Rush and that ghetto-ass Kimora, too. If me and Nelida hook up, we'd knock that power couple shit into a whole other stratosphere. I'd leave Trudy for this bitch in a fuckin' minute, for real, and anybody who knows me can tell you that ain't some shit I'd ever thought I'd do.

"So it's like that now?" I say.

Nelida leans against me and purrs, "Oh, it's all always been like that."

DISSED

K.j.a. Wishnia

One may smile, and smile, and be a villain.
                                                    Hamlet

One may smile, and smile, and be a doss wee cunt.
                                    Irvine Welsh's *Hamlet*

I always know it's some seriously *jodido* bullshit whenever they start off by getting my name wrong. It's either a telemarketer, or some charity calling me for the hundredth time because I once gave them a few bucks, or someone from the hospital's billing department telling me that, thanks to the latest health insurance screw-up, my last visit isn't covered and I'm responsible for the full fee of 350 bucks for a ten-minute consult. Whatever, it usually spells trouble.

So when the call came for *Ms Flomeena Buscarella* before I'd even had my coffee, I let the answering machine handle it. (*Latino* names are pronounced just the way they're written. Mine's Buscarsela. That's Bus-car-se-la. Not so hard, right?)

The call turns out to be a pre-recorded message from the Board of Elections telling me that my polling place has been changed from the junior high school I've been voting at for years to some address on Elmhurst Avenue that I rush to scribble down on a paper napkin.

Something doesn't sound right about that, but I'm not really awake yet. My daughter went to that school, and I still remember the first time I voted there because it was the year the presidential race came down to a couple hundred hand-counted absentee ballots in Broward County, Florida; New York elected its first woman senator, and a dead man won the senate race in Missouri. And if the first movie wasn't bad enough, then we had to sit through the lame sequel, *President Bush, Part II: It Lives.*

So all over the country the opposition is gearing up for the long march toward retaking control of the House and maybe even the Senate that begins with today's primary elections. But around here, everyone's watching the contest for City Council, District 21.

The challenger is Vivian Sánchez, a Dominican mother of four from the "heartland" of Queens who's running on milk money, matching funds from the Campaign Finance Board, and a small army of volunteers. She's running against incumbent James A. Rickman, Jr, son of a long-time party leader, and a polished product of the well-oiled party machine. The district is made up of parts of East Elmhurst, Jackson Heights, and Archie Bunker's old neighborhood of Corona. But times have changed since Bunker's day, when conservative hardhats ruled the blocks of row houses along 108th Street. Nowadays, the district is more than two-thirds *latino*, but so many of them can't vote legally that it's actually a close race.

After two cups of Ecuadorian coffee so strong the International Olympic Committee ought to ban it as an illegal performance-enhancing drug, I'm willing to brave the November breezes of these northern latitudes and walk to my tiny storefront office. It's conveniently located just off Roosevelt Avenue and out of the shadows of the number 7 train tracks.

I spend the first hour or so reviewing the case file on my newest paying client, a scrap metal dealer who's being charged with receiving stolen goods. He claims he didn't know the stuff was stolen. His lawyer wants me to dig up evidence to support that defense (scrap metal is one of the few businesses where it's pretty hard to tell the genuine article from the illicit kind).

So far I've interviewed a demolition crew that specializes in salvaging scrap metal, studied police reports on a pattern of recent thefts and other criminal behavior involving copper plumbing, and helped traced the stolen goods to a construction site on 106th Street, where the streetlights are always out at night. The modus operandi points to a couple of industrious but drug-addled schmucks after some easy money.

I mean, the thieves had to climb a steel mesh fence topped with a few hundred yards of razor wire, chisel through an eight-inch cinderblock wall and rip out the porcelain bathroom fixtures just to haul away twenty pounds of copper tubing worth about $40 in today's market, when they could have easily spent the day flipping burgers and making kissy noises at the women for the same money. Maybe their night work comes with a better benefits package.

I've got to expand my client base of paying customers because I do a lot of *pro bono* work, which makes me pretty popular around here. But I do so damn much of it I ought to be able to deduct half the people in the *barrio* as dependents.

My part-time assistant shows up around 10 a.m. I buzz her in and she flings open the door, jingling the bells left over from when this place was a knick-knack shop. The bells are kind of unnecessary at this point, but I never got around to taking them down and now I'm so used to them I guess they're here to stay, which is about as permanent as anything gets in my life these days.

My assistant's name is Cristina González. She's a sophomore at Queens College with a faceful of cinnamon-colored freckles that glow with a youthful perkiness that just about makes up for her slowly developing office skills. Apparently she had a fun weekend, going to the mixed-marriage wedding of her friends Jenn and Russell. I ask how that went, and she says that the whole Jewish–Catholic thing was okay, but the rivalry between the *Star Wars* crowd and the medieval role players nearly started a riot.

Kids today. Tsk tsk. In my day, the Trekkies would have kicked their collective asses. It just goes to show how Queens is a place that welcomes strangers of all kinds, although sometimes I think the motto over the golden door should be, *We've been fucked for 400 years. Now it's your turn.* Because every wave of incoming refugees brings a new set of problems, a new set of clients, and some new vocabulary. Besides *latinos*, I've worked for Croatians, Albanians, Indians, Pakistanis, Russians, and enough Orthodox Jews to bring my Yiddish up to about a hundred words. This came in handy one time when I had to stop a court-appointed defense attorney from presenting a Hebrew document in court that he had reproduced *backwards* until we corrected it.

Then there are the lonely old people who just call up every now and then to chat about their troubles. The private eye thing's a tough job, ministering to all those different people. But it still beats swinging I-beams around on a windy scaffolding, or running out the clock in some ratty cubicle, spinning my wheels and generating buckets of mindless flak for the six-figure-earning bastards three floors above.

Right now I'm busy with some routine forensic accounting (a skill I picked up at the P.I. firm of Davis and Brown), cross-checking binders full of invoices for anomalies, so I let Cristina set the radio to her favorite *rock latina*. It helps block out the other distractions. That is, until they take an ad break.

Suddenly the volume gets amped up and they start blasting some annoying infomercial about the latest in high-tech kitchen gadgetry—a computerized refrigerator that links to all your other appliances from its nerve center. Why would you need an air traffic control center in your icebox? Because, the pitchman says, "The refrigerator is the first place you go in the morning and the last place you go at night."

Uh, no. Sorry to spoil your party, but the fridge is *not* the first place I go in the morning. That honor is held by another location in the apartment.

Just as Cristina is turning down the radio, a man in a dark blue uniform appears outside the glass door, sucking the last drag from his cigarette. When the smoke clears, I recognize him as Harvey Limón, a security guard at the high school, and for a moment I think maybe something's happened to my daughter and I can't seem to hit the buzzer quickly enough.

But he comes in clutching an old-style audio cassette and says, "Filomena, you've got to listen to this and tell me if it's true."

He hands me the cassette. It's a battered old thing made of cheap, brown plastic, with room for about ten minutes of content, maximum. *Gee, it's been a long time since I've seen one of these, old timer.*

"And where did this tape come from?"

"I recorded it this morning on my answering machine."

"You still use a *tape* machine?"

"*Claro que sí.* It still works," he says, making me feel slightly ashamed for letting a phrase slip out that's so at odds with the traditional ways of the *campesinos* and their divine gift of being able to preserve the working life of expensive mechanical objects almost indefinitely.

Harvey left his hometown in El Salvador back in the 1980s, around the time the death rate started to outstrip the birth rate. He saw so much carnage that he can't even look at blood today. He once told me how the peasants used to give the soldiers water with finely ground glass in it to kill them in slow agony. He absolutely can't understand why the rival Central American gangs roaming around the school just can't get along with each other.

I shrug and pop the cassette into one of the tape recorders I use for formal interviews. I press play and listen to a decade's worth of hiss and dropouts, followed by an authoritative voice announcing that this message is for Mr. Harvard Limón, and that the Board of Elections is calling to inform him that since he is not properly registered to vote, he may be arrested if he shows up at his usual polling place.

I should tell you that Harvey is one of five children whose naïve and trusting parents thought that naming their kids after famous American universities would help them get U.S. visas quicker. His brothers Yale and Princeton did okay with their names, but his sister, University of Texas at Dallas, wasn't as lucky.

I tell him not to worry, it's a bunch of *mierda encima de más mierda.* They're just trying to scare him away from the polls.

Of course, this type of voter intimidation is one of the reasons he left El Salvador in the first place.

The irony is not lost on either of us.

And if we don't exactly have roving death squads up here, that's just a testament to the efficiency of our methods. Though I wouldn't try telling that to Amadou Diallo or Sean Bell.

"I'm being dissed," he says.

"You think? I mean, I agree that they disrespect you, but—"

"No, not disrespect. That other 'dis' word."

"Disturbed?

"No, that's not it."

"Distracted?"

"No."

It takes me a moment.

"Disenfranchised."

"That's it."

"Well, we'll just have to see about that, won't we?" I say, gathering up my coat and scarf.

"You know I can't afford to hire you."

I wave off his concerns. "Who said anything about hiring me? It's time for you and me to go vote. Crissy, watch the store till I get back."

I am a pitbull on the pantleg of opportunity.
                                        President George W. Bush

First we go to the address scribbled on my napkin, which turns out to be a vacant lot with a couple of broken streetlights overhead. So we head to the school, where it looks like business as usual. Volunteers are handing out fliers next to the POLLING PLACE signs posted about a hundred feet on either side of the front entrance. A home-less guy wearing clothes that seem to be made of strips of dried seaweed hands me a flier and a sample ballot with a thick black arrow pointing to Vivian Sánchez's name on Row A.

Long lines because of too few machines in the poorer neighborhoods? Maybe in Ohio, baby. Thank God the city still uses those reliable old clunkers that look like they belong on the set of some grade-Z mad scientist movie from the 1950s—solid metal booths with heavy levers that Iron Mike Tyson couldn't bend out of shape. None of this plastic touch-screen nonsense for us; none of those tricked-out video poker machines that swallow whole towns without a trace. No, we do election fraud the old-fashioned way.

We only have to wait a few minutes, but Harvey can't help being nervous about getting into trouble with the law, and he's seriously itching for a fix of his nicotine habit.

"They should let you smoke in here," he says, drumming his fingers on a rolled-up copy of the propositions on today's ballot. "Instead of banning smoking, they should just install brand-new ventilation systems in all public places."

"Come on, Harvey, this is New York. We can't even keep the firehouses open."

I get the next available booth, but once I'm inside with the curtain closed, I find that the party machine's candidate, James A. Rickman, Jr, is on Row A, and that the challenger, Vivian Sánchez, is on Row B. So either the sample ballot was wrong or else it was deliberately misleading. And I'm leaning toward the latter, since the other flier in my hand suggests that Kwesi Mfume, former president of the NAACP, endorses Rickman over Sánchez, and I know there's no way in hell that he did that.

And when I pull the master lever and jerk open the curtain, I learn that Harvey's been purged from the list of registered voters. The flustered poll worker, a middle-aged black woman, explains that he must have the same name as a convicted felon.

"Hold on," I say. "You're telling me there's another guy in Queens named *Harvard Limón* who's a convicted felon? You've got to be kidding me."

"*¿Qué hago ahora?*" says Harvey.

"Can he fill out a provisional ballot?"

"Not if he isn't properly registered."

"I've got to get back to work," says Harvey. "They only gave me an hour off."

I look at the poll worker, pleading for a favor.

"It'll take a lot longer than an hour to resolve this mess," she says. "Probably take a few weeks."

Back outside, I march straight up to the homeless guy, grab some of his fliers and scrutinize them for any signs of where they were printed. Of course, there are none. When I ask why he's doing this, he says he's getting fifty bucks for the job.

"Who's paying you?"

"Some dude I never seen before."

"He paid you up front?"

"You shittin' me? Half now, half when the job's done. Now get out the way, I got work to do."

"When's he coming back with the rest?"

"The polls close at nine, sistah."

One of the fliers says that the party machine-supported candidates are promising to cut taxes and increase emergency spending to stimulate the economy. And where is the new revenue supposed to come from? I guess they've decided to give the old "pot of gold" strategy a try (although the party faithful prefer to call it the "rainbow" strategy): apparently, a special congressional subcommittee is planning to monitor national weather patterns in order to locate the pots of gold that lie at the end of every rainbow in the country. Oh, and while we're at it, we'll have to round up all the undocumented leprechauns and render them unto the Faerie Queen of the enchanted castle of Avalon for safekeeping.

British Prime Minister Tony Blair promises to support the project.

I walk a couple of blocks out of my way so I can stop by the offices of a non-profit voter protection agency called Get-OffYourAssAndGetaMoveOn.org or something like that. The building's leaky roof is being held in place by what looks like forty yards of extra-wide duct tape. It happens to be right next to a bar serving the cops of the One-Ten Precinct, and just for the record, no car parked in front of that bar has ever gotten a ticket in the history of Western civilization.

Once inside, I check the water-stained ceiling tiles to see if they're about to cave in on me. When I'm satisfied that the ceiling might hold out a few minutes longer, I step around a big plastic bucket that's got five inches of standing water in it and a collection of nickels and pennies on the bottom that people have tossed in, transforming this mundane industrial plastic object into a wishing well of sorts. It's a pretty far cry from the sacred lakes where the ancient Celts once sacrificed barges full of precious metals to satisfy their capricious gods, but clearly the spirit lives on.

A dark-haired white girl named Lauren, who's gulping down a 24-ounce jug of Seven-Eleven coffee, asks if she can help me. When I explain the situation, she says that they've been getting calls all morning from people complaining that their polling places have been changed at the last minute. And oddly enough, all the people getting the calls have been *latinos* who are more likely to vote for Sánchez. Now *that's* what I call a pattern of criminal behavior.

"How widespread is it?" I ask.

"It's happening all over the city."

Ave María purísima.

I tell her, "I can't cover all five boroughs, but I'm sure as hell going to find out who tried to play me with that robocall."

"It's too late for us to hire you."

"Fuck that, I'll chase this one down for free."

I start with my caller ID history, which displays the "Unknown Number" message. But the guys I'm after aren't exactly the rebel underground trying to hide the source of their short-wave radio transmissions from the evil empire. I've got a friend who can trace the source of the call to an actual phone number in about ten minutes, which I can usually turn into an address using the standard databases, reverse look-ups and such. But he's not answering at any of his numbers. So I switch tactics and call the phone company and tell them that someone has been calling me at all hours of the night, waking up the kids and harassing me with sexual remarks, and I want to know where the goddamn calls are coming from.

The operator is sympathetic, but tells me she can't divulge the location of the phone number without prior authorization from the proper authorities.

I let her hear it in my voice that I'm nearly overcome with frustration and rage over being victimized like this, and that I'm about to break down and cry, when she whispers the number of an extension and says, "Hang up and call back. I'll get it in the other office."

Wars never hurt anyone except the people who die.
Salvador Dalí

The county headquarters of the party machine is a sleek, antiseptic building shaped like a chilled slab of cream cheese. They managed to dress up the main reception area by using the same walnut-to-brass ratio as any suburban corporate office, and I have to say that they've turned it into a sharp-looking place. It's certainly a long way from the brick-strewn alleys where their time-honored tactics were "test marketed" for the first time.

Back by the boiler rooms where the dirty deeds are done, they decided to go with linoleum tile and fluorescent lighting, and I happen to know that the contractor got a sweetheart deal on the fixtures, charging $4 per bulb *in bulk* when I can walk into any hardware store in the city and pay $1.99 for the same fixture.

When I tell them I called ahead about volunteering for today's get-out-the-vote drive, the receptionist directs me to a plucky young man who whisks me down a corridor and into a long, low room lined with banks of shiny white phones that are humming with activity. He hands me off to a woman with a mile-high hairdo and some mighty strong perfume who flashes a Kool-Aid smile at me when he tells her that I'm bilingual, and says that she's really happy to see me because they really need Spanish speakers working the phones. Really they do.

She sticks a Post-It in the paperback she was reading and clicks something on her computer screen. I look at the cover of the book and recognize the subgenre immediately. Ever-lasting love. You know, being in love with a ghost would present *a problem* for most people, but I guess that's the beauty of romance fiction.

She hands me a photocopy of a prepared Spanish-language script, then she accesses a few screens, highlights, clicks, and prints out a long list of *latino* names with matching phone numbers.

She leads me to an open phone and shows me how to work the scam—I mean, how everything works. She even makes me role-play a practice call, and the hardest part is trying not to blow it all by laughing at the mistakes they made in the Spanish. *Y'all couldn't find a native speaker in muthahfuckin' Queens, bitches?* And when she leans over to make sure all the cables are properly connected, a wave of clashing aromas hits me like a magazine full of perfume samples. I finally begin to get the hang of it, and she returns to her desk to find out how it's possible to fuck an insubstantial wisp of ectoplasm. Hey, just because he's been dead for 300 years doesn't mean he won't have fewer commitment issues than some of the guys I know.

I make about twenty minutes' worth of calls at their expense, deviating from the script as I see fit, until I feel it's safe to ask where the restroom is without attracting any attention. There must be some nice facilities for the party bosses upstairs, but us peasants get a rusty bucket next to the supply closet.

I take the long way back, listening at every door until I strike gold. Now, the polite thing would be to knock first, but since I'm currently suppressing the urge to draw my .38 and kick the goddamn door down, I figure they're getting off easy when I try the knob and swing the door open.

The kid sitting there has got pale, pink skin with eyebrows that are practically invisible, and short, reddish-blond hair that stands up at the sides as if he'd rubbed his head against a balloon. *This guy* is the menacing voice I heard on Harvey's tape?

But it's his voice all right, there's no mistaking it, and I've come in just as he finishes delivering the same threatening message to someone else.

Oh, and right next to him is a state-of-the-art robocall machine playing the same recording that I received this morning, telling people that their polling places have changed. At least I can say with some satisfaction that it's a shabby little room, and much more in keeping with this kind of set-up than the glitzy offices out front.

"Yes?" he says, smiling up at me with fresh-faced innocence.

"Wait a minute. You mean this *isn't* the Board of Elections?" I say, with mild shock.

The bright, still waters of his smile are gently rocked by a faint ripple of confusion.

"So I've actually got a shot at collecting the reward money for uncovering physical evidence of an organized plot to suppress the vote that results in a felony conviction? That's a couple hundred grand right there, and just think, I owe it all to *you*."

The corners of his smile wilt like the last rose of summer.

"And by the way, you've also violated the state laws against using pre-recorded calls to harass people *like me* who are on the federal Do Not Call Registry, for what it's worth."

And the waters become muddied with worry.

"So who paid for all this?" I ask.

He doesn't answer. No surprise there. But I can hear a pair of heels come clattering towards us on the freshly waxed floor.

"Oh, come on. Stop protecting them, kiddo. You think they wouldn't hang you to save their own asses? Now where'd the money came from?"

Madame de Pompadour arrives, borne along on a cloud of her overwhelming perfume.

"Never mind, we'll find out when we go through the financial records," I say.

"What are you doing here?" she says. "Are you trying to cause trouble?"

"Oh, I don't have to try, it comes naturally," I say, dialing a number.

"You'd better put that phone down."

"No, I'd better be calling the feds so they can come and bag this machine as evidence."

She tries to grab the phone from me, and when that doesn't work, she orders the kid to shut off the machine while she calls for security to come get me, and that's when I pull out my concealed weapon and calmly explain that a private citizen is allowed to use deadly force to prevent the commission of a felony or the immediate flight of the perpetrators therefrom. Dig?

They dig.

Of course, I don't tell them what *class* of felony. People rarely get shot over white-collar crimes. In fact, people rarely get *prosecuted* for white-collar crimes. I could steal a million dollars with a pen and never see the inside of a jail cell, but if I used a gun to hit a liquor store, I'd be looking at fifteen years' hard time.

The point is that all this reminds me of the kind of fraud committed in the "battleground" states like Florida and Ohio by the same people who want to make Reagan into a saint.

And my only regret is that I didn't bring a bigger gun.

Rights are free; social justice costs a fortune.
Katha Pollitt, *Subject to Debate*

The cynics are always saying that a New York D.A. could get a grand jury to indict a ham sandwich. Well, let me tell you, the ruling party machine in this town could *elect* a ham sandwich.

It takes the State Attorney General several months to build a case against the local party chairman, Al Crowley, one of those heavyweight party bosses who keep popping up in the headlines squinting at the camera and smiling like the well-fed kings and popes of the High Middle Ages.

In his defense, Crowley says that he was trained during his stint in the military to "disrupt the enemy's communications," as if it's perfectly all right to treat the opposing candidates in a representative democracy the same as a battalion of hostile troops in a war zone.

The real scandal unfolds after they subpoena the financial records, and find out that in order to pay for the disenfranchisement of thousands of voters, Mr Crowley siphoned money from the city's maintenance budget, including payments and supplies intended for Local 3 of the International Brotherhood of Electrical Workers. Those are the guys who take care of the street lights, which would explain why the lights were never working in our district. When questioned, Crowley says that he could have taken a lot more.

"My philosophy is never take a hundred percent of anything. Gimme twenty-five percent and I'm happy."

So now it's a *philosophy*. Move over, Spinoza.

The party is content to defend him from charges of "astroturfing," a method of funneling money to phony grassroots organizations created to pressure local politicians who believe that the groups actually represent the community. But they take it on the chin when it comes out that Crowley wasn't just corrupt in the service of party ideology, but also for his own personal gain. Imagine that.

He skimmed $5,000 from a children's charity to buy himself a big-screen TV. Really, Mr Crowley. I mean, at least spend the money on drugs and whores like everyone else, or do something relatively classy like stealing from the highway funds to buy a Mercedes for the wife and a little red Corvette for the girlfriend. But the *kids' charity?* Jeezus.

At least Vivian Sánchez won our district, even though Harvey didn't get to cast his vote for her (he still hasn't received official confirmation of his status as a legally registered voter), and we get to see Helen Marshall, Queens's first African-American Borough President, get re-elected to a second term.

But it takes two and a half years for the case to come to trial, by which time Mr Crowley has taken early retirement, so he is simply identified in the papers as a "former county party chair," as if it weren't a statewide conspiracy. So nobody gets punished for dissing half the population of Queens, and the party machine lives on to slime another day.

And I never see a penny of that reward money.

To borrow Mr Crowley's own metaphor, if this is war, then maybe it's time to start holding some war crimes trials.

I'm still waiting . . .

DEAD RIGHT

Ken Bruen

Twelve years. Yeah, that's how long she's gone. Nineteen years of age and as the old people say, "But a slip of a girl."

Here's the jig:

Move on/
Forgive and forget/
Time heals all/

Like fuck I burn. As I burned every day of those long awful years. Forget? Forgive?

Yeah, right. And move on? I'm moving alright. Right fucking now. I finally know who killed her. I've kind of always known . . . But to be sure.

My mother, one hard bitch, used to whine, "But to be sure to be sorry."

The fuck does that mean? When they found my daughter's body, they discovered a Claddagh ring lodged in her throat. I looked at my mother. Lying on her deathbed, her body raked by cancer, a set of rosary beads like handcuffs on her ravaged hands, she'd intoned:

"Forgive them, Jesus, Mary and Joseph, they know not what they do."

Like she believed that for one fucking second. They knew.
And she no more forgave them. Political all her life, she
knew how to play the filthy game—and if there was a God,
she was going door to door. On me daughter's head, if the
priest hadn't been there, I'd have strangled her with the
bloody rosary beads. And the priest? Touching my arm,
ordering, not asking.

"Tommy, make your peace with your Mam."

I gave him the look, last time a fucker put his hand on me,
he lost it from the elbow. Cleary, the priest, backing off, my
rep well known to him, trying.

"You'll feel better son." A slight tremor in his voice.

Son? I nearly laughed.

I had at least ten years on him and all of them bitter. My
amusement was choked by too much bile though. I moved
right in his face, asked, real quiet, "How the fuck would you
know what would make me feel better?"

He was backing away till he hit the wall, the portrait of
the new Pope above his shoulders. My mother, politician
that she was, soon as the old one bought the farm, she took
him down, dropped him in the trash and up with the new.
She kept the frame of course, she might not have had a
shred of loyalty but she wasn't stupid.

My fist was clenched and then I heard the death rattle.
You hear it once, you never forget. Cleary scuttled out from
under me, moved to her, began the last rites. The few
neighbors who'd gathered dropped to their knees like a Brit
patrol caught from three different rooftops, the Armalites
blazing.

I pulled open the door, went down the stairs. Mikey, the
last of my squad, asked, "Is she?"

I shook my head, said, "She's making a song and dance of
it."

He nearly smiled. The bottle of Jameson was fresh opened but not touched. He wouldn't begin without me. How we'd survived the SAS and the Prod death squads. I nodded and took two chipped china cups, Charles and Diana on one, John F. Kennedy on the other. My mother, playing both sides as usual.

It doesn't get more Irish.

Or ridiculous. Sorry, call it politics. I call it shite.

He poured, we touched rims, said, "*Slainte amach.*"

Drank deep.

Again.

Then he leaned back on the wooden chair, said, "I'm sorry about your young wan, them finding her, like that." And when I said nothing, he added, "Nothing like the Jay, 'tis the holy all of it."

I nodded, took out me worn pouch, smelt the rich tobacco, rolled two, handed him one and then that slight smile as I fired him up with the worn Zippo. We'd taken it off a squaddie from Manchester, an acne-riddled kid, barely eighteen and looked about twelve, his uniform hanging on him like the worst of bad news.

And worse it was going to get. Two days we'd held him, waiting for the powers that were to decide his fate. Midway through the second day, when he thought he might actually make it out alive, I asked him, "What do you know about politics?"

Mikey had given him a cup of tea. Two sugars and a chocolate digestive.

He thought it meant something.

It did. We don't eat biscuits.

He drank the tea, noisily, like a child, said, all eagerness, anxious to please.

"Paddy, me? I don't know nuff-ink."

My backhand knocked him clean out of the chair, I said, "Don't call me Paddy."

Mikey got him back in the chair, even gave him a rag to wipe the blood off his mouth and Jaysus, he began to munch on the biscuit, tears rolling down his cheek, melting the chocolate. I'd have thought the chocolate was the best bit but he was Brit, the fuck did I know what they liked, besides killing us.

He said, "I dunno *Sir*, I follow the football is all, Man U, like, it was real mistake to let Beckham go, jeez, he was mighty, see him bend a ball?"

Cunt. Overpaid pretty boy. Never knew a fucking moment's hardship his whole golden life. And his wife, the *Posh* wan . . . set her loose on the Falls Road, see how far that pout would take her.

My daughter, putting the Spice Girls poster up on her wall and my rage, tearing it down, screaming, "Don't put no English cows on the wall of my house."

Her mother pleading with me, "She's a child."

And furious, I'd taken all her CDs, fucking Brits all, threw them in the fire, said, "Not in my house," I think, but memory is funny, I think she whispered:

"Meant to be our house."

Unflinching. That's what Nora, my wife said I was. I looked it up and told her never use high-faluting talk with me again, we had perfectly good Irish words of our own.

When Nora had passed, the mason asking me what I wanted on her headstone, that's the word I used. None of that . . . Rest in Peace . . . your daughter dead . . . peace . . . sure . . .

But the squaddie, we never got his name, why would we? Mikey gave him a corned beef sandwich towards evening.

He took that as real good sign, said, "I love bully beef."

The call came about a half hour later, as he, all worked up, was telling Mikey about a memorable game with the Gunners.

I shot him in the back of the head, twice, *bully beef* still trailing from his mouth and if I didn't know better, I'd think Mikey was taken aback but he shrugged, gave that small smile, started to strip the body.

He found the Zippo, a logo: Man U rule.

I said, "That's dead politics."

Mikey, using the Zippo to fire a rollie, muttered, "Dead right."

Mikey had grown up on the Falls, watched his Da gunned down by the Brits in the early Eighties, his mother drink herself to death, had joined the Boyos early, getting hit by a rubber bullet when he was all of ten years old, and you get hit by one of those suckers, you hurt. And he was always quiet. Never said a whole lot but by the time he joined my squad, he'd a fearsome rep, totally without fear or remorse.

I'll be honest, I hadn't wanted him. Sounded like a wild card. Back then, the streets of Belfast, you had to know exactly what you were doing and an unknown kid, no thanks.

Shay had said, "Give him a chance."

Not a suggestion, an order and then, those wild crazy days, I believed in Shay, shite, I believed in a lot of stuff.

Mikey proved his mettle, in every way which counts, never backed down, never whined and when we were pinned down, most of our guys dead, the SAS all around us, he asked me, "Any bacca left?"

The guy had balls of brass.

When my daughter disappeared, he'd asked, "What can I do?"

I'd said, "Help me find her." We didn't.

And now, here we were, the old days gone, the brand new politics of peace beaming on us, sitting in the kitchen, sinking the blessed Jay, doing what we did best: waiting.

Mikey took another hit of the brew, then said, back to the discovery of my daughter's body, "Shay."

I drained my own ration, said, "I gave him the ring."

He put his second rollie under his Doc Marten, crushed it gently, asked, "When do we go?"

I shook my head, said, "A *cara*, this I do alone."

He buttoned his sea jacket, the same one he'd worn all those years, gave the half smile, said, "Bollocks."

The priest was coming down the stairs as we prepared to leave, said, "She passed peacefully lads."

I said, "Like the country."

Sitting in the kitchen now, Mikey took another hit of the Jay, said, "I'm real sorry about your girl."

I knew he was. Back when she'd first disappeared, it was Mikey who told me of the rumors that Shay was *seeing her*. Proof, I couldn't move without it and he was still my commanding officer and we were up to our balls in strife.

Her body had finally been discovered, ten days ago, a Claddagh ring in her throat. That ring, a tiny flaw in the heart, got me a discount on account I knew the ring belonged to Commander Shay, our op's chief.

Good guy.

I'd given him that ring when I was best man at his first wedding, a lovely wee lass from the Upper Falls, killed in a Brit *friendly fire* encounter. And now was married again, to a Dublin socialite. He'd become a leading light in the peace initiative, even had his photo in the paper with Clinton's arm round his shoulder.

Gobshites.

His shiny new wife, an interior decorator, Jesus. They lived in Foxrock. That's Dublin 4. The 4 tells you everything. Serious wedge. Cash and lots of it. It's Bono and New Ireland. A long sad bloody prayer from the Upper Falls. It's all I know of hell and sell-out.

Mikey and I drove over the border a few days later, went to a safe house on the north side of the city. I hadn't been to Dublin in a time and the area we were in was almost completely black, the flow of refugees swelling the population like a successful novena. Man, I felt for these folk, their black faces expressing bewilderment at the unexpected ugly face of Irish racialism. There was a whole new war brewing right here but I had my own fight and hell, if I survived, maybe I'd lend my support to these new outcasts, we had a lot in common.

I had the rage, they were getting the hurt, lethal combo. I rang Shay. He was all, what's the buzz word . . . *bonhomie?* Full of it. Would I like to drop by for drinks the next evening?

Would I the fuck ever.

His house was imposing, long driveway, beautifully tended gardens and what, were they fecking sprinklers? BMW parked carelessly at the door. Two heavies at the front.

He was still a Boyo.

These weren't wannabes. Gym tough, a whole different deal to the street.

They frisked me thoroughly.

Regarded me with complete contempt, one of them with a bar room complexion, sneered, "Thought all you mad dogs were dead?"

I went with, said, "Gone but to wash me."

Shay was standing in front of a log fire, I liked that if little else. He had a tan, white silvery hair, flowing carefully along the collar of his Armani suit. A slim Rolex, he kept shooting his cuff, lest I miss it. He was holding, and I'm not fucking kidding, a *snifter* of brandy, swirling it gently around, like some faggot on Stately Homes.

I wondered if Clinton taught him that. Golfing buddies now.

He gushed, "Tommy . . . lad, you're looking grand."

I looked like shite but so what else is new?

He said, "You'll be having something?"

He knew better than to shake hands. I said, to rile the prick, "Black and tan."

The drink named after our most hated enemies.

Old joke and never . . . ever . . . humorous.

As he mixed that, he asked, "How's your Ma?"

I let a beat skip then said, "Dead thanks."

He shook his head, said, "Ah Tommy, still with the bitterness, we've moved on from that, have to."

He handed me the drink in a Galway Crystal glass, the logs from the fire throwing sparks off the intricate design of the rim, almost like radiance. I didn't drink, put it down on a mahogany coffee table, said, "They found my daughter."

His eyes guarded, he said, "My deepest sympathies, she was a bright lass."

I said, "Brighter than you thought."

Now he put his brandy on the mantelpiece, asked, "How's that?"

"Before she died, she swallowed the Claddagh ring, she knew I'd know who killed her, you, you fucking animal."

He moved to a small table, said, "Ah Tommy, it was an accident, you know I'd never hurt her intentionally." Then he turned, his whole face changed, the old Shay in place, eyes like dead rats, a Browning held loosely in his right hand, his whole tone now was idle pity, he said, "Yah sad bastard, you came here, what? For revenge, with no back up, no weapons, where's that psycho who used to follow you like a fucking pathetic lap dog?"

The first bullet tore through his hand, the Browning flying from his shattered fingers, and Mikey said, "I'm right here."

Mikey's face was cut and I could see his left shoulder was bleeding, he said, "Them fellahs, they weren't worth a toss." He threw me a Glock and I said to Shay, "Kneecapping, you were always fond of that."

Later, before he died, I made him eat the Rolex.

Hope it stuck in his throat, it certainly did in mine.

You're thinking, I never told you my daughter's name.

The fook business is it of yours?

Back on the north side of the city, as I bandaged Mikey's wounds, he asked, "What now boss?"

I looked out the window, the passing black faces, I said, "Might have a new cause."

He gave the half smile.

THE MAYOR'S MOVIE

Sujata Massey

The Amrikans were the ones who sent the imam to Ahmedabad.

On the day the Stars and Stripes rose in Kabul, Imam Ghulam Ali Qadir crossed the Khyber Pass into Pakistan. He arrived in Ahmedabad with a dusty, hard-eyed entourage: Afghanis with Kalashnikovs, Arabs in ground-sweeping *djellebahs*, and other men in heavy army fatigues, citizens of a country that nobody dared ask about.

All of them were there under the protection of Abdul Khan, the *malik* who owned most of the area's poppy fields. Mama said it was a blessing that neither her parents nor Baba's were alive to see the long-beards dethrone Mustafa Khattak, the village's beloved old *nazim*, or mayor, shouting to everyone that they'd come as liberators. Liberate us from what, Baba had grumbled—the right to electricity? The load-shedding and resulting blackouts in Ahmedabad were worse now than they'd ever been, and what were the bigshots in Islamabad doing about it, and the rise of Imam Ghulam Qadir? Less than nothing.

Hush-hush-hush, Baba had murmured, lying back on the cushions after a skimpy dinner of rice, a sabzi of greens and potatoes, and lentils. *Hush*, her father had repeated, *even the walls have ears*. Amina's younger sister Zara had looked around then, eyes wide, as if the mud walls of the house had suddenly sprung to life.

When the sisters lay under thick, hand-sewn quilts in bed at night, Amina had explained that Baba just meant that life was dangerous now in a way that it hadn't been before. When Amina was Zara's age, girls covered their hair with loose scarves and dressed modestly in *shalwar kameez* suits, but they'd been allowed to walk outside unaccompanied. Amina had attended a girls' school in the next village, and shopped with her mother at the village market. But when she was twelve, the school officially closed, and now females couldn't leave their houses without a male relative, which was highly inconvenient, because Baba worked ten hours a day overseeing the farm fields he owned. And farming was tough these days, with Baba's usual labor force being siphoned off to better-paying jobs in the poppy fields. The produce that he did manage to grow often rotted before it got to market, and Baba lived in fear of the roadside bandits, who'd taken from him before, but so far spared his life.

Things had changed slowly for the worse, ever since the imam had made himself Ahmedabad's mayor. One of the first laws he'd enforced was that all females would wear a *burqa* with only a thin slit of veiling to let their eyes peek out. Girls could no longer go on the rides when traveling amusement companies set up carnivals in town, or ride on the backs of their fathers' or brothers' bicycles.

It was law. Sardar Asif Rashid, the town's police superintendent, had come by two years ago and taken almost everyone's bicycles away, because boys in outlying districts needed a way to reach the *madrassah*, the religious school the imam had established.

Baba rarely complained; Amina knew he was unhappy that the girls' school she and Zara had attended had been closed, but he seemed to think that not only the walls had ears, but the mountains and streams, too. Her mother had grown into herself, the anger curving her back prematurely, or maybe it was fear. They were all trying to look smaller, less likely to be noticed. Her mother carried herself like a grandmother now, and her face was pinched and dry, and not just because the Zadeh family's shop no longer carried Pond's.

Still, when Baba was away in the fields, Mama didn't seem to care if the walls had ears. One Monday morning, she kept up a grumbling commentary to her sister Roshmal, who had come for tea. Khala Roshmal lived near enough that she could scurry across the lane without being noticed, just as Amina did when she was visiting her cousin Wasila, who was also fifteen.

"Do you remember what you were doing at school at our daughters' age?" Mama asked Roshmal as the cook, Nasreen, brought in a pot of thick, milky tea. "Studying. All these girls are learning is to cook and clean. I tell you—we're training them to be maids!"

Roshmal raised her eyes heavenward. "Yes, maybe in a few years they shall be blessed enough to find positions working in the household of That One."

"Yasmin from the other side of the hill works there now," Nasreen said.

"Yasmin's working?" Amina turned with surprise to Nasreen; she hadn't expected that their family cook, who was in the house even more than they were, would have known anything about the doings of the mother of her old school friend, Farida. All Amina had heard about Farida's family was bad: that six months earlier, her father had died in a car accident on the way to Peshawar, and there were no nearby relatives to take them in.

"Yes, she moved in with her daughter, Farida, a few months ago. He has a large staff there, just for one person." Nasreen sounded disapproving.

"It's one thing to cook and clean for your own family, but can you imagine washing his underthings? Cleaning his bowl? Why, I couldn't trust myself," Mama said archly.

Roshmal's round face flushed pink. "If you poisoned That One, you'd hang within the day. Don't even joke."

"Jokes aside, what other way could there be to stop him from being re-elected?" Mama asked.

"But there's voting," Amina said. "Under national law, women can vote. You don't have to vote for him."

"What's the choice?" her mother answered. "Nobody is foolish enough to run against him."

"Mustafa Khattack should try. During those days, it was better." Amina thought about all the ways: there were still bicycles to ride, school to grumble about, and Indian movies to watch on the DVD players that had sat forlornly ever since the law changed to permit viewing only news, religious programming, and cricket.

"Even if there was a man foolhardy enough to go against That One, who would be brave enough to vote for him?" Khala Roshmal asked, looking with concern at Amina.

"Me, if I were eighteen. Women still can vote, Mama. It's Pakistani law."

"But who do you think counts the votes, checks the papers right after you drop them in the box? Asif Rashid." The town's chief constable was always eager to curry favor with the outsiders, if it meant more power for him. He'd sent Mustafa Khattak into exile shortly after the powerful foreigners rolled into town. It wasn't that the Sardar was so religious, either; everyone knew he drank *sharab* in the old days. But he didn't anymore. Just as he turned a blind eye on the newcomers arriving in town without so much as a visa. They didn't need them because they were the imam's guests.

"There are imams who are less severe. Of course, they are our *own* people," Roshmal said with a delicate raise of her eyebrows. Unlike Mama, she'd kept her eyebrows plucked, even though so few people ever saw her uncovered face.

"I'd like to see Farida," Amina said. "She was in fifth class when they closed the school. I talked about lending her my sixth-class books . . . do you think we could invite her for tea one day?"

"She's got no time for books, since she has a job now, Amina-*jaan*." Mama's voice, as she called her daughter darling, softened slightly. "At least you have Wasila to play with."

"Amir could go over there, maybe, to ask if there's a time we could visit Farida." Amina knew her eldest male cousin had plenty of spare time: his market for pirated Bollywood blockbuster films had evaporated, because of the new laws.

"I don't want you at that house." Mama put down her glass of tea with a clink. "You are too outspoken. I can only imagine you saying the wrong thing, and being overheard. Next thing, your father and I will be in prison or worse."

"I'm not nearly as outspoken as you," Amina said, and earned a light cuff on her ear. But it was all right. Amina had an idea. Later on, she would send the flashlight signal from her window to Wasila. It was a method of communication they'd created as small children. Two flashes meant it was time to talk; one cousin would patiently repeat the signal until it was answered. Whoever had the first opportunity would watch for an all-clear—no men on the street—and bolt across to the other's home, where the door would be unlatched. Often they'd scamper back before the parents even noticed anything had happened.

Amina didn't have any time to send a signal until after supper so it was dark, and her light bounced clearly to Wasila's room. Wasila signaled back after a minute—Amina imagined her groping for the flashlight under a large pile of the illicit, old Indian movie magazines. Wasila's signal of five flashes to Amina meant she was free to go, and would be the one to travel.

"Wasila is coming over," Amina casually announced to Mama and Baba, who were watching the news on television in the large, open room that served as their dining and living room. It was nine-thirty; the lights had been on for an hour, and would probably last another twenty minutes before shutting off. At this time, village-wide, almost everyone was watching television, on the internet, or pushing their DVD players to the limit, because once the darkness came, there was very little to do until dawn, and the call to prayer.

"I didn't hear the telephone ring." Baba looked puzzled, when he opened the door to his niece.

"The girls persist in signaling each other with lights," Mama said. "They're very mysterious, cloak-and-dagger sorts."

"The Famous Five," Baba said with a laugh, referring to the antiquated British children's novels that Amina and Wasila had traded before the new imam had ordered them burned. "Where are your other three members?"

Amina didn't dignify her father's weak joke by answering. She just whisked off with Wasila as quickly as propriety would allow. Tucked away in the little closet of a room which Amina shared with Zara, the girls talked in low voices.

"Do you remember Farida, from school?" Amina began.

"Oh, yes," Wasila answered. "The shy girl. I heard something about her father—"

"He died in an automobile crash. She and her mother have become servants at the imam's." Amina lowered her voice. "I think, to cheer her up, we should visit."

"Yes," said Wasila, who was usually game for anything. "Farida's sweet—I'd certainly be interested in hearing about what That One is really like. But what could we bring her?"

"How about my old sixth-form books? And do you think Amir would walk with us to the house, tomorrow following afternoon prayers?" Amina was thinking of the muezzin's three o'clock call to prayer. Everyone prayed five times daily, whether they were at home, in the field or mosque. After the sunset prayers, it was important to be home.

"I'm sure he will. And if anybody stops us on the street, he'll say you're Sharifa." Wasila was talking about her older sister, who was married and living thirty miles away—one of the lucky ones.

The next evening, Amir and Wasila came to the door and requested that Mama let Amina accompany them on a walk, ostensibly to gather mushrooms. A walk was more or less the truth, since they were going about three kilometers, some of it through the woods. Mama unsuspectingly let Amina go, adjusting her *burqa* and checking that her fingernails were short and free of polish—fingernail polish was a vanity that Wasila and Amina indulged in constantly. When life was so boring, changing one's nail color was the least that could be done, although there were no replacement bottles left to buy in Zadeh's Goods Shop.

"So, this Farida, is she pretty?" Amir asked, between puffs of his Goldleaf cigarette. Ever since the imam had established a rule against watching films, Amir's business had evolved from film to what he called "number data"—gather-

ing the names and account numbers of people with credit
cards and using them to untoward ends. Such a waste, Baba
had said to Mother; if Amir had been admitted to university, he would have learned ways to use computers for
good. But now Amir was his family's biggest earner, and the
thought of him leaving to attend university in Islamabad or
Karachi seemed impossible.

"She was quite pretty back in school—how old were we
then, though, twelve?" Wasila said.

"Yes, and Farida was eleven, which would make her
thirteen now. But don't try your *filmi* lines on her, not
with That One in the house." Amina felt vaguely excited to
be coming close to the architect of her family's misery, but
she didn't have a death-wish.

In this section of the Northwest Frontier, telephone
service was spotty, so people communicated primarily with
mobile phones, although that was problematic given the
towering mountains that rose between villages. The imam
had a land line, as did several other officials, but few
households did. Amina couldn't imagine Yasmin had a
private telephone, so she'd already sent over Amir to
arrange an appropriate time for the girls to visit. The three
cousins walked four miles to stand before a buzzer that had
been set into the great stucco wall surrounding the imam's
house. It was the grandest home in their town, comprised of
a *hujera*, or main house, with a great room, parlors, the
imam's bedroom, and a kitchen in the back. There was a
separate house for women, where Yasmin and Farida slept
with the other female servants, and an extra guesthouse for
male visitors.

Shortly after the buzzer sounded, Yasmin's voice came
tinnily over the intercom, allowing them to proceed through
the high iron gate to the main building.

"Your timing is excellent," Yasmin said, offering to take the girls' heavy black *burqas* as they entered the house. "The imam is at Dr. Khan's home, attending an election planning meeting. You two go can go through the hall without worry and join Farida in the kitchen. I'll make you girls tea. I'll bring you tea as well, but please wait in the side garden," she added to Amir, because of course he couldn't socialize with Farida.

"Thank you, Khala Yasmin," the girls chorused; then, holding shoes in hands, they walked along the cool marble floors that were so clean their bare feet squeaked. At the end of the front hall was an arched open doorway that led to a garden. There, amid a struggling array of small palm trees not suitable for the northern climate, they left Amir to wait.

Inside the main house they located Farida in the kitchen, squatting on the floor. She was sorting lentils, carefully placing the perfect ones in a bowl and the inferior ones on a cloth on the floor. Farida may have been thirteen, with her long, silky black hair worn in braids just like their own, but there was an exhausted sorrow in her face that drew down the bow-shaped lips that Amina had remembered.

"Farida! It's been too long," Amina cried, moving shyly forward. The girls clasped hands, and Amina was surprised to feel how rough Farida's palms were; like those of a mother, not a girl. Wasila, too, moved forward to greet their old friend.

"Sorry, I need to get this finished before That One returns," Farida said, dropping her hands and sitting down again with the lentils. "Such a pretty *hijab* you're wearing, Wasila. It's not from here, is it?"

"No, Peshawar. But it's old," Wasila answered, slipping the grape-colored scarf off her head and shoulders, and over Farida's. Amir had business dealings that sometimes resulted in gifts. In the old days Amir had given both girls movie magazines and CDs; now it was socially appropriate clothing.

"How lucky you are," Farida sighed. "Please take it back. I don't want to make it dirty."

"We brought you something." Amina showed her the parcel of books. "Wasila and I don't need these anymore. They're from the sixth-class curriculum, maths and literature."

Now Farida laid aside the bag of pulses and took up the literature book. "Oh, my. Thank you. I can read in the evenings, *Inshallah*, when my mother and I are in our quarters."

Yasmin came with tea, and after exclaiming over the gift of the used books and smiling warmly at the three girls, melted away to the scullery area where the sounds of vigorous washing commenced. The girls chatted leisurely, and when the tea was finished Farida said she needed to hide the books. This was understandable, Amina thought; probably, the imam didn't approve of women reading school books, even in the house.

"I have a special place," Farida said, leading them through the marble halls and toward the sunlight of the garden. Under scrubby weeds circling a walnut tree, she found a flat stone and lifted it. Underneath lay the flat top of a brass box. Farida took a key attached to the string of her *shalwar* trousers to open the box. Inside were banknotes bundled together with rubber bands, identity papers, and a mobile phone.

"I can't believe you're showing us this," Wasila said. "Your secret treasure box!"

"I want you to know where it is," Farida said, laying the books down. "Just in case anything happens to us."

"What could happen?" Amina asked.

"I'm—I'm not sure I want to stay here."

"Yes, the work seems very hard—"

"No, it's not the work. It's That One."

"Is he cruel?"

Farida gave a shudder that was so delicate her *hijab* barely moved, but Amina noticed it.

"What is it, Farida?"

"He—he's begun asking me to be the one to always bring him things, serve his meals. If Mama was there I wouldn't mind but he—he frightens me. I cannot say no to him. If I did—can you imagine?"

Amina and Wasila exchanged glances, and then Wasila said, "Amir has his own cell phone. You must call us on that, right away, if you need help. That mobile phone—does it still work?"

"Yes. We recharge it when we have a chance, and check messages every day, when the men are gone. If you want to meet again, call me at this number." She wrote it down on a corner of one of the notebook pages the girls had given her, and tore it off and gave it to Wasila.

"What's his daily program?" Amina was thinking about returning to see Farida, but she certainly didn't want to run into the imam.

"Well, every day he spends mostly at the mosque or the *madrassah*, but he's home most evenings. Except Wednedays, which is the political meeting."

"Who's at those meetings?" Amina realized it would be useful to know exactly who in the village couldn't be trusted.

Farida named Constable Asif Rashid, a couple of minor clerics, a representative of the district council who lived in the next town, and the town's doctor. Amina was mulling over the significance of these men when a rattling sound came from the house.

The three girls turned sharply to see Amir standing in the doorway. He nodded awkwardly toward them, his eyes finally moving from Farida.

"You fool!" Wasila screeched, as Farida turned to fling the scarf that was draped loosely about her shoulders over her head and face. Amina did the same, even though she was somewhat related to Amir and had known him since she was born. Amir disappeared from the doorway just as the sound of Yasmin's voice rose from the side garden, asking him if he would try a few sweets.

"I'm sorry for my brother's boldness," Wasila apologized.

The girls were subdued on their walk home, though Amir was full of commentary. Yasmin had given him a short tour of the first floor, and he'd seen something you wouldn't expect an imam to have: a big-screen television with a satellite channel box.

"The television was off, but the name of the channel he'd been watching was on the box. It's the adult channel," Amir said. "What a hypocrite!"

"Oh, dear," Amina said. "Now I know why Farida's so worried about the imam asking her to serve him alone."

"Serve him alone?" Amir suddenly seemed less jovial. "But that's against the rules!"

"The imam makes rules for everyone else, maybe," Wasila said. "But not for himself."

The next day it rained, but the town punishments were still on schedule for three o'clock in the afternoon. Everyone over the age of twelve was expected to fill the stands of the cricket stadium. The sides of the stadium were decorated with election signs for the imam. On a platform set up in the field's center, two unlucky people awaited their respective punishments. There was a man who'd stolen bread—"for his children," Mother had murmured under her breath—and a shrouded woman nobody could recognize or knew anything about.

The girls shut their eyes tightly, as Mother instructed, while the man lost his hand with an anguished scream. And they kept their eyes closed too, while the woman was caned by one of That One's deputies for immodest behavior in public. When her name was given before the caning commenced, Amina gasped aloud. It was their old third-form teacher, a married mother of two girls. She'd removed her *burqa* while weeding her garden in the summer heat, and been reported by passing newcomers. The sound of the blows, and the teacher's choked cries, made Amina writhe. But there was nothing anyone could do.

The punishments were over; the imam took center stage. That One stood in all his glory, long scraggly silver beard hanging over his black robe, his hair hidden in his large, twisted, gray-red turban. The Koran passages he was reciting went unheard in Amina's brain. She was thinking about what the imam had done to the man and woman; what he was doing to all of them. Three years he'd been in power, and all this had happened; if the imam stayed, what would life be like in ten years?

That night something Amir had said about the imam stuck in her mind as she tossed and turned, trying to get to sleep. Hypocrisy. And by the time she'd woken up, she had an idea.

"Amir, what do you know about bad movies?" Amina asked the next morning. She was visiting Wasila and Amir's house later that morning; the mothers, covered by their *burqas* despite the midsummer heat, were in the garden hanging laundry.

The girls were rolling chapattis for lunch, and Amir, who was supposed to be downloading virus protection on his computer, had come in to badger them to make him a cup of tea.

"Bad movies? You mean, where the acting's terrible . . . or the story is immoral? There's plenty of both, often in the same film." Amir took his cup with a nod of thanks.

"Can you buy bad movies through mail order, just like you did all those Bollywood films when you were running that business?"

"Yes, of course. Not that I'll buy one for you! Even if there weren't rules against it, you shouldn't be thinking about things like that."

"Amir, since you know so much . . . what do you think might happen if the imam was discovered to have ordered such type of films?" Wasila asked, on cue. She and Amina had already discussed the plot in detail; enlisting Amir was the last part of it.

Amir made a *you're-crazy* circle with his finger, around his sister's head. "Well, he watches that filth on the TV already. He doesn't need to order anything."

"But if a package addressed to him came into the post office . . . and there were bad films inside, and somebody found out . . . what would people think?" Wasila persisted.

"What if he opened the package in his house? Nobody would see at all," Amir pointed out.

Amina sighed. Her elder cousin was so slow. "If he opens it at home, he'll surely take the time to view it before he throws it away. If he throws it away at all—don't you think?"

"Somebody from the outside would have to see it." Amir's voice came slowly.

"Yes. How about his election committee?" Amina said.

"It's complicated," Amir said, after a pause.

"Well, we've got Farida on the inside. She can just tell us what he's doing."

"If Farida's caught, she would receive a lot more than a caning," Amir said.

They all would. That was left unspoken.

The details were surprisingly simple. First, Amina and Wasila shopped for a film; being good girls, they didn't download any images that were offered to them, just tried to judge by the DVD's cover. Amir got the number data on a Visa cardholder in California; a few strokes of the keyboard brought a pleasant confirmation email that the goods had been purchased and would immediately ship to one of Amir's old black market contacts living in India close to the Pakistan border. Because of the challenges in cross-border smuggling, Amir's contact thought the venture might take two weeks. The election was two-and-a-half weeks away, which meant that the timing was close, but Amina was hopeful. She'd been in telephone contact with Farida, who assured her that she would keep a close eye on the imam's behavior and the location of any packages he might bring into the house.

The imam's assistant, Iqbal Shad, made a sweep of the post office several times a week, and with the election coming he'd step that up. Sixteen days after the order was placed, Iqbal Shad picked up a flat, plastic-wrapped package for the imam. "Probably a campaign contribution," he'd reportedly said to the postmaster, who'd naturally commented on the Islamabad postmark. When Iqbal Shad had gone to pick up the imam in the center of town, he'd handed him the package with a flourish that had been noticed by two shopkeepers, six children and even Mama, who had been walking with Baba home from the market.

"The imam was strange today, opening a parcel and then quickly shoving it into his clothes," Mama recounted as she was talking to Baba before supper. "I wonder if it's bad news from the government?"

"Not likely," Baba said glumly. "More likely it's drug money."

Amina could hardly bear to wait until supper finished, and she'd have a chance to get over to her cousins' house to use Amir's cellphone to call Farida. But finally, it happened. To her surprise, her call didn't ring into Farida's voicemail but was picked up by the girl herself.

"I saw the package arrive," Farida said by way of greeting.

"Does he—has he thrown it away?" That was Amina's secret fear, that all would be wasted.

"I'm not certain—he doesn't seem any different in demeanor. He came in, said he didn't want supper, and asked Iqbal Shad to drive his whole entourage to Peshawar to look at some weapons."

"Tomorrow?"

"No. He sent Iqbal Shad right away. Iqbal grumbled to my mother about it, because who wants to drive in the dark just to go somewhere and look, not buy?"

"So he's home alone with the film." Amina pondered the significance of this.

"Yes. He went into his study with the DVD player straightaway. He forgot his five o'clock prayers, can you imagine that? Mother said he must not be feeling right."

"Really?" An idea was forming in Amina's head—there was a great chance of failure, but success would be so sweet as to make the risk worthwhile. "Farida, do you know Dr Khan's telephone number?"

Dr Khan was not at home, but at a fundraising meeting at the mosque. Amir, posing as Iqbal Shad, reached the physician on his mobile phone. "The imam's not well," he intoned, making his voice sound extra panicked, to help mask his voice. "Please come to the house, see what you can do."

Dr Khan had wanted the imam to come to the phone, but Amir insisted that he had lost consciousness. "Please, sir, just come to the house and see for yourself."

There was no ambulance in Ahmedabad—what would you expect, with no hospital?—so the vehicle that rushed up to the house was Dr Khan's Land Cruiser. Out of it sprang not only the town doctor with his bag, but the cleric, Ibrahim Raza, Chief Constable Asif Rashid, and two other senior members of the community. At the sight of everyone, Farida melted away into a corner, realizing just how dangerous things had gotten. The other servants were scared, too; old Yusef, the sweeper who was half blind and senile, opened the door to the visitors, but it was up to Yasmin to answer to them. She stammered out that she had heard nothing about an illness from the imam. When questioned further by Dr Khan, she had to admit she had not seen him in the past hour, because he'd refused supper and told her to take her daughter to the women's quarters. All the servants had been sent out of the house to their quarters, so nobody had known the imam had been taken ill.

"Know-nothing woman!" Asif Rashid roared, and pushed past her, standing at the doorway. The other men thundered past, kicking off their sandals behind them, raising a tiny cloud of dust that made Farida cough. Still, she followed, a tiny black shadow that nobody noticed.

As everyone drew closer to the imam's private study, strange sounds came faintly through the door—a kind of frenzied breathing, and the most peculiar groans Farida had ever heard, as she was to tell her friends later. Asif Rashid broke open the locked door with a hard movement of his shoulder; then, as the doctor and his colleagues entered the room, the grunts turned to shouts, first from the imam, and then from Sardar Asif Rashid.

From her hiding place, Farida saw the big-screen television, a glowing image of bare golden limbs spread akimbo. The imam was writhing on the floor, almost mirroring the screen, seemingly oblivious to his visitors until the last minute. The DVD package lay face-down on the carpet, and Farida could clearly see the picture of half-naked women and the film's title: *Hot Girls in the City*.

Yasmin fled the room with Farida. Holding hands, the two ran out to the garden to scoop up their hidden possessions. They then crept under the cover of darkness across the fields and forests to Amina's house in Ahmedabad.

The knocking on the back door awoke everyone. The guests, in hushed voices, told about what had transpired at the great house. Mama and Baba seemed startled, but agreed that Yasmin and Farida should take shelter, and perhaps be moved to a safer location the next day.

But while the women were sequestered in Amina and Zara's room the next day, waiting for Mama to organize transport on a friend's van to another town, a surprising thing happened. At noon prayers at the mosque, the district representative, Muhammed Ali Khalil, made a startling announcement. The imam had been relieved of his duties, and the district representative would serve as temporary acting leader of the town.

"What about the election?" The crowd, at first shocked into silence, began asking questions.

"Well, the imam cannot run for mayor anymore. It's not my decision, but a matter of abiding by sharia law."

A ripple of confusion seemed to course through the men, along with whispers. After a call to silence, a hand was timidly raised. One of Baba's friends asked, "But who will lead us?"

Khalil answered, "I have consulted with our local member of parliament, and have agreed, at his suggestion, to oversee the community during the trial and interim. However, we invite new nominations for mayor from the community."

"What trial?" somebody called out from the back.

"The imam's trial. He will be tried by the *jirga* at three o'clock this afternoon on charges of acquiring and using pornography." And with a sharp gesture of a hand, Representative Muhammed Ali Khalil cut off the flurry of resulting questions and swept out of the mosque.

The stadium was full that afternoon, as everyone in town aged ten or over was required to witness trials. And though the imam sputtered and blustered, the case against him was short and sweet. The postmaster and the imam's assistant, Iqbal Shad, recounted the details of the package and the imam's secretive behavior once it was in his hands. Sardar Asif Rashid, Muhammed Ali Khalil and Dr. Khan described their shock and sorrow at discovering the imam with the film. The sentence laid down was the same as for adultery: stoning to death, a punishment that had always existed on the books, but had never been enforced until the imam had taken charge.

When the sentencing was carried out, Amina kept her eyes tightly shut and her hands clamped on her ears. But after the imam's body had been carried away, there was a roaring sound in the street. She opened her eyes to see a convoy of cars, the imam's entourage, leaving town. Iqbal Shad ran after them, calling, and the car door swung open. He and the Sardar scrambled inside.

237

A cloud of dust hung on the street after they'd left, and then everything broke lose. Women came out on the streets, gathering in groups, laughing and smiling underneath their *burqas*. The coffeehouse down the street filled with men, talking animatedly over who should run for mayor. The shopkeeper, Zadeh, was going to run, and perhaps even Mustafa Khattack, who was considering returning to Ahmedabad. Inside the houses, women gathered and buzzed. Children outside shrieked with laughter and played tag.

"This is not what I expected," Amina said, when she, Farida and Wasila had finally settled down after the revelry to tea and biscuits. "I never intended to *kill* anyone."

"You didn't kill him; the law made it happen," Wasila pointed out.

"Be quiet, we must never speak of it again," said Farida. The three girls pricked their fingers and let their blood run together, enacting an oath of silence.

The next morning, all three girls took turns riding on the back of the new bicycle Amir had bought. Amina felt wobbly at first because of the years of inactivity and the burden of her *burqa*. Amir grumbled until Amina gained her confidence and was sitting in a secure sidesaddle position. Then, as he picked up speed, Amina felt a laugh start inside her, something crazy and deep that she wasn't afraid to let out, for once.

SWIFT BOATS FOR JESUS

by Gary Phillips

Rudy Garza broke a shoelace as he tied one of his Botticellis. He held the torn end to his face, glaring at it like a building inspector looking for cracks in masonry work. It was just a goddamn piece of expensive coated thick string when you got down to it. A lace that matched the rubbed cordovan of his shoes made of ostrich hide. The silver-haired salesman, his buffed nails gleaming, had patted Garza's hand in a fatherly way. He'd insisted Garza simply must buy the extra laces only from his store. It just wouldn't do to get those mismatched replacements from the local supermarket, now would it, sir, he'd gushed.

"Certainly not cheat you out of the ten bucks more you were able to add onto the bill, oh no," Garza muttered, smiling lethargically. Well, he did respect a hustler. Garza retrieved the new lace from the dresser drawer and finished tying his shoes over his herringbone-patterned sock. He checked his profile in the built-in mirror on the inside of the bedroom door. He'd gone with the dark Ralph Lauren slacks and the camel tan Oleg Cassini sport coat over the flyaway-collar burgundy Zegna shirt and the Belisi silver silk tie with matching pocket square.

Garza patted his gut, worried that he'd already had Luis, his tailor, let the pants out. Too many damn gin martini lunches with this contractor or that vendor.

"Man's got to know when to cut back," he reminded himself in a gruff imitation of his long-gone father's voice.

"Rudy," Lettie called from the kitchen below, "can you take Rosie in? I have to be out in Playa earlier than it was originally planned." His wife sold corporate real estate.

"Not a problem," he called back as his cell phone chimed. He notched an eyebrow, knowing the familiar number on his screen all too well.

"What you doin' up this early, fool?" he cracked to Jason Prichard.

"Shit might be comin' down, son," Prichard said coldly and efficiently. He was a city attorney in Compton, assigned to the neighborhood prosecutor unit. That meant he targeted gangs and gang activity.

"What's wrong?" He willed himself to remain composed.

"I got a tip the feds are sniffing into the Burkhalter business," his friend said. "That dipshit cousin of Jaime's, you know the one I'm talkin' about, the one I almost had to put in check over at the Peacock that time."

"Yeah, I know," Garza said, dreadfully expectant.

"Well that *pendejo*, got himself arrested coming back across the border carrying some Ingrams with their serial numbers filed off and inserts in the barrels to throw off ballistics."

"Fuck," Garza swore softly. Then his daughter called up to him.

"I got to go, Papa G. I need to help Amy set up her exhibit for science class."

"I'm on my way, sweetie. Just finishing this quick call."

"You're always finishing a quick call. Don't make her late," his wife warned as he heard the front door close.

"So Homeland Security got on his ass," Garza surmised.

"Naturally," Prichard confirmed. "Way I understand it, Jaime T's primo was transporting for the Crazy Nines. But of course he wet his pants once he was caught, and said anything and everything he could to make a deal to keep from getting put on the Gitmo express."

"Daddy," his daughter peeled.

Garza started for the stairs. "I'm coming, *mija*. You got your backpack and lunch?"

"Yes," she drawled, as only a put-upon twelve-year-old could. Her older brother had slept at a friend's house.

"Look, I'm running late," he said to Prichard. "Call me back when you know more."

"You make sure there's nothing else laying around to back up the testimony of a lame loser like that cousin, dig? Because I have no desire to get in the wind at my age, my brother." Prichard clicked off.

Father and daughter left. As he drove her to school in the Land Rover, Garza half-listened to Rosie's usual drone about some creepy boy or a squirrel she saw munching a hot Cheetoh. Automatically he put in a "Wow," or "Really?" at the right intervals. He also assessed how much damage Jaime's cousin, Hector Rivas, could do. He concluded that what he had to say would make those buzzdicks at the Bureau salivate, but Hector didn't have shit in the way of convicting them.

Sure he'd shoot off his mouth about Garza, but Hector couldn't be that scared of the government that he'd roll over on his cuz. Jaime was the leader of the Crazy Nines. Hector had to be terrified that between here and whatever cell he was rendered to, Jaime would reach out and touch him with a knife across the throat.

He kissed his daughter goodbye and watched her saunter into St. Cecilia's with the other children. The Catholic school was a funky assortment of Sixties-era buildings contrasted to the new playground equipment that fronted the state-of-the-art computer lab. Both courtesy of a fund drive seeded by a generous donation from SubbaKhan, the mega developer who'd won the bid for the new complex of shops and theaters being built adjacent to the Happy Trails casino.

Their bid was higher than the others, but Garza had convinced the council that SubbaKhan was worth the investment. The work was done right and usually ahead of schedule, and there was the cherry of the sweet percentage of a local hire and training agreement he'd hammered out on the project. With an under-the-table kickback to him for his efforts. Garza as Bell Park's city manager lined his pockets, but he never forgot he was a homeboy who'd fallen into clover.

Not that SubbaKhan would gain much initially in erecting this project here in this part of Southeast L.A., where the 710 Freeway cut through. Bell Park was all of 6.6 square miles with a forty-three-person police force, and had to contract for fire services from the county. But the deal with them allowed the developer to own part of the leased land. In the long run then, given there was a steady traffic of patrons to the Happy Trails from the other small municipalities in the surrounding area, the swollen coffers of SubbaKhan wouldn't grow any leaner. And a happy international conglomerate was a giving international conglomerate during elections, and at special times throughout the year.

On his cell behind the wheel, he tried to get Mayor Sharpe on the line, but it went to message. Garza checked the time on the dash: 8.20 a.m. He veered off the main avenue and drove slowly through a residential section. Dammit. He could see Emil Rojas' people were already out door-knocking.

"Look Abel," Garza said after hurriedly calling and connecting with Chief of Police Ramirez, "I need you to get some of your uniforms talking up the mayor. Rojas' people are out thicker than cock-a-roaches." He pronounced it just like Pacino did in *Scarface*. It wasn't just juiced up rappers who liked to sample that movie.

"I will, Rudy," Ramirez assured him, "and I've got some firefighters coming too. But you better get Don Pedro out of the Pearl Blossom."

"The fuck."

"He's been holed up there since about three this morning." He didn't go on. He didn't have to.

"Why didn't you call me?"

"I didn't know until an hour ago. Shit, you're his keeper."

Garza admonished himself and drove over to the massage parlor located exactly two blocks and a hilltop outside of the city in a DMZ of unincorporated county. Tradition held that if a sheriff found a body here, and the case load was high—and when wasn't it?—then maybe said body might find itself moved a few hundred yards into Bell Park. Sometimes it worked the other way around if the city cops could get away with it. After all, what was a corpse among friendly rivals?

He parked on the side of the three-story building. The Pearl Blossom personnel conducted their trade on the first two floors, with the second floor reserved for their renowned specials. The neon sign in fancy script announcing authentic Thai deep tissue message was off, its tubes dingy and splattered with bird droppings. He knocked forcefully on the back door security screen. Footsteps on the rear stairs, then Fanny Xa opened the inner door and after a beat the outer one. She was in sweats and a tank top with a picture of a collie on it. Her graying black hair stood up and out like a fright wig.

"How far gone is he?" Garza asked, moving past the bleary-eyed woman and onto the stairs.

"Good morning to you too, fuck head."

"Not today, Fanny."

"Whatever," she mumbled, shuffling outside in her bare feet to spit.

Upstairs on the third floor, Garza entered her bedroom, which was painted in purples and black for accents. She had one of those old fashioned vanities in one corner, its make-up table overflowing with small bottles of perfume, eyeliner, lipsticks and a tube of Ben Gay, he noted. Mayor Pete "Pedro" Sharpe snored on his back in the bed, his girth tangled among the purple silk sheets and dark lavender duvet. Garza smiled, shaking his head. In the late Eighties, Sharpe, a former football and track hero at local Israel Bissell High, had taken his cue from Dylan's song and knew which way the wind blew. He adopted the Mexicanization of his first name when he was running that first time for re-election. The mayor knew from being out and about, let alone from a census chart, that the demographics of Bell Park, once the hillbilly haven of Dust Bowl-era migrants, were irrevocably changing.

The city had seen an influx of African-Americas in the Sixties, and there had been a resulting power struggle for who got what seat at the table. Sharpe, who was black, emerged from that fight and came to office backed by a shaky coalition. This happened just as the next ethnic wave was coming on strong in the city—Latinos. But it didn't hurt that Sharpe spoke Spanglish with ease. On a Spanish language station he verbally outmaneuvered his Latino opponent in his first re-election contest. That candidate had been earnest, but he was a *pocho*, a Latino who didn't speak Spanish. He didn't go over well with the new majority.

"Pete, time to rock, baby." Garza shook him and only succeeded in interrupting a snore. Sharpe smacked his lips but didn't otherwise make an effort to wake.

"Like Dr. Phil says, how's that workin' out for you?" Behind him Xa laughed and hacked. She began searching in a nightstand beneath a shelf upon which was a stuffed red-and-black-feathered rooster before a sun painting. These were some sort of religious symbols reflecting her Muong heritage.

A couple of light backhand slaps to the whiskered face roused the mayor. The whites of his eyes were as red as spoiled apples. "Hey," he managed.

Xa found her half-smoked joint and fired it up.

"Let me hug up on a little of that, will you, my dear?" Sharpe held out a large hand. A ring with a dark gem that sucked up the light was on his pinkie. She handed the joint across and he took a healthy drag. He didn't cough and his hand didn't quiver as he blew out a steam of narcotic smoke. He handed it back to Xa, who leaned over and gave him a peck.

"We got to filet gumbo, Pete. You've already missed the breakfast at the old folks home. But you can swing by there on your way back from the VFW hall speech." Garza wasn't the mayor's campaign manager, but knew his schedule more intimately than hizzoner did.

"Ah, what the fuck for, Rudy?" Sharpe pushed himself up so that his back was to the headboard. He folded his muscular arms across his broad chest. "Maybe Rojas should get it. I've had a good run and so have you. Let's golf and play poker in the afternoons and let Mister Reformer find out just how fuckin' hard it is to run things. Let reality kick him in the ass and smack that rose-smelling piety out of his mouth."

"I'll make some coffee," Xa announced, puffing on her joint as she ambled into the kitchen. "I've heard way too much of this already."

Sharpe was in his late sixties, Rudy wasn't. The older man might be at the end of his string, but he damn sure had more to give and get. Bell Park's mayor and city council were part-time jobs, the city manager a full-time post. But it was a position that served primarily at the mayor's pleasure, so Garza needed Sharpe back in the saddle this one last time.

"We have certain obligations, you and I, Mr. Mayor. Certain fulfillments that we are direly responsible for their completion, *comprendes, carnal?*"

Wearily Sharpe began, "If you can't eat their food, drink their booze and fuck their women . . ."

". . . and still vote against them," Garza said.

". . . then they shouldn't have gotten involved in politics in the first damn place," they finished together. Sharpe smiled, self-satisfied.

The city manager's cell phone chimed again. "Look, you only think you want to laze around and count your liver spots. But that's for old men, Pete. Not men like us. Not men who make it happen on the streets and in the sheets."

Sharpe gave him a sideways appraisal. A slight smile creased his seasoned face. He didn't say it, but wanted Garza to go on.

"We can't let this prick Rojas set the terms for when you exit office. He's some kind of headline-chasing substitute teacher who the holy rollers and a few prune-faced pedophilic priests have propped up."

"That's right," Sharpe agreed, getting into it.

"This is trench warfare we're talking about," Garza continued, "this isn't a game for punks and *chulos*, am I right?"

"Hallelujah!" Xa cracked from the doorway. The joint hung from her mouth as she wiggled her fingers.

"Right on," Sharpe added, sitting more erect, wiping a hand across his face.

Garza paced about the room, putting the evangelist into his spiel. It used to be it was only twice a year, usually around the Fourth of July and Christmas time, which was when Sharpe's wife had died five years ago, that he had to give him the rah-rah. But this current campaign seemed to have really taken it out of the mayor. He didn't have the fire in the belly for it like before. He really was getting on.

Garza stood before the window, backlit by the morning sun as he spread his arms. "So what are we going to do, champ? How we gonna rumble?"

"Rumble like thunder and strike like lightning," Sharpe said. He was sitting on the side of the bed in his striped boxers, scratching his nuts.

"And what are we going to unleash on our enemies? What shall we smite them with?"

"We shall bring them low with the power of our words and mightiness of our deeds." Xa helped him stand on his wobbly legs.

"For who is the captain?" Garza said, silencing his ringing cell phone.

"He is," Xa yelled, slapping Sharpe on the shoulder.

"And does he not lead our swift boats through treacherous waters?"

"I do," Sharpe vowed, giving him a quick salute.

"And do we let slip the swift boats against our enemies simply for our own selfish reasons?"

"No sir," Sharpe and Xa said in unison.

"For who do we guide our swift boats to victory?

"The people," Sharpe said solemnly. "Our swift boats are for the people."

"Amen," Garza said. "Now get your funky ass showered, shaved and dressed and let's get back in the game, son."

"Most assuredly," Sharpe said as Xa, arm around his waist, led him to the bathroom.

Back on the road, Garza returned the two calls he'd gotten from Sharpe's campaign manager. He told her where to fetch him.

"Don't we need to go over some last-minute strategy?" Cerna Chacon then said, chuckling.

"No doubt," Garza answered. As he drove back through town, he was pleased to see the mayor's volunteers were now canvassing as well.

"Who are these wholesome young women you have out on Portillo?" he inquired. He knew the regular volunteers.

"Don't you go getting any ideas of inviting one or two of those dewy-eyed females to your Politics 101 sessions, teach," she warned. "They're part of a poli-sci course over at Cal State. Nice, huh? Their professor and I attend the same AA meetings. Fact I'm his sponsor."

"You're such a creative woman, Cee-cee," he complimented sincerely.

"Then you better reward me. I need to relieve some stress having to deal with our man." She sighed heavily.

They set a time at their usual place and Garza headed for the Happy Trails, passing back through part of the north side. The base for Emil Rojas' support had come out of the precincts here. This was where a grassroots group called the Local Justice Initiative, a bunch of community college drop-out Che Gueveras, had organized members of congregations about the proliferation of liquor stores in that area.

The residents became activated on that issue, getting some ink and results. Indeed the north side contained more than its fair share of liquor stores. After all, Garza had seen to several of those permits being okayed by walking the paperwork over to council and doing some horse-trading.

One of those galvanized residents was Rojas, who, because of service as a medic in the Gulf War, got the attention of the mau maus and the sanctified, and it was off to the races. St. Cecilia's was located in one of those northern precincts, but its leaders knew who buttered their bread and had held two pancake breakfasts for the re-election of Pedro Sharpe.

Inside the casino the SSIers and the day walkers—those old-timers who recharged at home at night to be ambulatory in the sunlight—were already vigorously tapping the keys of the video slots or getting ready for morning bingo. Jules, a former vato now working the security detail, gave Garza the high sign. On the side of his neck was a faded tattoo of an eagle grappling with a python. Like the others decorating his body, he was in the process of having it removed via laser treatments. The city manager moved past him and into the outer office of Neils Weaver, the manager of operations.

"His lordship available?" he asked Berta Yanez, the receptionist. As with Jules, he'd gotten her this job at the casino.

"Let me check, Rudy." She buzzed the inner office either for show or as a heads-up. Weaver did like his morning toot. "Please, go on, good sir," she said, smiling, and did a flourish with her hand, indicating the inner door.

Yanez, a high school dropout, had done six and three-quarters years on a ten-year bid for aiding and abetting in the transportation of a truckload of ecstasy. But she was one of the few who took advantage of her time. She not only got her GED, but took coursework that she was now completing toward becoming a paralegal. The fact she'd been incarcerated in a minimum security facility instead of the max lockdown prosecutors initially wanted to send her to was due to Garza's intervention when he was on the city council.

In the office, Weaver, a lanky individual with thin glasses and thinning brown-blonde hair, stood and held out a fist. "What up, homeboy?"

Garza knocked his knuckles against the other man's and remained standing. "We might have a problem on the Burkhalter thing." He explained the call he'd received that morning.

"So far it seems like the feds are stirring the waters to see what floats to the surface. But we shouldn't ignore this," Garza added.

Over the years Bell Park's administration had been the focus of several inquires by the District Attorney and the Bureau. There was the allegation of their injudicious use of highway checkpoints to bust undocumented drivers so as to impound and sell their cars to raise municipal funds. Or that Crazy Nine shot callers had been tipped-off about impending police raids. These and various other allegations Garza, Weaver and several other interested parties could ill afford to have proven in court.

Weaver asked, "You talk to Jaime T?"

"Not yet and not likely if I can avoid it," Garza admitted. "I've got an election to secure and don't need him and his crew out and about causing consternation.

Weaver pursed his lips and blew air. "If this investigation gains momentum, I'll have to alert Al."

"That's why I stopped by. We need to make sure he doesn't, you know, go all native on us."

Weaver laughed dryly. "Shit."

Alfonso Jardine was a Mexican Jew. His father was from Cuernavaca and his mother had been a World War II refugee whose family snuck into Mexico escaping the Nazis out of Poland. Jardine originally made his money in the discount mattress racket, and due to family ties on his dad's side here in Bell Park, had opened the Happy Trails Casino more than twenty years ago. The casino drew patrons from all over, and accounted for some two million plus in salaries and tax revenues for the city. This was not an insignificant sum to the small municipality, and thus Jardine was a player in local politics as he was a backer of Mayor Sharpe.

Jardine had also dabbled in the internal affairs of Israel, supporting Labor Party members, as well as owning land over there. At one point a few years ago the gang situation was getting out of hand in Bell Park. This was due to the rival Rolling Daltons, a black gang with some Latino membership, encroaching on the Nines' drug territory.

Innocents were getting cut down in the crossfire, and naturally the residents were demanding action from the outgunned and outnumbered police force. Jardine, from his compound on the beach in Baja, sent a group of mercenaries into town, some of them former Shin Bet and African campaign veterans. It did not go well with these para-chute-in, parachute-out types, used to slapping around the populace and letting the Good Lord sort them out later. Even in Bell Park, civil liberties couldn't be that blatantly ignored. Particularly as the media latched onto the story.

"If he gets a mind to send those yahoos back this time," Weaver noted, "he'll have our pictures in their target files."

Garza said, "It's not going to get to that."

Weaver leaned back in his seat. "It can't, Rudy."

Promising to keep him in the loop, Garza was back on the road. The radio ad they'd done for the Spanish language station was running. The minute spot had the voices of two middle-aged women talking as if over coffee at the kitchen table.

"Why yes," one said, "that Mr Rojas seems nice. But with all the abuse problems of the church, why did he have that young girl sitting on his lap?"

"I know," the second one replied, "reading her a story," she snorted incredulously. "*Qué lástima*, didn't he know better? What kind of teacher is he anyway?" There was no campaign mailer of Rojas with a child on his lap. Perception was everything.

"Sweet," Garza said to himself as he kept an appointment in nearby Santa Pico, a city even smaller than Bell Park. In a modest stucco home with hand-sewn curtains, he met with the heads of several block clubs throughout the southeast area. These women, ranging in age from their forties to their seventies, would be on duty tomorrow at several election booths in Bell Park. Each had a son or daughter, grandchild or great-grandchild, who Garza had helped in some way. They had long memories and a peasant's sense of loyalty. These were women like Garza's dead mother, and he was like them.

"Have some tea, *mijo*," Mrs. Almirez greeted him as he stepped inside the kitchen from the side door. She turned to pour from a steaming ceramic pot.

"Thank you," he said, nodding his head and greeting the others, some thirty-seven in all. This was a quick overview of tomorrow's plan. Nothing crude to potentially raise a red flag like misplaced ballot boxes or having the dead on the voting rolls. Through the normal *chisme*, the drama, and the back-fence gossip leading up to this election, plus the use of the traditional phone banking to tabulate how people were voting, these women had been given names of their friends and neighbors ID'd as Rojas's supporters.

"We're ready," Estella Rencinos said after Garza finished with last-minute details. Rather than try to stuff the ballot box as Garza had arranged in the past, these women would, when feasible, merely punch another hole in an already punched card of some of Rojas's supporters. An over-voted ballot was as invalid as an unmarked one.

"Now, no one overdoes it, right?" he said to the ladies. "We can't have any of you going to the pokey." That got nervous laughter. The idea here was these women knew a lot of people or were known by a lot of people. The older ones, the neighborhood *tías*, the community aunties, would engage the opponent's voters. The election was predicted to be light, so a backup was unlikely at the polls. Therefore it was natural that there would be more time for casual conversation.

The person was distracted talking to the older woman while handing the ballot in its paper sleeve to the younger woman. When this one tore off the perforated top of the punch card for the voter, fumbling a bit to expose that other part of the punched card, they'd use a punch on the end of a ballpoint pen to put another hole in the card, then tap it back into its sleeve. The distracted person, after chatting up the *tía* about her child's progress in school or that recipe for the Christmas *tamales*, would, as required, place that altered card in the sealed ballot box's slot.

Garza had rehearsed the punch move with the selected punchers, and he was impressed at the level of sleight-of-hand these old gals had mastered. They had few reservations about committing larceny in the service of La Causa.

In a close race with low turnout, a one- or two-percent spoilage could be the margin of victory. He gave a finishing pep talk, making sure to crank it down from the sermon with Sharpe, and was off again.

At his desk in his City Hall office, which was a squat unassuming cinder-block bunker of a structure tucked into a corner of Bolívar Park, Jason Prichard rang him on his cell.

"They found Delia," he said without introduction. "She's living down there in Tucson near the college. In fact she's shacked up with, of all things, an adjunct professor of late

nineteenth-century French fuckin' literature. I guess her
thing with Burkhalter turned her on to nerds or some shit,"
he said contemptuously.

"Fuck," Garza said.

"Double fuck," his friend concurred. "The good news is I
learned from another source that she got popped a few
months ago on a meth charge, so she's still tweaking."

"And if she's tweaking, she's as unreliable as Hector to a
jury."

"Yeah, hopefully. But that might not stop an indictment
from coming down," the lawyer noted. "The Bureau has a
hard-on for you, Rudy." As was their custom, they were
using disposable cell phones. They switched them out every
other week.

"True that, my brother," Garza said, suddenly upbeat.
He'd been sent an inter-office email and had opened it while
they talked. He told Prichard the good news. "The poll we
did Saturday has Don Pedro up by five points. When we get
over this hump tomorrow, then I can concentrate on how I'll
tarnish their images and cause doubt and confusion before
the feds can spit-shine their shoes. Don't worry."

"Uh-huh, be happy."

"Exactly."

Telling him he'd report in if there was any other pertinent
news, Prichard rang off. For the next two hours or so, Garza
did the City's business. From adjusting gaps in the sanita-
tion budget to meeting with the city-sponsored after-school
program, he was in his groove.

Then, crossing the parking lot for city employees, he saw a
familiar car come around the long way. He couldn't mistake
the vehicle for anyone else's as it was a fully restored, and
fully modernized, maroon 1935 four-door Packard touring
sedan. It was one gorgeous machine but Garza wasn't

pleased to see it now. The car slowed in front of him and the rear window slid down on its electric motor. In the back was Jaime Torres, the Crazy Nines chief. Due to a mystical conversion brought on while on peyote getting a lap dance two years ago, he'd taken on the Aztec last name of Teculciztecal. No one, not even Torres most of the time, could pronounce it. So he remained Jamie T.

"My friend," the gang leader said, pointing one of his long black nails at Garza. There were rings on three of his fingers. "I understand we have a problem." He was sitting nearest the passenger window in the Edwardian gear he favored these days, complete with owlish sunglasses. Whatever the hell that had to do with the Aztecs, nobody dared ask him.

Garza explained in a smooth and calm way why he didn't see the Hector and Delia situation as a problem.

"Let us hope," the other man said. "For I am most vexed that this situation my cousin is in may have come from an inside tip. A snitch you'd say."

"Why do you suspect that?"

"Elemia has seen it."

Next to him was an Eight Ball chick Garza didn't recognize. Though he did note her ample breasts strained against her skimpy top. A stylized skull was tattooed on her cheek. Beside her on the car's bench seat was an older woman who went by the Elemia tag. She was Jaime T's personal *bruja*, a witch and spiritual advisor, but Garza knew her when she was Suzanna Rios from the projects.

"Shit," Garza said, looking directly at her, "she couldn't see pale-ass Paris Hilton naked in a room full of Zulus."

Rios had a hand on Eight Ball's thigh. She raised that hand and languidly gave Garza the finger as the car glided away. Jamie T might be all ancestored up, but he did love his three-ways. Back on the streets, he ate two *carne asada* tacos from a cart vendor and headed over to the Royal Viking motel for his assignation with the mayor's campaign manager, Bell Park Police Sergeant Cerna Chacon. She'd texted him to be at the motel at this time. It wasn't their first such meeting at the VK, a few freeway exits further south of Bell Park.

"Don't be shy, stud," she teased. They'd barely entered the room and Chacon was tugging on his zipper. She was dressed in civilian clothes but had brought her department-issued equipment bag. This she tossed on the bed.

"Please, I do have my standards," he joked, pretending to pull away.

"You better get that standard at attention, soldier." She gave his crotch a squeeze and undid her shirt, revealing a lavender bra and her feathered serpent tattoo that began on her abb'd stomach and disappeared below the belt line of her pants. Soon she was down to her thong and moving toward the bed, Garza close behind her, naked and excited.

On the bed they snorted some coke she'd brought along to charge their batteries. The two then got busy with various efforts at exchanging body fluids.

"You like that, baby?" she murmured, nibbling his inner thigh.

"You know I do," he moaned as he reached back to the equipment bag. Given what she was doing, she didn't see him reach inside. He withdrew an old-fashioned revolver with a six-inch barrel. Chacon had her eyes closed, gobbling him up, and he slapped the warm steel against her scrunched forehead.

Startled, she halted and gulped hard.

"Get on your back," he commanded, the gun unwavering on her.

She did as commanded, keeping her legs closed like a chaste school girl.

"Open them," he barked, using the business end of the ancient police special to tap her knee.

"What are you going to do with that?"

"Don't you worry about that. You just do as I say." He rubbed the barrel along her inner leg, moving it steadily upward.

"Please don't," she pleaded. "I'll do anything else you want." She put her hands over the area he was intent on reaching.

Garza's heavy breathing drowned out the din of horns and brakes outside the motel room. The two were in lustful thrall.

She grabbed his wrist, but his other hand was around her throat and he worked the tip of the gun past the material of her sheer panty and inserted it in her vagina.

She gasped. "Do me, Rudy," she said as she tongued his ear and lobe.

He worked the barrel of the gun in and out of her as she bucked in pleasure, her strong arms holding him tight while she bit into his shoulder. Almost there, she told him to stop and they came together using the tried and true method.

Cooling off, she asked him, "Are you getting jammed over Burkhalter?"

"How do you know about that?"

"I have my ways." Her cell rang and, noting the number, she answered and listened. "Okay, Pete, I'm on my way." She clicked off. "The mayor demands my presence."

"How's he holding up?"

"He's got the spirit again, Deacon Garza. He's on the warpath. I'm going over with him to fire up the Delta phone bankers." The Deltas were the remaining black sorority in town.

"As long as he makes it in this last stretch."

SWIFT BOATS FOR JESUS

"Don't you worry your pretty little head about it, sweetheart." She grabbed for his limp member through the slit of his boxer, giggling.

He returned to City Hall and, after tidying up a few matters, made his rounds. He dropped off campaign literature to the parking enforcement crew on late lunch break, delivered Braille call sheets to the home for the blind, and trays of Pollo Fiero chicken to the soccer club whose members would be out doing evening canvassing.

Somewhere past seven that night, he knocked his tumbler of Jameson's against Jason Prichard's at the Peacock Inn.

"Nice work, home," he toasted his friend.

"Good thing I remembered Collier had retired to Phoenix. He put her on the run." Prichard smiled broadly and quaffed his drink. He referred to Bob Collier, a former captain with the Compton Police Department, when Compton had its own department before contracting with the sheriff. Prichard called in a chit and got him to drive to Tucson and flash his badge in Delia Gomez's face. He growled that those nice clean-cut FBI agents who contacted her were the least of her problems. That all sorts of nastiness with this hush-hush branch of law enforcement he represented was about to befall her for narco-trafficking. He'd be back with a warrant, he'd advised her. He'd watched from hiding as she tossed a suitcase in a raggedy Camry and took off from the adjunct professor's house.

With her gone, Hector Rivas could play his tune to the cheap seats, but the feds knew they had nada. Burkhalter had been the comptroller of Bell Park. Three years ago there'd been another reform push and the mayor and his allies on the council were forced to fire his crony and hire the stick-up-his-butt Burkhalter. He began to dig up money streams best left alone. Jardine was unhappy, as was Jamie

T and Prichard. Using selective prosecution, Prichard helped clean up the gang problem in nearby Compton, but also kept the Rolling Daltons from expanding. And there had been cash thank yous from Jamie T regarding this.

Fortunately the forty-something Burkhalter, a bachelor, was a lonely man.

Garza had Delia, an aging neighborhood chick, dress like a square and made sure she bumped into Burkhalter in City Hall. He tumbled, hard. Soon she had a key to his apartment. One evening, she let Hector in with a replacement computer tower just like his. Only this one contained beaucoup downloaded bestiality images. Naturally some of the images were leaked to the media. Burkhalter protested, but to no avail. His credibility was toast, as was his investigation.

Prichard talked with Garza some more, then left for a date. The city manager did some politicking in the working-class bar of laborers, copier salesmen and receptionists. He glad-handed and gabbed, bought a couple of rounds, handed out buttons and reminded them of their polling places.

Out in the warm evening, walking to his car, Chacon phoned him. He'd stopped near a gardener's old pick-up truck laden with lawn equipment.

"I know you're insatiable, woman, but I've got to get home."

"Rudy," she said in a rushed tone. "Where are you? I'm in my car and coming to get you."

"What are you talking about, Cee-cee?"

"Jamie T thinks you're the snitch."

"Why the fuck would he think that?"

Two men dressed in working clothes exited the bar.

"Because that silly bitch we have undercover was on the hot seat and came up with a story implicating you. She's the one that provided the tip leading to Hector Rivas' bust."

The two working men stood close to the pick-up.

A chill cooled Garza's body. "She got a skull tattooed on her cheek?"

"Yeah. That way our unis would know who she is. But she was able to phone in tonight and told me she was about to be exposed this afternoon and panicked. I was her training officer so she's close to me, that's why she felt she had to get it off her chest in case it caused problems. Problems," she snorted. "That goddamn Elvira or whatever the hell she calls herself had a vision that someone close to him was snitching. I've got to get you to a safe house, then we can work this out with him."

The two men closed the gap to where Garza stood with his back to them.

"Okay. I better come up with an excuse for Lettie. I— "

Garza didn't finish his sentence as the first of the fifteen stab wounds entered his body, piercing his lungs and kidneys and stomach.

"No, wait, it's not—" he tried to tell his assassins, but they were coldly and quickly efficient in their mission. They left him curled in his blood on the sidewalk, Chacon yelling into the cell phone in his now slack hand. As they drove off in the pick-up, sure not to stand out like say in a lowered ride with spinner rims or the like, Rudy Garza rolled over on his back on the blacktop, his Botticellis unstained and at attention. He stared peacefully at the stars.

One star in particular seemed to get brighter and bigger, filling his vision. In the heart of that brilliance, forms materialized. The swift boats were swooping down from the heavens to lift him up and take him away.

Hallelujah.

CONTRIBUTORS

Black Artemis [aka **Sofía Quintero**] is the author of several novels and short stories that cross genres. Her works include the hip hop novels *Explicit Content, Picture Me Rollin'* and *Burn*, and she is collaborating with illustrator Urban Envy on a graphic novel series. Sofía is also the author of the novel *Divas Don't Yield* and has contributed novellas to the anthologies *Friday Night Chicas, Names I Call My Sister* and *Juicy Mangos*. She is the president and owner of Sister Outsider Entertainment, a multimedia production company that produces quality entertainment for urban audiences. To learn more about Sofia and her work, visit www.*black-artemis.com*, www.*sisteroutsider.biz* or www.*myspace.com/sofiaquintero*.

Ken Bruen lives in Galway, Ireland. He has two daughters, a doctorate in metaphysics, and has had 21 novels published. He's won the Shamus twice, and the Barry and Macavity Awards.

Mike Davis lives in the San Diego neighborhood of Golden Hill and is the author (with Kelly Mayhew and Jim Miller) of *Under the Perfect Sun: The San Diego Tourists Never See* (New Press, 2005). He has also recently published *Planet* *of Slums* (Verso, 2006) and *In Praise of Barbarians* (Haymarket, 2007).

Robert Greer lives in Denver where he is a practicing surgical pathologist, research scientist, and professor of pathology and medicine at the University of Colorado Health Sciences Center. He edits the *High Plains Literary Review* and reviews books for KUVO, a Denver National Public Radio affiliate. He has published six mystery novels featuring Denver bail bondsman CJ Floyd, two medical thrillers, and a short story collection. His latest CJ Floyd novels are *The Fourth Perspective* and *The Mongoose Deception*.

Pete Hautman has written 16 novels for adults and teens. Awards include three Minnesota Book Awards for *Mrs Million* (2000), *Sweetblood* (2004), and *Godless* (2005), and the 2004 National Book Award for Young People's Literature for *Godless*. His crime novels *Drawing Dead* and *The Mortal Nuts* were selected as *New York Times Book Review* Notable Books. Two of his novels, *Mr Was* and *Snatched*, were Edgar Award nominees. Hautman lives with novelist and poet Mary Logue in Golden Valley, Minnesota, and Stockholm, Wisconsin, where they are collaborating on *The Bloodwater Mysteries*, a middle-school mystery series.

Darrell James is a California writer living in Pasadena. His short stories have appeared in numerous mystery magazines, and in the anthologies *LAndmarked For Murder* and *Deadly Ink*. He is the winner of the 2004 Fire To Fly competition and 2007 Deadly Ink. His gathered short stories, *Body Count: A Killer Collection*, garnered a 2007 Reader Views-Reviewer's Choice Award.

Jake Lamar was born in 1961 and grew up in the Bronx, New York. He is the author of the memoir *Bourgeois Blues* and five novels: *The Last Integrationist, Close to the Bone, If 6 Were 9, Rendezvous Eighteenth* and *Ghosts of Saint-Michel.* He has lived in Paris since 1993.

Michele Martinez is the author of the critically acclaimed thriller series featuring Manhattan federal prosecutor Melanie Vargas. Her books—including *Most Wanted, The Finishing School, Cover-Up* and the forthcoming *Notorious*—have won awards, been named in numerous "best" lists and been published in many languages. A graduate of Harvard College and Stanford Law School, Michele spent eight years as a federal prosecutor in New York City specializing in narcotics and gang cases. She now lives in New Hampshire with her husband and children.

Sujata Massey is a journalist turned mystery writer. She is the author of the ten-book Rei Shimura mystery series set in modern Japan, which has won the Agatha and Macavity Awards, as well as being nominated for the Edgar and Anthony Awards. She lives in Minneapolis with her family, and is currently at work on a historical thriller set in India.

Before turning to writing full time, **Twist Phelan** was a plaintiff's trial lawyer and a commodities trader. She has written four mysteries set in Pinnacle Peak, Arizona, featuring Hannah Dain and Joe McGuinness, lawyers who are also endurance athletes. Her short stories have appeared in anthologies and major mystery magazines. Her next book will be something different, a big novel set in the financial world. Her only experience in politics was at 11 years old, when she transported a paper bag full of money from a real estate developer to a zoning commissioner. Find out more about Twist and her books at: *www.twistphelan.com*.

Gary Phillips writes stories of misdeeds and shenanigans in various mediums from the deceptively sunny shores of Los Angeles. His current work includes a coming-of-age graphic novel, *South Central Rhapsody*, a serialized political thriller, *Citizen Kang*, on *www.thenation.com*, and he is co-editor of the *Darker Mask*, a collection of edgy prose super-hero stories from Tor. Please visit his website at: *www.gdphillips.com*.

John Shannon was born in Detroit and grew up in San Pedro, California, the gritty port of Los Angeles. He has worked on a newspaper, taught school in Africa and lived several years in England before returning to L.A. He has published 13 novels in the US, England and France, including *The Taking of the Waters*, a three-generation family saga of the American Left, and *The Concrete River*, the first in a series of mystery novels featuring Jack Liffey, a laid-off aerospace worker, which together build a jigsaw picture of the multi-ethnic city.

K.j.a. Wishnia's first novel featuring Ecuadorian-American P.I. Filomena Buscarsela, *23 Shades of Black*, was nominated for the Edgar and the Anthony Awards, and was followed by four other novels, including *Soft Money*, a *Library Journal* "Best Mystery of the Year" and *Red House*, a *Washington Post Book World* "Rave" Book of the Year. His short stories have appeared in *Ellery Queen's Mystery* magazine, *Alfred Hitchcock's Mystery* magazine, *Murder in Vegas*, and most recently, *Queens Noir*. He teaches literature and creative writing at Suffolk Community College in Brentwood, NY. You can find out more about him at: *www.kjawishnia.com*.